"I'm sorry. It's just that everything seems so uncertain. I know I agreed to what we discussed, but now I'm not so sure," Lauren said in a whisper.

Michael watched her mouth tremble slightly and could think of nothing else but the kisses he wanted to place there. His gaze slid down to her bare shoulders and his pulse began to race. It was their wedding night. He'd waited months to stand before Lauren as her husband.

"You shouldn't worry about any of that tonight, Lauren. Regardless of what happens this week, this month, or several months down the line, we can make things up as we go along."

He realized, as he spoke the words, that it could possibly set them up for complications, but he also knew how much he loved the woman standing before him.

Michael wrestled with the things going through his mind and wondered if she knew how much he wanted to put his arms around her. Stepping forward, he kissed Lauren, her lips warm and incredibly soft. He remembered the first time he'd ever kissed her and all resolve to be rational, to hold steady or to diminish in any way the feelings he so desperately needed to keep on a short leash, left him. He pulled her to him tightly, crushing her breasts flat against his bare chest as the softness of her negligee accentuated the feel of her against him. They were man and wife, for now. . . .

He clenched her body to his and realized that for the second time that day, there were tears on his face. This time, he couldn't be sure if they belonged to him or to Lauren.

LINDA WALTERS

A Matter of Time

BET Publications, LLC
http://www.bet.com
http://www.arabesquebooks.com

ARABESQUE BOOKS are published by

BET Publications, LLC
c/o BET BOOKS
One BET Plaza
1900 W Place NE
Washington, DC 20018-1211

All Kensington Titles, Imprints and Distributed Lines are available at special quantity discounts for bulk purchases for sales promotions, premiums, fund-raising, and educational or institutional use. Special book excerpts or customized print-ings can also be created to fit specific needs. For details, write or phone the office of the Kensington special sales manager: Kensington Publishing Corp., 850 Third Avenue, New York, NY 10022. attn: Special Sales Department. Phone: 1-800-221-2647.

First Printing: January 2005
10 9 8 7 6 5 4 3 2 1

Printed in the United States of America

I'd like to dedicate this book to the memory of my mother, Ethel Beatrice Thom, whose life both inspired and influenced me immeasurably.

Mom, you were right: water does seek its own level!

Acknowledgments

I would like to take this opportunity to say a sincere "thank you" to my family, whose support, patience and understanding I am never without. Thanks to Nikki, Lance, Teylor, and to my sisters, Gloria, Delores, and Connie. Thanks to my niece Bonnie, my copilot. You guys are all the best . . . I love you.

Thank you to all the folks back in New York City (you know who you are) for every ounce of grit, grime, and sincerity you've instilled in me. I couldn't do it without you. Thanks also to Donna Hill—you're still my idol!

Thanks also to the team at BET. Your continued guidance has helped produce the quality product that is typeset here. Thanks, ladies—you're all incredibly talented!

And most of all, I'd like to thank God, who makes all things possible.

Chapter One

The whitewashed gazebo sheltering the wedding of Lauren Traynor and Michael Townsend was set amidst one-hundred-foot Casuarina palms whose planters had never even dreamed of the twenty-first century. A breathtaking view of the Caribbean Sea, which surrounded the island of Barbados, was practically ignored by the people present. Their eyes and attention were fixed on the couple who stood before them. They sat in witness as the future unfolded.

"From this day forward, for better or worse . . ." The minister's words drifted through the air as waves crashed against the shoreline in unison, in rhythm, almost as affirmation that the universe was in sync with the nuptials taking place. Flaming torches lined the perimeter, creating intimacy in the open-air forum as the sun set slowly, its orange glow adding a warm intensity to the depth of its hue. A hush fell as all in attendance watched the couple take steps which would bind them eternally.

Lauren and Michael gazed directly at one another. Michael appeared calm and resolute, his handsome face remarkably composed. He'd planned the ceremony hastily but meticulously, with the resort where their wedding was held taking care of everything but the rings. Part of a chain that prided itself on its delivery of full scale excellence, The House was the pinnacle of six properties owned by the Elegant Hotels Group. Privacy, luxury, and above all, attention to detail were its mantra—and it delivered on all fronts. For this wedding, every detail—down to the magnum of the finest champagne, a basket overflowing with tropical fruits, gourmet cheeses and specialty crackers, and complimentary all-cotton terrycloth robes as an additional takeaway gift in each room—had been carefully planned.

Lauren's hand shook slightly as Michael slipped the diamond-encrusted band over her finger. Lifting it to his lips, he looked into her amber eyes and smiled. Lauren's heart beat faster, her pulse quickened; then she tore her eyes away, a single tear winding its way across the planes of her cheek. She felt overwhelmingly complete, but also knew she was on the brink of a total loss of composure. The day had come so quickly and she felt breathless as she stood in front of the man who was her world, and her future.

Michael's gaze never left her. He took in her beauty and drank of it. The creamy white of her dress, veil, and headdress accentuated the caramel tone of her skin. The gown's sleeveless bodice was enticing, yet demure, while the slim satin skirt hugged her waistline and curved hips. Lauren Traynor-Townsend glowed, her beauty enhanced by the heightened excitement visible in her cheeks. Her skin radiated health, and the sun-burnished bronze she'd acquired over the last twenty-four hours only enhanced that glow.

She breathed slowly, shallowly, as if trying to remain conscious. Every few seconds, she inhaled deeply, though it was all but invisible to anyone but the groom. His never-wavering stare caused her to look again into his gray eyes. They remained unreadable but his resolute gaze confirmed that the

promises they'd made in the past weeks would be upheld—
no matter the consequence.

Seemingly in the distance, Lauren heard the words, "you
may kiss your bride," and felt herself move forward into
Michael's welcoming arms. The kiss was soft, tentative,
nondemanding, yet their lips clung together as if by design.
Lauren was mindful of the presence of both her mother and
father, could almost feel them looking on. She experienced a
small glint of triumph knowing that she'd managed to bring
them back together, if only for the occasion. That fleeting
thought was replaced by a slight rush of desire as she responded to the groom's kiss, despite resolve, despite an audience, despite an unwillingness to do so.

She opened her eyes as their lips parted, hoping there
were no telltale signs of her inner struggle. This day would
be long, much longer than any twenty-four hour period she'd
ever experienced.

Lauren heard the applause of their friends and family and
knew the ceremony was over. More accurately, she knew what
would now begin and wondered if she had the inner strength
to weather all that was sure to come. She'd barely had the
necessary resolve to get through her wedding day. The next
twelve months would be a true test of her faith and beliefs.
Now, she needed to suspend her fear of failure and try to
move forward.

Earlier that day, her usually calm demeanor had disappeared as the realization that today was *the day* had become
a steadfast reality. After showering, Lauren had ordered a
light breakfast that she'd been too nervous to eat. She'd managed to nibble on a hard-boiled egg and drink half a cup of
coffee before heading for the beauty salon. Hair and nails
seemed like a priority at first, although, as each hour passed,
it made the need for such trivial details less crucial.

Luckily, Gloria, Lauren's former roommate and maid of
honor had helped her dress carefully and overseen the hotel's

preparation of the reception. She was the one responsible for coordinating the placement of flowers, double-checking that Lauren had Michael's ring, and generally doing everything in her power to keep her best friend calm. The day before, both women had luxuriated in a facial and a massage, and now, after having undergone several hours of hands-on beauty, Lauren's outward appearance seemed peaceful. But in reality, nothing could alter the feelings she had meticulously hidden from herself, feelings she had shared with no one and which even she had trouble acknowledging.

Each of the guests in attendance had watched in silence as the ceremony progressed to its ultimate conclusion. Duke Hayes, the best man, Michael's business partner and college roommate, whose expression was now strangely unreadable, was ecstatic. Duke had initially doubted his partner's ability to commit to one woman. Ultimately, he'd come to champion the union. Marriage hadn't worked for him, but he definitely looked forward to his partner settling down. Maybe now that the wedding was over, they would be able to focus on their newly formed business alliance with Cityscape Broadcast Network, one of the fastest growing radio networks in the United States. CBN's acquisition of their independent radio station had allowed them to move into markets which now reached the Sun Belt and the Midwest.

Mentally chastising himself for even thinking of business on a day that was clearly a personal triumph for his best friend, Duke forced himself to switch gears. He smoothed his beard and straightened his tie. Glancing at the maid of honor, he smiled slowly. He could get used to looking at Gloria, he mused. He'd felt like that from the first time he'd ever met her. And although he wasn't at all sure of how he was going to make it happen, he was more than one hundred percent confident that he could.

Morgan Pryor stood in Duke's line of vision. He'd managed to remain expressionless throughout the ceremony, but as the bride and groom turned to face their guests, he suddenly smiled. Duke wasn't sure what the sudden change in demeanor meant, but he registered it in his mind, then immediately dismissed it. Now was not the time to focus on anything other than Michael and Lauren's happiness. He could focus on Morgan, their new partner and the Chief Operations Officer of Cityscape Broadcast Network, at some other time.

Duke smiled as he moved forward engaging Michael in a bear hug. "Congratulations. May you be blessed with nothing less than unwavering happiness and the patter of many little feet. Now when do I get to kiss the bride?"

"I guess now is the best time, 'cause after today, keep away from my bride. I don't trust you radio types," Michael said, laughing, as he continued to hold Lauren's hand. Though he could still sense some nervousness on her part, he knew she was glad the ceremony was over with. Michael hadn't had time to be nervous. Knowing how uncertain Lauren was, he was relieved that he'd gotten her to the altar.

"Oh, so now you don't trust me—your best friend since college days and your partner for life. Oh, ye of little faith. Actually, I understand your insecurities, my brother, competition being what it is," Duke countered, smoothly taking Lauren by the shoulders and planting a quick and brotherly kiss on her upturned lips.

"You two are like competitive teenagers," Lauren teased as Michael gathered her in a possessive embrace.

Kissing her softly, he turned her face up to his and shook his head. "Not since college has this guy offered any real competition—and even then he had to pull out all the stops to keep up with me," he quipped. Lauren smiled then, and Michael knew a tightening in his chest that had become familiar to him. The love he felt for her flowed like kinetic energy between them. It never stagnated and continued to move, grow, and change each day. She remained a mystery to him, although he felt he understood her every emotion. He watched her face light up, and turned to see her parents approaching.

"Get your own girl. It's about that time anyway," Michael told Duke then. In the innocence of his statement there was a healthy wish for Duke to know the happiness that he had just secured. He wanted only the best for his partner.

"I'm working on it," Duke offered with a wink. Michael looked at him, shook his head, and laughed.

"If you're thinking along the lines of what I am, please watch your step. The road is extremely rocky and lined with pitfalls, if you get my drift," he said in a cautious tone.

Lauren overheard the exchange and smiled politely. She glanced around the room, found the object of their conversation and wondered if Gloria knew of Duke's interest. Michael had mentioned that he thought Duke had a crush on her from their first meeting. She knew that he would have his work cut out for him if he was seriously considering any attempt to date Gloria. But it was not her place to alert him to that fact. She continued greeting her guests, smiling while she wondered if the marriage that had just taken place was doomed to fail.

Eva and Colin Traynor had been politely waiting to greet the newlywed couple and at that moment, her father walked forward. Salt-and-pepper hair adorned a distinguished carriage that was lean and hard from many years in military service. Standing under the gazebo with his only daughter clad in a beautiful wedding gown, one arm intertwined possessively with her new husband, the scene nearly brought tears to Colin's eyes. Even with his ex-wife standing stoically beside him, managing her emotions so well, he found it difficult to keep his response to the day's events under control. In his eyes, Lauren was still his little girl.

Eva moved closer and folded Lauren in her arms, holding her tightly for several seconds as Colin looked on proudly.

Both women were teary-eyed when they parted. Neither spoke, afraid a torrent of emotions and unstoppable tears would overtake them at any moment. "The Colonel," as Lauren's father was often called, cleared his throat, and they turned, including him in the intimacy of the moment. He embraced Lauren and relished in the fact that his baby girl had, in fact, finally grown up. Lauren looked at him, her eyes shining with tears, and he thought he saw true happiness in her face. He held her away from him and scanned her head to toe.

"You look so beautiful. But then you always do. You're my daughter," he added with obvious pride. He reached out to Michael and shook his hand. He almost embraced him, but held back. The realization of just having met the young man who would hold his daughter's future in his hands settled over him heavily.

Lauren and her mother once again embraced as Colin realized just how much both he and his ex-wife had to be thankful for.

"Mom, don't start. If you do, I won't be able to handle it," Lauren whispered in a voice quavering with emotion.

"Honey, weddings make everyone cry. If you have to shed a few tears, don't be ashamed of it. Everyone here loves you tremendously, and a few tears only let us know how much this means to you," her mother added quickly.

Lauren nodded and turned to her dad. She did not trust herself to continue the conversation without doing just the thing she was so desperately trying to avoid. Although she hadn't seen the Colonel in over a year, he still looked exactly as she remembered.

Tall, trim, and commanding, he'd flown in from Colorado on a military hopper that morning. His uniform fit him perfectly, the distinct lines emphasizing his flawless physique. He held the regulation hat in one hand, sometimes switching it to the other as nervousness seemed to overtake him in waves. His duties on the base in Denver were minimal but complex. And although he was certainly eligible for retirement, that did not seem a viable option to him now, or at any time in the very near future. Colin Traynor intended to remain a military man for all of his days. He loved the regimen, the discipline, the organization. He most certainly loved his country. But above all, he loved his daughter who now stood before him shrouded in white, looking more beautiful than he'd ever seen her. And he remembered, in that moment, that she had been extremely beautiful to him when he'd held her in his arms some twenty-eight years earlier.

"Lauren, sweetheart, are you okay?" The question was asked quietly and her answer would mean everything to him. He'd done a lot he was not proud of and he'd unintentionally hurt her in many ways. Still he'd always wanted happiness for her. The divorce had hurt her immensely and for that, Colin had been sorry. But he'd also known that Lauren's strength would allow her to handle the disappointment of her parents' broken marriage. Now, staring into her almond-shaped eyes, the lashes beaded with the tears she was trying to keep from falling, the realization of just how much he'd missed her laughter and her smile hit him squarely in the chest.

He blew a sigh of relief when she nodded her answer. "Baby girl, you've grown into a woman," he exclaimed as he folded her into his arms. Lauren was overcome by a surge of emotion again. This was her father, whom she loved and respected. She remembered the many military ceremonies they'd attended during which he'd received each and every one of the medals he now wore proudly. Both she and her mother had witnessed his acceptance of them, knowing the heightened responsibility they carried, as well as the commitment and performance they represented. She couldn't remember feeling more proud of him, more connected, than at those times.

Michael watched the interplay between father and daughter, saw the resemblance, and knew he wanted to get to know Colin Traynor better.

"You must be a very persuasive young man to have won my daughter's heart. I congratulate you wholeheartedly," Colin said, realizing then that Michael was watching him intently. He meant the words he'd spoken, remembering that Lauren had kept her distance from the opposite sex for a long time. He never remembered her dating in high school or college, and wondered when she'd finally come into her own. In looking at Michael, he noticed a self-assuredness and confidence that told him more than words ever could. He saw a young man who could take care of himself and, hopefully, a wife too.

Michael watched his bride's father struggle with the transition, knowing that whatever he said in the next moments could quite possibly make all the difference in his relationship with the colonel. "Yes, sir, it took a lot for me to convince her that nothing she said or did would alter our future together. She's about as stubborn as some of the Midwesterners I went to school with," he added, a grin spreading across his face. "But you know, the challenges she presented only made me come to love her more. I realized she was a prize the first time I saw her handle herself on a coast-to-coast flight," he added.

"Oh, you two met in transit, much like her mother and myself. Only I was being sent overseas with the military and her mother was a student at the Parsons School of Design in New York City. We bumped into each other on a Manhattan street. It felt a little like I'd been hit by lightning," Lauren's father described, the memory bringing a smile to his face.

"Lightning, that's a good description. I think it was more like a bolt of cynicism when I met Lauren, sir. She berated me for being a pain in the neck, kindly told me to take my seat, and then ignored me all the way across the country.

Three thousand miles of torture, but I never took my eyes off her," he admitted candidly, while his bride stared at him. Lauren blushed then, knowing that Michael was doing his best to make fast friends with two of the most important people in her life. He'd charmed his way into her heart and was doing a great job of it with her parents.

"Call me Colonel. Everyone else does," Colin said.

"Colonel it is. . . . By the way, I'd like you both to meet my dad, Sergeant Townsend. He's also signed up for active duty, only it's with the New York City Police Department. He's been there so long, they probably wouldn't know what to do without him," Michael added as his father approached. The two men shook hands briefly, realizing that they were now part of an extended family by virtue of the union which had just taken place. Michael stepped aside, and his father kissed his new daughter-in-law quickly on both cheeks.

Lauren looked into the face of a man who looked exactly like her husband except for the smattering of gray at the temples.

"Michael told me you were beautiful, but I figured he was prone to exaggeration. If anything, he didn't do you justice. You are gorgeous, Lauren," Walter added, memories of his late wife, Maria, suddenly filtering through his mind. "Welcome to the Townsend family. We're not a large clan, but we do honor our women."

The young woman who had just become his daughter-in-law was breathtaking. Tall and slender with auburn hair streaked with golden highlights and stunning almond-shaped eyes that were amber in color. He could immediately see how his son had fallen in love. She had to be intelligent too. Michael never dated girls without brains. But he sensed there was even more to her as she focused her full attention on her new father-in-law's face.

"Well, thank you, Mr. Townsend. Your son has your good looks and maybe a little of your charm too," she added. Her smile was genuine. She recognized that her father-in-law was a powerful man within the ranks of one of the most well-run, yet challenging, police departments in the entire country. Lauren looked at her husband and father-in-law, comparing the similarities between the two men and recognized they were both exceedingly attractive.

Michael's gray eyes conveyed an unmistakable message. One that Lauren returned without a blink. Her pulse quickened and a healthy glow moved its way up her body. To the other guests, she represented the quintessential "blushing bride." Only Michael recognized that she had responded to his unspoken communication.

He silently calculated how much longer they would have before they would be alone, and realized that even minutes would be too long. He wanted her *now,* wanted to feel her within his arms, responding to his kisses with his ring on her hand. They'd both agreed to postpone lovemaking in the two months prior to their wedding day. It had been a difficult decision for him to make, but he'd done it knowing that the remainder of their lives would be filled with passion, a lifetime of lovemaking. That and only that had convinced him to agree to the eight weeks of celibacy they'd recently endured. It had been torture, but tonight would be the end of that. He smiled at the thought.

"Okay, folks. We're going to let the bride and groom take some photographs while we begin the cocktail hour. If you'll just come this way," Gloria announced as she ushered the guests into the intimate room reserved for the reception and dinner. Tall white calla lilies in crystal vases had been placed in the middle of each table, with circular wreaths of baby's breath surrounding each arrangement. Pale yellow linen tablecloths with satin napkins crowned the middle of each table setting. The room overlooked the ocean with a clean sweep of glass forming one entire wall. Several potted palm trees stood near a sitting area with plush white sofas, and a grand piano. A three-piece combo played softly as hors d'oeuvres were served and champagne was distributed to each table.

Later, when photographs of the groom's father, the bride's parents, the maid of honor and best man had been taken, dinner was served in four courses: a rich, she-crab bisque, asparagus almondine with smoked salmon, then a main course of lobster tails fra diavolo serve with grilled summer vegetables and finally, the wedding cake filled the guests' stomachs. Then, the newlywed couple danced several times with the wedding attendees joining them on the dance floor as the night wore on.

Lauren couldn't remember when she'd been more fatigued, but she was also extremely excited. Becoming Mrs. Michael Townsend had meant more to her than she wanted to admit. The groom had made it exceeding clear that he was more than happy to be legally bound to her, and that was all that mattered. Michael's vows to love and cherish her for the rest of her days promised to play themselves over and over in her head as she got ready to throw the bouquet.

Lauren took a last furtive look over one shoulder, spotted her mother and her best friend, noted their positions, and let it fly.

"Oh my goodness, Lauren, honey, you must have done that on purpose. I definitely should not have caught this," Gloria said quickly as she looked frantically around in search of another person to hand the delicately bound yellow and white bouquet of roses off to. As she nervously passed the arrangement from one hand to the other, Eva Traynor congratulated her and kissed her on the cheek.

"I am so glad that Lauren didn't throw it in my direction. The first marriage is charming, and all others may very well be overkill," she added, her voice lowered so that her ex-husband did not overhear. At the moment, he was engaged in conversation with Morgan Pryor, discussing the nation's current policy on the Middle East. It was a topic no one else at the table had any interest in.

"Mrs. Traynor, in all honesty, I have to tell you that I will never marry. My dad recently passed away, but before his death I constantly did battle with him. Trying to carve out an independent existence when you're the daughter of someone like Gino Sorrentino is not easy. My big brother, Morgan, saw to it that I was never far out of either of their sights. A husband spells a repeat of that kind of monitoring, in my mind. So no thanks, thank you very much." Gloria took a long drink of champagne and smiled demurely, hoping her best friend's mother would not judge her unkindly because of her unique stand.

Truth be told, Gloria liked men, loved the idea and feel of being around them, and longed for a relationship that she could feel comfortable in. The problem was that anyone in her immediate circle was usually intimidated by the past history of the Sorrentino family. Knowing that she was the daughter of a deceased "wise guy" who had reportedly been one of the most powerful men on the East Coast didn't really assist her in getting dates. And Morgan still did everything in his power to keep an eye on her, though he did his best to remain inconspicuous.

"You say that now, but let me tell you something," Eva said, leaning in closer to Gloria. "Lauren had her beliefs about marriage too. Looks like it's one down and one more to go." Her smile did little to detract from the look of a mother who knew more than she was willing to admit. There was something about the declaration Gloria had just issued that simply didn't fly.

"I'm really happy for Lauren. She's with one of the nicest guys I've ever met. Every now and again, I date, but I do my best to keep my private life just that: private," she whispered, mindful of her brother's presence at the very next table.

Unbeknownst to Gloria, her every move, her exact emotions, and her posture were being observed. While she defended her anti-marriage stance to her best friend's mother, Duke watched her, unable to focus on anything or anyone else in the room.

He'd held his breath while the wedding party photos had been taken earlier, wondering if Gloria could feel the hammering in his chest as she stood beside him. He'd wanted to say something but nothing seemed appropriate. There were too many complications. He couldn't bring himself to say anything that was meaningful so he remained silent, all the while thinking she looked more beautiful than anyone in the room. Her maid of honor gown was a mixture of pale yellow satin trimmed with a sheer netting of yellow chiffon. Tea length, its spaghetti straps and square neckline emphasized her tiny waist, and the color only enhanced the rich darkness of her hair and brown eyes.

Duke swallowed the last of his drink and turned to watch Michael and Lauren lift their glasses in toast. Champagne was poured and each of the guests lifted the crystal flutes in tribute.

"To my bride and to an eternity filled with love," Michael offered, kissing Lauren quickly on the lips.

"Here, here," was chanted throughout the intimate room as each guest drank to the couple's happiness.

Duke stood gallantly and indicated his intent to toast, as another round of bubbly was poured into each flute.

"As the best man, I'd like to offer a special toast. . . . To Michael and Lauren, may you always have love in your hearts, laughter in your voices and one another on your minds." Applause, laughter and the clinking of glasses could be heard as Duke made his way around the room. His final destination was the table where Gloria sat. She was seated beside Morgan. Duke knew he was breaking every rule that he'd set up from the first time he'd laid eyes on her.

Before he reached her, he stopped by the table of the bride

and groom, who were seated at an oblong table facing their small number of guests.

Michael hugged him then clapped him on the back heartily.

"Man, you're the best," Duke said, meaning it and wanting Michael to know that. He then kissed Lauren's hand and bowed slightly. "And you're his queen. I didn't ever think I'd see this day, but now that it's come, I am really happy for you both. You each have something special that the other not only complements, but actually duplicates too."

"Thanks, man," Michael said. "I appreciate that and your friendship. You know how much we've been through since we started WJZZ."

"It's been a long time, Mikey. The ride has been a good one. I've never regretted our partnership and I know you feel the same way. I just wanted to wish you and your bride happiness. You're both exceptional people," Duke added.

"I know you want the best for me. That's what I've got too: the best," Michael said, glancing at Lauren, who was showing her father her rings. Turning back to Duke, he continued, "Okay, now you can sit down before we both get any more mushy." There was laughter in his voice but a serious look on his face.

Duke smiled and made his way across the room, finally coming to Gloria's table, where he raised his glass and then touched hers ever so slightly. Gloria was surprised, but managed to conceal it. Instead, she smiled and raised her glass even higher.

Morgan looked on in silence but took note. He'd brought his new assistant along just for the heck of it, and wondered if Noelle realized she was watching history unfold. Duke clasped Morgan's hand, and the two men acknowledged one another much the same way they would at any business meeting. There was no easy exchange, no friendly banter, and Duke sensed that Morgan would be a hurdle to overcome. He swallowed the last of his drink and made a decision.

The bride and groom prepared to leave the reception as cake was distributed and wedding favors were discovered in small ribbon-clad boxes. Sterling silver picture frames, with "Michael and Lauren Townsend" engraved across the bottom of each, created a cherished keepsake.

Lauren watched as the guests opened their takeaway gifts as the memory of a conversation she and Michael had long ago replayed itself in her mind. *Look, I know I love you and I suspect you feel the same way too,* he'd said. *You're just too stubborn to admit it. With what we just went through together, we both deserve a chance to find out if what we have is real. Just trust me, Lauren. If it's not working, we'll go our separate ways and never look back. If not, we'll be together."*

She'd watched him closely, looking for any sign of insincerity or humor, but had seen none. His gray eyes were locked onto hers and Lauren knew in that moment that whatever happened, he was prepared to gamble it all on their future together. And so, she'd agreed to a marriage, with a time line—after twelve months, they could part with no questions asked if either of them was in anyway dissatisfied.

It seemed they'd just completed day one of 365.

Chapter Two

Michael watched as Lauren removed the pearl-encrusted headband, her hair tumbling about her face. He remained silent, suddenly overcome with too many thoughts and not enough words. She looked enticing, which only increased his desire. But he hesitated, knowing that he had, in fact, almost bullied her into the ceremony. Theirs was a marriage born of true circumstance, as desperate times called for desperate measures. He'd done all he could to convince Lauren that it was the right thing to do, and at the eleventh hour, she'd agreed. They would be married, they would cohabitate, but there was a contingency plan in place. He watched and waited while his bride of only six hours moved toward the master bathroom. Lauren reached behind her, struggling to remove her gown. He hesitated for a microsecond, crossed the room and gently lowered the zipper. The effort required to mask the naked hunger on his face was monumental. He wanted her; he'd always wanted her. After enduring a day filled with happiness and good wishes from their most treasured friends and their closest loved ones, his first reaction to his new bride was an unexpected one for him. Behind closed doors with the woman he'd exchanged vows with only hours earlier, he found he simply wanted to take her in his arms and allow the impact of the day's events to sink in.

Michael literally breathed a huge sigh of relief—relief that the wedding was over, but more importantly, that it had finally happened.

Lauren was a hard case. Her ability to be pigheaded often presented a major barricade. Michael knew that. But he also knew she loved him. Now all he had to do was convince her that it would last a lifetime. The chemistry they shared remainend alive. Often, Michael was almost certain that the woman in his arms had as little control over her body as he had over her mind. Their lovemaking had always been passionate and mutually pleasing.

Despite everything they'd been through, all they'd shared, Lauren had been prepared to walk away from it just to avoid the emotional challenge it represented. Her reverence of her parents' marriage and complete devastation over their divorce had landed a crushing blow to her ability to believe in everlasting love. She'd grieved silently and deeply for what had been lost in the decomposition of their union. Even her mother's reassurance and adjustment to life without a husband, who seemed to prefer military life to the standard nuclear family, had not truly convinced her. Michael realized that he had to somehow show her that theirs was not a prototype for disaster. If he could do that, their mutual happiness would have a solid chance, he reasoned.

Michael remembered the first time he'd seen Lauren. She'd held his heart hostage ever since. He'd watched her walk down the aisle of a Boeing 727 after blowing him off with the grace and charm that still remained intact. Then she had calmly instructed him to take a seat, and proceeded to do her job handling the other two hundred or so passengers on board flight 234 en route from New York to Los Angeles.

His thoughts shifted as he now watched the gown slip from her hands and fall in a pool of gathered silk at her feet. His intake of breath was inaudible, only his ears and his inner soul realized how loudly he breathed, how fast his heart beat inside his chest. The familiar scent of her fragrance reached his nostrils and he knew why men were often called dogs. He felt he could recognize her anywhere, and it always affected him the same way. He responded to her on all levels: mentally, physically, and emotionally.

He wanted tonight to be more than special; he wanted it to be memorable. He knew that he'd made an irrevocable promise. To pledge that their marriage would be perfect and without any strain for a year had been foolish. He had no doubts about his promise to love her for a lifetime. The coming months would be difficult enough without having to live up to something which no man in his right mind would even entertain. If he were to reveal even the most minute detail of their agreement to any one of their friends or relatives, they could both be signed into the nearest mental institution.

During their first long weekend stay in Barbados, Lauren had told him she was pregnant. As soon as he found out, Michael insisted she move in with him right away. Lauren, unable to hold down food and even water at times, weakly resisted him. The pregnancy made work difficult so she reluctantly took a short leave of absence from her job as a senior flight attendant at Worldwide Airlines. She hoped that in another month or so, she would be able to return, if only for a little while.

Looking back, Michael realized he cherished those months. Although Lauren usually spent a small portion of the day not feeling well, by the time he arrived home from work, she'd been able to get the nausea under control. They'd leave the house, dine at a restaurant in the area or see a movie, and spend the remainder of the evening enjoying one another's company. If she was really feeling well, Lauren would prepare dinner and they'd spend the evening exchanging ideas and listening to Michael's extensive jazz collection.

They were two people committed to making things work, although one of them was more optimistic than the other.

Lauren believed that Michael loved her, she just didn't believe that love would last forever. Even so, Michael's persistence that it would prevailed for the time being. After Michael convinced her to get married and they'd made their special pact, the wedding was scheduled for only two months later. It would be intimate, with only their closest relatives and friends in attendance.

Michael suggested they fly back to Barbados. It had been the birthplace of the late Maria Townsend, his mother, and where their unborn child had been acknowledged. Though the family had a home there, he insisted the entire wedding and honeymoon should take place at one of the island's most stunning resorts so that their guests would enjoy the elegance and intimacy of a world-class property.

Some forty-eight hours after their plans had been made, Michael and Lauren were both jarred by the events which occurred. Lauren's moans had awakened him during the night, instantly alerting him something was wrong. Some nine hours later, Michael came to know the true meaning of heartbreak. The child Lauren had been carrying was no more. That event sealed even more solidly his determination to bind her to him. Lauren emerged with a slightly different perspective. She fully expected that with the end of the unplanned pregnancy, the need for the hastily planned wedding would no longer exist.

Surprising Lauren, he insisted they go through with the original plans. Day by day, she was worn down with his insistence. Thoughts of guilt and non-deservance plagued her. She began to show signs of her inner turmoil and looked haunted, developing dark circles under her eyes which showed clearly through her honey-colored skin. Michael's initial worries turned into steely determination as he watched her wrestle with demons he was unable to help her conquer. They continued to haunt her even up until their wedding day, and Michael wondered how far back in the recesses of her mind the memory of the child they'd lost really was as she stood before him, her beauty irresistible.

There had been many nights that she sobbed herself to sleep as he held her in his arms. He suffered as well, but recognized that Lauren's experience was understandably more devastating. He held his own emotions in check, never revealing how deeply the miscarriage affected him. They nursed each other through that time, with Michael being the support that Lauren needed and her needs shielding him from facing his own reaction to the loss.

"Why do you continue to blame yourself, Lauren?" he asked softly one day as they were sitting in the den/music room. Michael watched Lauren's face closely as strains of smooth jazz played in the background.

"I guess it's because the pregnancy was unplanned. The fact that you wanted me to live here with you and you kept badgering me about marriage and you know my feelings about that." Her voice trailed off. "I was so confused all the time. I keep wondering if my feelings of ambivalence contributed? I don't know, maybe my thoughts somehow caused the miscarriage."

"Lauren, honey, that's ridiculous. Stop punishing yourself for this. We'll have plenty of other times to start our family. I promise you that," he stated emphatically.

Michael's enthusiasm about marriage and starting a family was contagious, and eventually Lauren found herself responding positively, even as the painful memories of her lost child and parents' divorce still resided in her mind. She knew he believed what he'd said. She also knew he'd been deeply affected by the events, but had handled it stoically for her sake.

He had thrown himself into his work at Cityscape Broadcast Network, committing himself to conquering his latest business challenges. In his mind, the miscarriage was certainly regrettable but not the end of the story. He was determined to make Lauren Mrs. Michael Townsend regardless of the loss of their child. Each time he pledged his loyalty to her, the decision surprised and unnerved Lauren.

"Michael, are you sure?" she responded one time. "Think about it, and please know that if you want to cancel, I understand. Emotionally, we both have a lot on our plates right now," she added, her brow furrowed. They had just finished dinner and were having a cup of coffee in the den, the fireplace crackling as each log burned intensely, giving off a wealth of heat.

"Lauren, there's nothing to think about. Right now, after what we just went through, there's no discussion I need to have, other than to iron out the details of our wedding plans. I know you're still grieving and so am I. I don't know and I can't explain it," he said ernestly. "But I do know one thing. You are the woman I want to spend the rest of my life with. It had nothing to do with the pregnancy—that only put my plans on a fast track. I love you."

Lauren looked at him then and her eyes filled with tears. "Yes, yes," she whispered as she moved toward him.

They embraced for a long while, each filled with thoughts of what they'd just been through, some memories too painful to share, too deeply ingrained to describe.

"So, you'll go through with it. Say yes, Lauren. I know you want to and I do too," he said as he kissed her lips softly, wiping the tears from her cheeks with the tips of his fingers.

Lauren looked down, trying to get a handle on her emotions, then looked directly into his eyes. What she saw there filled her with hope, love, and something else: fear. The resounding question that remained within her mind was *What if our love can't last?* Buoyed by Michael's energy, and his love, she buried her insecurities that night and finally agreed to get married after Michael had presented her an easy out if she was unhappy in any way. In the morning, Michael confirmed the reservations he'd made weeks earlier. The wedding would take place as planned.

Now, as Michael finished unzipping the gown, he swallowed in an attempt to quell the rising desire which always enveloped him whenever Lauren was nearby.

"Thanks," she whispered stepping out of the gown and placing it on a chair. "You know, I can't believe we really did it. It feels unreal. When we were standing there talking with our parents, it felt so strange. And I had no idea you and your dad looked so much alike. It's uncanny. Is his job with the police department dangerous?" Lauren realized she was jabbering nervously, but could not help herself. The man standing across the room was now her husband, legally bound, and that simple fact made a tremendous difference.

Lauren's question hung in the air for a few moments while Michael attempted to pull himself together. At the moment, Michael's thoughts were not on his father, the NYPD, or anything even remotely related to either. They were tied up with the swell of Lauren's breasts against the strapless bra she wore. Reluctantly tearing his eyes away, he cleared his throat.

"Dad is a lifer, much the same way I suspect your father is. They're both committed to something that is much larger than they are," he added without conviction. It wasn't that he did not believe what he was saying, it was just that the torture of watching her without touching her was getting to him.

With that statement, Michael walked closer to Lauren. "Much the same way I am committed to you" he uttered, unable to stop himself from taking her into his arms. He reached for her and encircled her waist from behind. Kissing her neck softly, he relished the feel and fit of her. He heard her sigh and knew that she too felt the chemistry that was a constant whenever they were together.

There was no resistance from her, which only fueled the fires already burning within him. He no longer wanted to make small talk. In fact, he didn't want to talk at all as he turned her in his arms and their lips met in a kiss that began as a mixture of passion and resignation.

Lauren's surrender to the marriage was complete. It had come at a high price, but she had no intention of kidding herself about its outcome. They'd had innumerable conversations about what they each thought the union would accomplish, and in the end she'd consented to become his wife with one small caveat. Her efforts to convince Michael their union might fail had been stonewalled each time she'd brought this up, especially after the miscarriage. In fact, it had taken an incredibly glib speech and pure determination for her to convince him to acknowledge it was even a possibility.

He'd once again explained that his marriage proposal had had very little to do with an unplanned pregnancy and more to do with the very real love he felt for her, equating it in some ways to the commitment he had to his work.

"You know how important the station is, especially right now when we're still building the platform to increase our market concentration," he'd argued. The intensity with which he spoke served to convince Lauren of his sincerity. She'd watched him take on the huge task of merging the station he and his partner Duke Hayes had built from a struggling operation with a tiny market share to what now represented almost regional proportions.

When the merger of WJZZ and Cityscape Broadcast Network had taken place, it was a dream come true. With that kind of backing, a change in personality, perspective, and, perhaps, direction was also a possibility. It had also given Michael new adrenaline to solidify his personal life, now that he'd accomplished one of his biggest professional goals. He'd encouraged Lauren to spend more time at his Upper West Side brownstone after the merger, often claiming that he couldn't sleep well unless she was at his side.

Now, as he held her in his arms, Michael realized he had just a year to convince her that his love was unbreakable, would withstand any challenge. He intended to do everything in his power to strengthen the relationship so that there were no second thoughts, misgivings, or other roads that could possibly lead to her trying to enforce even the slightest degree of separation when the twelve months were complete.

With these thoughts in his mind, their kiss deepened as passion overcame them. Michael's hands touched Lauren in places that elicited soft sighs. Her response was all he needed to give him further encouragement, and when they broke apart, each was breathing rapidly. A peach-colored flush crept its way toward Lauren's face and she looked at Michael with a defiant pout.

"You definitely do not play fair," Lauren said, her voice uneven with passion and exasperation at her inability to resist her husband's attention. She struggled with the desire his kisses evoked and the control she felt was necessary to keep in place. Although this was their wedding night, Lauren was still not one hundred percent sure of her decision to marry. She felt she needed more time, a moment to catch her breath. The day had passed so quickly, she hadn't made the mental adjustment from lover to wife, and felt as if she'd missed a step. She looked at Michael, an unspoken plea in her eyes for understanding.

Michael placed a crooked smile on his face, and took a step backward. "You're right. But don't forget that I am caught up in the same trap. You're irresistible, but you're absolutely in charge." He smiled sadly, turned and walked toward the living room of the suite. "I need a drink. A real one, not champagne or that other bubbly, pretentious stuff," he added, heading for the bar which had been stocked with every imaginable spirit known to man.

Lauren knew regret then, and sadness too. There was no place she'd rather be than in his arms, but her own inner demons stopped her from telling him that. Her love for Michael was something she struggled daily to control. She feared it would be her undoing. That was what she told herself on good days. On bad ones, she acknowledged that she was already in a world of trouble. Her attempt to rein in her feelings, to deny her response to Michael and gain a true hold on the pace and depth of the relationship, had been railroaded long before her wedding night.

Lauren began removing her makeup, the realization that she had married a man she had come to care about despite her reservations about love, staring back at her in the mirror. She felt she had one last chance to avoid the pitfall so many women fell into. Even her own mother had succumbed to the tragedy that awaited any female who was unwary of life's most unfair challenge.

She felt she knew firsthand the sorrow and the pain, even if it was through her mother's eyes that she'd experienced it. At a very young age, she'd learned the lesson and she had no desire to repeat what she'd seen her mother go through. At sixteen years old, she'd acknowledged that everlasting love, the one thing every human being on the planet searches for relentlessly, sometimes even to their own doom and detriment, was simply not a reality.

Lauren did not believe in lasting love. So she vowed to keep her life from being ruined by the intrusion of an elusive, if not nonexistent, phenomenon. Sure, she reasoned, one could experience euphoric infatuation, earth-shattering sex, and once in a great while, fabulous compatibility. But in all honesty, she did not believe that any one of those things could coexist in the same relationship simultaneously for any length of time. And that was the problem. Lauren refused to allow her life to unfold based on something which was unobtainable—especially when it could very well involve bringing children into the world who would also experience the devastation that a broken home would foster.

In the same way she'd experienced pain and disappointment when her parents had thrown in the towel on a marriage that spanned more than fifteen years, it was her goal to avoid that kind of unbearable heartache. Seeing them together at the ceremony had brought a fresh set of tears to her eyes. Lauren wondered now what each was doing at that very moment. She hoped, in spite of their differences and their divorce, that they were at least able to enjoy their stay on the island. She could not imagine that they'd travel this far and then not even communicate.

The rich timbre of Michael's voice interrupted her thoughts. It was their wedding night, she remembered suddenly. Sleeping in the same bed with Michael would be difficult, especially when she was trying to keep her feelings for him from overwhelming her. She ruefully acknowledged that her body had a mind of its own when she was in his presence. Their first date had been her undoing.

Prior to that, Lauren had wanted nothing to do with Michael—or any other man for that matter. She'd made up her mind that dating would be something she just would not do, especially not passengers. It was sometimes difficult to turn down the daily offers she received as she went about her duties as a senior flight attendant. But she stuck to her guns for the most part. It wasn't until she'd looked into a pair of stormy gray eyes, watched their owner walk away from her, and felt the blood racing through her body that Lauren had succumbed to her first bout of Michael Townsend. Now, more than a year later, she'd just walked down the aisle and pledged to be his wife.

"Are you coming out of that bathroom, or am I going to

have to come in there?" Michael called to her again from the other side of the room. Lauren laughed, knowing he was probably ready to do just that if necessary.

"I'll be out in just a minute. Anything worth having is worth waiting for," she returned, knowing full well that he was probably pacing the floor.

She continued to undress and then reached into the box that she had placed in the room earlier. The satiny white gown she lowered over head had been a gift from Gloria. Its chiffon skirt flowed from an empire waistline and the satin top was held in place by two satin spaghetti straps. The lace bodice had tiny satin-covered buttons, which she painstakingly fastened. The sheer fabric left little to the imagination while it enhanced her body, its diaphanous folds swirling erotically.

Lauren pulled her hair into a high ponytail, sprayed herself lightly with her favorite perfume, and walked into the master bedroom.

Michael was nowhere in sight.

Chapter Three

Michael walked the beach, a man in search of himself. If anyone had told him more than eighteen months before that he would have responded to any female on the planet like he'd responded to Lauren, he would have laughed. But the reality was that love had found him and taken him to task. Instinct told him that perhaps it was justice. He'd certainly caused enough heartache and anxiety in numerous females long before he met Lauren. The question that kept his mind racing was why and when did I change my attitude, my goals, my mission? He wasn't sure if he was seeking an answer, or if the mere examination would be enough, so he continued to walk, aimlessly.

Michael found it hard to believe that on this night of all nights, barefooted and with the neck of his tuxedo shirt open to the ocean air, hands in his pockets, he would still be attempting to solve the mystery of the woman who was now his wife. He wondered if she was worried, or if she had even noticed that he'd left the suite. Out of nowhere, he found himself picturing Lauren as she became frantic upon noticing his absence. The mental image brought an unexpected smile to his lips, and he chuckled softly. Then he refocused and realized that perhaps he was being unjustifiably cruel, a thought which surprised him. He knew his thoughts could not be a sign of something good to come. The ink was barely dry on the marriage license, and they were already encountering a major hurdle: Lauren, he thought, did not want to consumate the marriage.

Michael knew if he pushed the issue, he would win. But that was just it: he didn't want to have to convince his own wife to make love with him. Hell, he wanted her to initiate things, much like she'd done before everything had changed. But then, he realized that Lauren had always fought with herself over all aspects of their relationship, and that tonight's development was nothing beyond the norm for her. *So why did I insist on this marriage?* he asked himself repeatedly, but no answer was forthcoming.

The swell of the ocean seemed to mirror his inner turmoil. He watched the waves crash against the shore as he thought. The realization that only time would heal the wounds from which his bride suffered came to him, and he silently vowed to wait for that to happen. If that was what it would take to deliver her to him one hundred percent, then so be it. He also vowed to put in the time, the energy, and the patience to see her through whatever it would take to produce a whole, healthy and happy union.

As he thought through these things, he noticed his surroundings, acknowledging that he was indeed in the midst of nature's bounty. Through the pounding of the surf against the rocks, Michael noted that many were worn away at the specific spot where the powerful ocean surf made contact with the shoreline. The natural occurrence suggested many things to him, and as he stood, watching a timeless routine take place, a new understanding suddenly occurred to him. *Just as the rock is worn away by the pounding of the surf, so would be the heart of a human being.* It sounded like he'd heard it phrased that way in the past, and it made him want to discover the brilliant mind who had supplied those exact words. He had quite possibly come up with the antidote to his problem. He also realized that it was time to face reality.

Michael walked into the darkened suite, his heart thudding in his chest. His disappointment was genuine as he realized that Lauren had not waited for his return. He held his anger in check, telling himself she was understandably tired from all the preparation of the day's events and quite possibly exhausted. But the feelings of uneasiness still nagged him and he undressed quickly, took a shower and silently slipped beneath the sheets.

Lauren was asleep, but felt the movement of the king-sized bed and awoke immediately. She lifted her head and smiled sleepily.

"You're back—I got a little worried you know," she said, instinctively moving closer to the warmth of his body. Michael groaned inwardly, uncertain of what his next move should be. He wanted to take her in his arms. He wanted to make love to her and let her know there was nothing to worry about. His need to exhibit the emotions that had been straining to be released throughout the day almost overwhelmed him, yet he held back. His interest in the long-term effects of their union overrode the immediacy of anything that he could now think of. He wanted the future, not just a moment in time.

Lauren sleepily wondered why he'd left the room earlier, worried if it was the first sign theirs was a marriage doomed to fail. She already thought it was, but didn't expect to be proven right on her wedding night. With that thought, an overall sadness filled her. Suddenly she noticed the smell of Michael's aftershave and found herself suddenly more than a little awake. Throwing one arm across his body, she lay her head on his chest. She could hear the steady beat of his heart, and wondered if he knew just how difficult it had been to do without the feel of him these past two months. She breathed in the scent of the man whom she'd slept with every night, whom she'd wanted to make love to for all sixty of those nights, had wanted to be in his arms for every moment she was in his presence.

"Where were you, anyway?" she asked quietly. He remained silent, and with each additional moment, Lauren felt an eternity pass as she waited for his answer.

Michael's mind was racing, his every nerve on edge with the restraint he was exhibiting. Somehow, through teeth that strained to let out a scream, he answered slowly, "I went for a walk on the beach. You should have seen the moonlight, it was beautiful."

"I thought you might have decided that the marriage was not going to be worth it," she answered, hugging his body beneath the sheets. She longed for him to deny her words. To tell her she was wrong.

At that moment, his every nerve tightened and Michael knew the true meaning of torment. Why was she still unconvinced of how much he needed her, how thoroughly he wanted her, and just how much she too needed him.

His silence was so loud. "Is it possible that we've made a terrible mistake?" he heard her ask, her voice filled with concern as she quickly sat up and turned on the bedside lamp.

Light flooded the bedroom, filtering softly through the sheer negligee that Lauren wore. Michael's eyes feasted on the beauty displayed before him and he knew an even greater agony. He forced himself to turn away, ashamed of his inability to tolerate looking at his own wife, but knowing he was most certainly reaching his limitations. She had to come to him.

"Of course it's not a mistake, Lauren, we love each

other," he said sincerely. "Look, let's just get some sleep," he said, closing his eyes, though the vision of her had already burned itself into his imagination. He didn't know what to do, wasn't sure that he would be able to sleep next to Lauren in the condition he was in. The one thing he knew for sure was that he would never be immune to the woman at his side, would most certainly never be able to ignore her.

Lauren turned out the light, slipped back beneath the sheets and wondered what she'd done wrong. Why had he left her alone on their wedding night? Was he having second thoughts too?

With his back turned to her, Michael wondered if he had figured all the angles wrong. Will this marriage work, he wondered. He shook the doubts from his mind. He was determined to make it work.

He heard a noise and listened intently. When he heard the sound a second time, he recognized it. Lauren was crying softly.

"Honey, what is it?" he asked, as he reached and drew her into his arms.

"It's nothing, it's everything, it's silly," she sputtered as she buried her wet face in his chest. Michael reached over, gathered a few tissues, and offered them to Lauren. She wiped her eyes, looked up at him, and felt an instant rush of emotion.

"I am so sorry I fell asleep. It's just that I was so tired and I'd been nervous all day. I laid down to wait for you and before I knew it, I woke up, and you were back already," she explained quickly.

"Don't worry about that. I'm enjoying your being awake now, even though you are drenching me," he said, laughter just beneath the surface of his statement.

"I'm sorry. It's just that everything seems so uncertain. I know I agreed to the plan we discussed, but now I don't feel so sure." Her voice trailed off with unspoken words and undeclared thoughts.

"You shouldn't worry about any of that tonight, Lauren. This is our wedding night, and regardless of what happens this week, this month, or several months down the line, we can make things up as we go along. I want to be the best husband you could hope for. And I want you to be my best wife, my only wife," he added quickly.

"Michael, I know you're right, only please give me some time to convince myself. I don't know if we've made the right choice."

He listened to the words coming out of her mouth and wondered if she realized that even as she spoke, her body belied her excuses. The tips of her breasts rose with each breath she took, and Michael knew from past experience that she was physically excited. He looked into her eyes and saw desire mixed with hesitancy. He knew that it would take time to secure the trust, the faith, and the commitment which he felt their union deserved.

Lauren was responding to Michael despite her resolve. Her feelings for him were confusing and disturbing, placing her in a quandary that seemed unsolvable. Michael's face was almost unreadable in the moonlight as the sound of crashing waves meeting the shoreline created a natural melody in the background. Lauren sensed that he was totally in tune with her, which only exacerbated the feelings she so desperately wanted to suppress.

Unable to stop herself, Lauren kissed him then, her lips warm and incredibly soft. He remembered the first time he'd ever kissed her, and all resolve to be rational, left him. He pulled her to him tightly, crushing her breasts flat against his chest as the softness of the sheer fabric she wore accentuated the feel of her against him. Michael groaned and began to slowly explore the planes of her face. He wanted to remember each moment of this night, every nuance of her body, and planned to take his time in an effort to savor each and every second of the hours going forward.

Lauren sighed softly as his hands wound their way down her shoulders, tracing the fine definition of her clavicle before finding her breasts. Michael's touch elicited an excitement that took her breath away. Each time he reached another sensitive spot, Lauren gasped in pure pleasure. She held onto him almost as an anchor in a storm; the desire that raged between them, sweeping each into a maelstrom of current, as Michael took his time relishing the feel of her within his arms. He feasted on each area of Lauren's body, so that when he moved on to the next, there was no question as to his thoroughness.

Michael continued his exploration, placing soft kisses from her neckline to the top of the sheer gown she wore. Slowly he began to pull down the spaghetti straps, revealing an expanse of smooth skin. A course of pure pleasure filled her body, and she felt herself preparing for him even as she marveled at her response.

"Do you want me to take this off?" she asked shyly. Michael shook his head and looked her straight in the eye.

"Not really. I think it's more interesting with it on actually," he answered with a devilish glint in his gray eyes. He laughed then, and Lauren did too.

Michael lowered his head to kiss her again. The heat between them reached scorching temperatures, the earlier tension dissolved by the passion that had taken its place.

Michael continued his exploration of Lauren's heat-filled form, placing kisses anywhere exposed skin was present, removing the sheer fabric from her as he explored every nuance.

Lauren sighed as she reached out one hand, pulling herself up and over Michael's body. He succumbed to her domination gladly, smiling to himself as he realized that he'd once again underestimated her. He shouldn't have assumed she was holding back from him so quickly. He chastised himself as he recalled that though they still had many issues to overcome, their mutual desire for lovemaking was not one of them.

Planting several soft kisses along his jaw, Lauren made a trail with her lips from his face to his neck, soft, tiny kisses punctuating the journey. Michael groaned in pleasure and Lauren knew that he too experienced an inordinate amount of pleasure when making love with her. The chemistry between them existed whether they wanted to acknowledge it or not. Her body knew what her mind would not accept.

Emboldened by his response, she placed both hands on his chest and lowered herself onto him. Michael closed his eyes, his hands cupping her rear end gently. Lauren felt powerful, in control, and extremely sexy. She wanted the night to last forever, wanted their lovemaking to last an eternity, and truly hoped that their marriage would survive. At the moment, that issue seemed very, very far away. His arms, his hands, his lips were very much in the present.

Michael could only entertain one thought as his wife rose above him—bringing him to ecstasy with each movement of her hips. It was how he could prolong the miracle of having her there in his arms, in his bed, in his life. He would do everything in his power to make the marriage work. And although they had lost their first child, the tragedy had brought them together even more solidly. Sure, he'd had to cajole, convince and otherwise calculate to get Lauren to walk down the aisle with him. But, in his mind, the fact that they'd still taken the steps to become man and wife said quite a lot.

Lauren cried out in ecstasy at that moment, and Michael too found the release he'd been holding back. The joy he felt was like a weight being lifted and replaced by the firm pressure of the body of his wife above him. He clenched her to him and realized that for the second time that day, there were tears on his face. This time, he could not be sure if they belonged to him or to Lauren.

Chapter Four

Morgan's decision to take Noelle to the wedding had been a last-minute one. He'd hired her to be his assistant three months earlier, after she'd walked into his office and blown his whole concept of "assistant" to smithereens. Noelle typed at breakneck speed with no errors, cleaned up his stilted grammar without mentioning it, and took notes like she read his mind. However, the thing that had gotten her hired was none of those. Not the typing at ninety words per minute, not the correctly placed commas. In the final analysis, it had been her legs. Dressed in a charcoal gray pinstriped suit with a short, tight skirt, she'd strode into his office and acted like she belonged there. Morgan wasn't quite sure what to make of her, but clearly didn't know how to do without her speed or her accuracy. In a relatively short period of time, she managed to carve a niche for herself. These things surprised and even slightly annoyed him because they also made her irreplaceable.

Noelle also managed to keep the office running without chaos. She was the first to notice if anything was amiss, a true sign of a good assistant, in Morgan's mind. Her tactics

made him think of Janice, his stepfather's first and only secretary, who had given him her two weeks notice just after
Gino's unexpected death. Morgan felt a true sense of loss
when she quit, as his stepfather had brought her on board
with the start of the Sorrentino corporations more than
twenty years earlier. She'd known more about the day-to-day
operations of the business than many of the partners.

Initially, Morgan thought he'd be better off not hiring
someone new, because he didn't trust anyone. It wasn't until
he'd misplaced several crucial documents, overlooked a
meeting that almost cost him a major network decision, and
nearly pissed off the entire board of directors that he made
the decision to hire someone new. An assistant would either
spell clarity and organization, or disaster and exposure.
Morgan gambled as he picked up the phone and made a call.

Noelle Stephenson was the name he got. She'd come with
the highest of recommendations and a stellar resume. Morgan
had been prepared not to like her, probably not to hire her,
and to resort once again to his own tactics. That was before
she'd walked across the room, looked up at him and blinked
coldly through the horn-rimmed glasses she wore.

By the end of the first week, he realized she was more
than competent. By the end of the first day, he knew he
wanted to find out more about her. By the time the invitation
arrived to Michael and Lauren's wedding, they'd gone to
lunch twice. Neither date had been spectacular. In Morgan's
opinion, she was playing hard to get. In Noelle's estimation,
he was a) her boss, b) not her type, and c) probably a felon.

Those factors made it even more annoying when he asked
her to accompany him to the wedding of one of the newest
partners. When Morgan mentioned it would take place in
Barbados, Noelle figured he either really liked her or, at the
very least, was determined to get her into bed. So she turned
him down. But just two days before he was scheduled to
leave, she decided to take the trip.

It was the first sign of real progress the Federal Bureau of Investigation had detected in the investigation they'd recently begun. Noelle Stephenson was in effect a "weapon of mass destruction," which had been unleashed as a last-ditch effort. Cityscape Broadcast Network would either crumble under the weight of undercover scrutiny or emerge like a shiny new penny; it all hinged on the reports scheduled to be filed by one of the department's most effective agents, who happened to be packaged in the body of a female R & B star.

Morgan's confusion over Noelle's change of mind was short-lived. He was glad that for once he'd taken steps to enhance his personal life. However, he did remember that when he'd initially brought the wedding up, her reaction had been more than puzzling.

"I'll have to get back to you on that," was her only response, as if he'd asked her to block out a Friday night for a movie. The following morning, as he dictated notes to be added to the week's upcoming agenda, she looked up, stared intently at him, and swallowed.

"What are your intentions?"

The quietness of her voice in combination with the look on her face told him she was dead serious. No smile, no coy toss of the hair, no slight hesitation in her delivery. Morgan decided the best response would be to ignore her. Though he hated to admit it, he was bitter over her nonchalant attitude to his offer. He continued his dictation and summarily dismissed her. "That's it for now," he said, turning his chair toward the expanse of windows that offered him a panoramic view of Madison Avenue.

"I asked you a question." Her statement hung heavily in the air. She remained standing, obviously waiting for something that Morgan was reluctant or unable to give. He'd expected her to leave, figuring she wasn't ready for what he had in mind anyway. He knew she wouldn't have the guts to admit it, though, and would probably take the easy way out.

"Yeah, you did," he answered, turning toward her abruptly, suddenly becoming more than a little angry. Just who the hell did she think she was anyway, putting him on the spot like that?

"Look, Noelle, you don't have to come—it was simply an invitation. My intentions are to attend the wedding of a business partner, who just happens to be marrying my sister's best friend. Not that any of that is your business. I figured it might be a kick to take a date along. It wasn't a marriage proposal or a signal that you're on your way to becoming my lifelong companion." He delivered the last line with strong emphasis knowing it would probably cause her to either quit or tell him to go to hell, maybe both. He was more angry than he'd been in a long time, and he suddenly wondered why.

"I asked a simple question. You are my boss, and by accepting a date that spans a weekend, I'd just like to get the ground rules on the table so that I know exactly what to expect." She was calm and continued to stand her ground, which unnerved Morgan even more. He wasn't used to people asking questions he wasn't ready to give the answer to. He hadn't really thought about what he wanted from Noelle or from the weekend; her cross-examination forced him to give careful consideration to his true intentions.

All the time she had been taking notes, he'd done his best to keep his mind on the information he needed to include in the correspondence they were working on. Now that it had been completed, he realized he liked her sitting across from him. Even if it was in confrontation.

Noelle smoothed her pants and looked Morgan in the eye. "Thanks for the invitation, but I don't think it would work." She picked up her notepad and ended the conversation. He watched her walk toward the door, unable to look anywhere else. She'd worn pants for the first time that day and although she did things to him in a skirt that he hadn't been prepared for, pants were not a bad thing on Noelle either. She was built—there was no other way to describe it. Five foot nine inches of sinewy muscle, legs that seemed to go on forever and breasts that nicely filled out the gray angora sweater she was wearing, Noelle was a total package. He turned away as she closed the door and admitted two things. One, he really wanted her to accompany him to Michael and Lauren's wedding. And two, for the first time in a long while, he wasn't altogether sure of his intentions.

Some twenty minutes later, the silence in his office was interrupted by the loud buzz of the intercom. It was Noelle. Morgan picked up, knowing she had already moved on to the next tactical position.

"Three days, right?" she asked.

"Three days," Morgan responded in the same emotionless tone, giving none of his true feelings away. Though he did not see it as a game, he knew due to his long-standing business experience and Gino's former training methods that rule number one was "never give yourself away." Not to anyone, under any circumstances.

He clicked off the phone then and found himself smiling as he did so. He knew he'd won.

Chapter Five

Lauren held the phone to her ear, her jaw dropping in disbelief as she listened to her mother recount events that had taken place at the wedding.

"I was actually in shock. All throughout the day, the man I'd lived with for almost three decades flirted shamelessly. It was subtle and not at all apparent to those around us, but more than obvious to me. But instead of feeling flattered, the unexpected attention made me very nervous," her mother explained reluctantly.

Lauren listened quietly, not knowing how to respond to her mother's revelation. The fact that all this had been going on while she and Michael honeymooned during their three days in Barbados was unbelievable to her.

"Mom, go on. I don't know what to say, but please don't clam up now."

"No, I want you to know, because it's important. As the day wore on, I slowly recognized that standing before me was a different version of the man I'd shared my life with so many years before. This was a kindler, gentler Colin Traynor. Surprisingly, the changes were not altogether reassuring."

Lauren continued to listen, finding some of her mother's disclosure uncomfortable, some simply thought-provoking. She wondered if her mother was trying to tell her she had reconciled with her father. She doubted it, but she could always hope, right?

"He paid constant attention to me throughout the ceremony, only leaving my side as he escorted you to the altar, delivering you into the hands of the man who would be our new son-in-law." Eva smiled warmly at the thought.

"Lauren, I thought I would be immune to your father's charm after the divorce had become final. If someone had even hinted that he'd show up years later and affect me in any way, I would have denied it was possible."

Eva's admission was bittersweet. She was grateful that she'd been able to move on in her life, yet looked at the past with some nostalgia, if only for the familiar. She continued, her voice taking on a determined edge.

"On a day when our daughter was taking one gigantic step in the journey to becoming a woman, a wife, and a partner to someone she obviously loved, the immunity I'd built over the years was slowly being neutralized by your father's presence. I have to tell you, Lauren, that I was not at all sure I was ready to forgive or to forget."

"Mom, you don't have to explain anything to me. I understand," Lauren interjected, unable to remain silent any longer. *Where is she going with this*? she wondered.

Eva began speaking in a voice that was barely above a whisper, yet its clarity commanded Lauren's full attention. "You should know why I don't know what to do. I know you never got over our divorce. I know how it affects you to this day. I can't deny there's still a lot of pain when I think about your father and I."

Lauren wasn't in the mood to replay the past. "Mom, can we talk about something else?" she asked.

Eva ignored her and continued her story.

"Colin had initiated the divorce out of the clear blue sky. Just like that, without any warning, he lowered the boom. He phoned from the base, said he would be home early, and showed up some forty-five minutes later. I thought it odd, but pushed it to the back of my mind."

Eva took a deep breath and then went on. "When he came through the door, I immediately sensed something dark was about to happen. In retrospect, I suspect that I should have known. He'd changed his clothing before leaving the base—he no longer wore his uniform. It seemed odd but I dismissed it as not being important.

" 'Where's Lauren?' were his first words he spoke. He took off the lightweight jacket he wore and threw it over the back of a kitchen chair. I remember what I said to him almost as if it were yesterday." Eva murmured quietly.

" 'Study class, after school every Tuesday,' I responded. 'She won't be home for about two hours,' I answered quickly, wondering if this was something to do with you instead of me. Then shame flooded me when I caught myself thinking that it would have been a relief if it was about you. But I knew better. Somewhere deep inside me, warning bells were ringing, whistles were blowing, and a sixth sense was giving me every indication that the reason for his question was anything but routine." Eva hesitated, exhaling slowly.

"I want you to know. This isn't easy for me but I think it's important for you, so bear with me," Eva said evenly.

"In all the time we'd been married, he'd never come home early for any reason. Suddenly, I knew what was about to happen. With the first words from his mouth, my husband confirmed all of my worst fears. Through a very uncomfortable series of disclosures, I learned of his long-standing unhappiness. I felt nothing, aside from nausea. There were no tears. My emotions—" Eva's voice broke off and Lauren held her breath, unable to speak.

Was this what Michael and I will go through?

"The divorce became final one year later," Eva explained, finding her voice. "Until then, I simply went about the daily routine of living: handling the necessary tasks, completing the mundane chores. Inside, it felt as if I were dead, though I did my best to keep it hidden. In some way, I hoped that your father would come to his senses and change his mind. I felt that if I kept absolutely still and quiet, he'd recover from whatever form of madness had obviously taken over his mind and will." She let out an insecure chuckle that did little to hide the pain she was reliving.

Lauren's threshold broke then, and she sobbed once. Out of respect for her mother's endurance, she stopped herself from breaking down totally. "Mom, I am so sorry. I knew you were going through a lot then, but I really was clueless as to the depth of your pain. I only knew I missed my father, missed the life we all had shared, and wondered what to make of it all." She grabbed a tissue, dabbed at her eyes, listening for her mother's next words.

"Well, I suspected as much. We were all going through an incredible amount of mental pain. Unfortunately, your father never returned to the mind-set that we should remain a family unit. That very same night we had our discussion, he packed a few things and moved to the barracks. I think it was probably even worse than he imagined, but he'd never admit that. Lauren, I can say now that I know the decision to leave his family was not an easy one to arrive at.

"Actually, he told me years later when we had the opportunity to really talk to one another with no holds barred that months had passed before he gathered the courage to bring the subject of a divorce up. It had taken a long while before he'd come to the realization that it was the right thing to do," Eva explained.

"After he moved out, your father received orders to return to the United States. Since we were still legally together, we had to leave the south of France too. I packed our things quickly, and we moved from our off-base apartment overseas to New Jersey. It was near the water. Something we'd all grown accustomed to in Europe. The schools were reportedly excellent too, and we agreed that your education was a high priority," she explained. Lauren heard her mother take a calming breath, steadying her emotions.

"Colin filed for legal separation almost two weeks after we got to New Jersey," Eva added matter-of-factly.

Lauren felt her eyes burn, as tears threatened to overtake her once more. "Mom, you don't have to say any more. Only if you want to."

"Yes, I do. This has been so long in coming. I should have told you sooner. It's good for me to talk about this," she continued, knowing that she had bottled her emotions for too long.

Lauren was silent on the other end, stunned by the revelations that her mother seemed unable to withhold now.

"You were an only child, a beautiful young girl who was also bright and sensitive. I knew you would have real difficulty accepting the fact that the father you had loved for so many years would no longer be there. I was extremely worried about you." Eva's voice ended then, her overwhelming pain evident to her daughter.

Lauren spoke quietly, mirroring her mother's somber mood, eager to add her own epitaph to the story.

"When I entered high school that fall, my biggest worry was that I had done something to cause my father to walk away from the family. I blamed it on something I had done wrong. It wasn't until I'd graduated college that I understood how little my behavior could have contributed to the failure of your marriage. By then, I'd already formulated a course of action in my own life that would almost surely spell disaster."

Lauren felt somehow relieved to share her innermost feelings with her mother, and wondered that if she hadn't married, how long it would have taken for this exchange between them to take place.

Eva kept thinking of the day her husband decided to end their marriage. The tears she'd shed had long since been forgotten. In their place, calm resolve had taken residence. The pride she had once possessed in being a military wife slowly dissipated, and a new sense of accomplishment took its place.

By the time the Traynor family returned to the United States, settling in southern New Jersey, Lauren was more than capable of fitting in anywhere in the world. While Eva dreaded the transition inherent in relocation, Lauren learned to genuinely love the challenge. Eva watched as her daughter did everything in her power to assimilate as quickly as possible, making friends with lightning speed and keeping in touch with many whom she'd recently left, but had spent valuable time getting to know.

She treated life much like a board game, and as she approached the end of high school, the challenge took on even more significance. Her freshman year was a breeze and she'd had no problems until her parents' divorce had become final in her sophomore year—the difference in her grades, her attitude, and her entire demeanor changed. By that time, Colin had transferred to another state.

After the divorce, Lauren was aware of the damage and the effect that the end of the marriage had had on her parents. As such, she was of no mind to duplicate their errors in judgment. She put dating in the category of "extremely dangerous." Even when boys in her high school began dropping by her after-school job at an ice cream parlor located on the boardwalk of the Jersey Shore, she'd done her best to ignore them. And she'd continued in that same mind-set all throughout college.

After college, Lauren's love of travel had led her to Worldwide Airlines. With its constant interaction with the public, it served as Lauren's introduction to a world that she could no longer hide from. On a daily basis, she was bombarded with attention from businessmen, athletes and entrepreneurs. She'd vowed not to date anyone, especially not a passenger. And she'd kept that promise. That is, until she'd run into Michael Townsend.

Eva cleared her throat, bringing her daughter back to the present. "Lauren, as we all left the reception area at your wedding, I have to tell you that I realized you'd finally grown up. No matter what had occurred during the years when we were desperately trying to manage our own personal demons, things turned out all right. And for that, I gave thanks."

"Mom, I never knew you went through all of that. I mean the details. . . ." her voice, filled with emotion, dropped off.

"I know. You were a child then, Lauren. My main concern was to help you grow up healthy and strong."

"Well, don't stop there," Lauren said playfully, attempting to lighten the mood. "I want to know what else happened at the wedding."

Eva laughed. "Your father asked if I'd like to see some of the island before we called it a night. I think he realized that his request had quite probably caught me off guard because I didn't answer for awhile. He was taking a hell of a chance asking me to spend time with him."

Lauren listened, her mind filled with a thousand questions, her heart filled with pride. This was her mother speaking, and although there had been a time when she would have thrilled at the thought of a reconciliation between her parents, she was pleased to know that her mother had made peace with the past. No matter what had happened during the weekend of her wedding, she knew Eva would be fine.

On the other end of the phone line, thinking of Lauren's wedding day and all that had transpired, Eva's eyes filled with tears, which she quickly wiped away.

"Mom, I don't want you to tell me anything that you're not prepared to, but did you and Daddy come to terms with things?" Lauren asked, her voice filled with concern.

"Lauren, I wouldn't have brought the subject up if we hadn't. It was a good thing, us being together. And yes, we reached what I like to think of as a 'new deal' in terms of our relationship. It's as if I've found a very good friend again, and so has he. For now, that's enough," she ended.

"Good. I have always wanted you guys to be friends. That was probably the hardest part about the divorce for me."

"Yes, loneliness is a difficult thing. My job at the architecture and design firm keeps me pretty busy, but it doesn't compare to human companionship. Anyway, I hope you'll understand. We care for each other but a lot of time has passed. . . ." Eva's voice trailed off with unspoken thoughts.

She did not want Lauren to misunderstand or misinterpret. Colin Traynor would be in her life for all of her life.

"I do Mom, and thank you."

"Lauren, you don't have to thank me for anything. I'll always care about your father. Maybe not in the same way I did before, but care nonetheless."

"I was thanking you for sharing with me. I'm glad you feel I'm mature enough to handle the details." Lauren laughed then, relief washing over her. Maybe when she and Michael parted ways, they could still be friends like her parents had become. She hated being so pessimistic, but her mother's story had just confirmed what she already knew: love is not everlasting.

Chapter Six

Michael's desk looked like a recently detonated mine-field. The office, decorated in stark black and white with splashes of aluminum and touches of slate gray, was located on the same floor as Morgan's. At the moment, chaos was in residence, and Michael knew something would have to be done soon to rectify it.

In the three weeks since he and Lauren had said their vows before God, the sun, and their guests, he'd come to several realizations. Unfortunately, he still had not found the right time to share this information with his bride.

In the three full days and nights of the honeymoon, Michael had spared no expense and given his total concentration to Lauren. His intention was to create a lasting memory—something neither of them would ever forget. After the first few rocky hours of their wedding night, their honeymoon had been near perfect. They'd strolled the beach hand-in-hand, shared sumptuous candlelight dinners and made love all over the Renoir Suite of the hotel. They'd also shared a pleasant tryst in a cove near their hotel. Just the thought brought a smile to Michael's face.

But now that they were back in New York, Michael was beginning to wonder if they would ever achieve a normal lifestyle, assuming the role of husband and wife without a degree of tension. He was starting to realize that a happy marriage might not be as easy to pull off as he'd originally thought.

After the honeymoon, they'd returned to Michael's townhouse and moved the remainder of Lauren's belongings to their marital home. All was well for forty-eight hours. Then, the bliss went bust.

Michael and Lauren were sitting Hindu style on the floor of their den with their white sheets wrapped around them like togas. Though they were laughing at how incredibly silly they were being, they agreed that it was also more fun than the traditional formalities inherent in a normal sit-down dinner.

"I think you look great in that sheet. It reminds me of some of the frat parties we used to attend at Northwestern." Michael laughed as Lauren paraded in front of him, obviously pleased with his statement.

"Oh, frat parties. Hmmm. I'll bet you were a hell-raiser even then," she teased knowing he'd probably had any girl he'd wanted. She wondered if she'd met him in college, would the same set of sparks have been present? Then she realized that she would have probably always been attracted to this man. His steel gray eyes, long, lean body and ever-present confidence held her in a grip that was impossibly magnetic. And though she was hard-pressed to admit it, she could not help but acknowledge his power over her.

"Hey, I said I attended them, not organized them. Duke and I would just how up and it would already be on," he stated looking very much like a Roman orator preparing to address the Senate as he crossed the room to get a bottle of wine from the refrigerator. Lauren smiled as he continued.

"That's the way it is at schools in the Midwest. I think the East Coast guys tend to procrastinate and postulate more, trying to impress a girl instead of coming right out and asking for what they want," he ended, a devilish smile on his face.

"I think that's awful, Michael," she said, furiously shaking her head. "Most young girls have a cautious attitude because it has been drilled into them at an early age. And even more so just before they leave for college. I remember some of the discussions at my house. My mother expected that I'd change my whole demeanor when I got to college. I probably surprised her, and my dad too, when I didn't date for the first three years."

Michael continued to watch Lauren, thankful that she was open to discussion on important topics, even if they didn't always agree. Her statement let him know one of the reasons why she had been a virgin when they'd met. He was glad to have been her first lover, and he wanted nothing more than to be her last. He also knew that if he was not able to help her get over some of the hurdles she now faced, due to the divorce and her miscarriage, their future was most definitely in jeopardy. Michael remained silent, listening to the things Lauren said, and wondered if they'd ever arrive at the place he most wanted them to be—in complete unison.

"You know, I don't think the sexes will ever be on equal footing," Lauren continued matter-of-factly. "And we'll always have double standards, until men can actually take more of the responsibility of planning and raising a family."

"You're probably right. That is only one of the reasons why it was so important for us to tie the knot immediately. I am dead set on being involved in the planning and raising of our family. In fact, I plan to see you barefoot and pregnant at least a few times before it's all over," he deadpanned.

The look of shock on Lauren's face told him that his words had hit pay dirt and he howled. "Boy, you should see yourself. If looks could kill, I'd be a dead man. Honey, I was only kidding. But I do want children—lots of them—the sooner the better. That way we can grow with them and not be in our fifties when they reach those difficult teen years," he ended quickly.

"Michael, I'm not sure of what I want right now," Lauren said quietly, a look of uncertainty on her face. "Especially after all that we went through with the miscarriage. I'm definitely not looking forward to another pregnancy for awhile. Don't you think we should wait awhile to see how things go? You know, give it time?"

Michael wondered if she realized just how beautiful she looked at that moment. The logs in the fireplace crackled and the glow that the flames cast in the room as the sun lowered in the sky was lovely. Nightfall would only enhance the effect.

Lauren's radiant beauty caused Michael's heart to beat faster in his chest. He loved this woman, loved her and wanted to make love with her all throughout the day. He couldn't imagine a day or a time when that desire would change, but he feared the issues Lauren was grappling with would have too much of a negative impact on their relationship. He also felt it was his job to turn things around because he'd been the one pushing for the marriage.

"Listen, I know you thought I wanted to marry you mainly because of the pregnancy, but that's not true—not even a little. I wanted to make you mine from the very first time we kissed. I just didn't know how to handle it. The pregnancy was actually a blessing. And although it terminated for whatever reason, we'll have plenty more pregnancies. And I mean that."

Lauren watched the handsome lines around her husband's mouth, the determined look on his face, and the stoic position of his jaw. In Michael, she saw everything she'd ever wanted in a man. Only one other man on the planet had ever moved her to tears, laughter, and then made her smile: her father.

She realized that aside from the unexpected separation and hastily arranged divorce from her mother, her father had never disappointed her. Could Michael have as solid a track record? And if not, when and where would the crack occur? Just how long would it take for their fragile union to decompose, ultimately resulting in a devastation she was not prepared to endure? That Michael would inevitably disappoint her, was her greatest fear.

Lauren knew that the questions that haunted her were also creating the environment she most wanted to avoid. She felt torn between her fears and her hopes; confused about the future she most wanted, but was unlikely to get.

Lauren looked around the room, remaining silent. She wondered if Michael knew just how deeply she didn't buy into his theory of everlasting love, unknown numbers of offspring, and the ultimate success of a marriage. Her arguments, thus far, had fallen on deaf ears.

Michael could be persuasive, extremely determined, and more than a little driven. He was one hundred percent sure their marriage would be successful, positive in his direction, and dedicated to the cause. The fact that he was willing to forge ahead with their union despite her misgivings gave Lauren little comfort on that night, though. His last words rang in her ears, and the pain of the miscarriage brought a flood of emotion.

"How can you say that?" she asked, raising her voice. "We're not even sure if we'll be able to make it to the next month, much less the next year. Raising a family, having children, and staying together is not a game Michael. It's a challenge," she yelled. Lauren rose from the floor at that point, her disbelief at his incomprehension evidenced by her stance and the serious look on her face. She waited for Michael's retort, her body language screaming mortal combat. Michael knew that no matter how he responded, it wouldn't matter. Defeated, he gave up momentarily. It was only the first week of their marriage and he was already starting to falter. Lauren's pessimism was becoming contagious. He had to get out of the house before he gave in to Lauren's negativity.

"Lauren, I can't do this right now," he said softly.

Standing, he walked toward her, kissed her gently on the forehead and headed toward the bedroom. He needed to clear his head, or at least think about something else. He decided the next best place for him would be the office. In silence, he dressed quickly.

Lauren remained standing in the exact same spot for the next ten minutes. Long after she'd heard Michael's Jaguar XJ6 leave its parking spot and longer still after the realization hit her that he had, indeed, left the house. Finally recovering from her shock, she stormed into the bedroom and got dressed.

She fumed as she set about unpacking another box of her belongings. Her anger propelled her to keep busy though her sadness fueled tears which went unshed. Too many words had been spoken, but too many things were still left unsaid.

After Lauren finished placing her lamps, ceramic vases and accessories around the townhouse, she didn't know what to do with herself. She sat down at the kitchen table and called her mom. The two chatted about mundane things, and Eva gave Lauren a simple recipe for broiled salmon that she had recently tried. Lauren listened, rationalizing that dinner might give her and Michael a chance to resolve the issues they'd grappled with earlier.

When Michael returned home late that evening, Lauren was waiting for some response, an explanation for his abrupt departure. But he seemed not to notice. He was too busy with his own thoughts.

The broiled salmon, green beans with mushroom caps, and green salad were consumed quietly with Michael and Lauren each miserable but committed to keeping their thoughts to themselves for the time being. It was an uncomfortable meal punctuated by polite comments. Michael complimented Lauren on its preparation and she thanked him as she removed the plates and loaded the dishwasher, wondering how much longer they would continue this way.

As they prepared for bed, the real challenge reared its head. Michael did want to talk before they retired, but took his cue from his bride and said nothing. He realized that by walking out earlier, he'd effectively silenced her, though that had not been his intention. Unspoken words churned inside of him, but he assumed Lauren was in no mood to discuss anything.

Lauren put on a pale blue nightgown and pulled her hair into a ponytail. She was tired, more tired than she had been in a very long time. She was also angry. Michael's lack of conversation throughout the dinner had affected her immensely. It wasn't that she wanted to be uncommunicative; it was more that everything she said was misunderstood. And although Michael had weathered the storm of the miscarriage like the trooper that he was, Lauren had second thoughts about the possibility of having to handle that same kind of issue at a later date. For her, one pregnancy was enough. She never again wanted to experience the kind of physical or emotional pain she'd known during and after her miscarriage.

"Are you asleep?" Lauren asked Michael as she got into bed. Out of habit, she immediately sought out his warmth.

"No, not really," Michael answered, his voice filled with reservation.

"Good, because I just wanted you to know that I understand what you were saying earlier today. I even agree with you in many ways. But if you are honest with yourself and with me, you'd have to acknowledge that childbearing changes lives, it changes people. I'm just not sure it's always for the best. Think about it."

Michael let out a low chuckle at that moment and smiled in the darkness, knowing Lauren would never stop trying to make her case. He missed her voice when she didn't talk. He also realized that the discussion underway was long overdue, and of great importance. Once and for all, they needed to get their act together so that going forward, they would be on the same page.

"Listen, I'm done trying to convince you of anything other than whatever it is you have a mind to believe. You see, I too have my idea of an ideal relationship, and this is clearly not it. But I also realize that there are reasons you would feel the way you do. So, until such time that you feel differently, and are able to articulate that change to me either through your actions or your words, I have resigned myself to the fact that we are involved in a marriage of sorts. It's not what I wanted, but I now know that in this world, nothing is ever what it looks to be," he said, his breath coming in short bursts due to the powerful feelings he was expressing with every syllable. "I'm in this for as long as it takes to reach the desired result."

Michael paused, blowing out a ragged breath as Lauren remained silent. He wasn't sure how she would handle this next statement. "Honey, I guess now is as good a time as any to tell you that I was notified at the office that I probably have to complete some last-minute audit functions on the West Coast offices of WJZZ. Morgan wants to make sure that everything is straight with the books. Duke will stay here in New York to keep the operation side of things running smoothly. We're still on the executive board, which is why Morgan wants our input. He's one shrewd businessman." As he rambled nervously, Michael leaned on one elbow, gazing at Lauren intently, hoping she would understand.

Lauren was quiet for what seemed like an eternity. She sat up and looked over at Michael as he folded his arms behind his head. A knot of fear had formed within her stomach, holding her words in check. *So this is why he was so absent during dinner,* she thought.

Lauren knew the station that her husband and Duke had built and then sold to CBN had been Michael's life. He would do any and everything in his power to see that it continued its lucrative existence. But she was also aware that the fragile state of their union had just been issued its death warrant. Lauren had never really expected the marriage to last, but she also never expected that distance would be their downfall.

"I don't know what to say, other than that I don't like it. And, of course, I'll probably miss you incredibly." The pause that followed her words was awkward, filled with emotion on both sides. "When do you leave? How long will you be gone?" she asked finally, her words sounding hollow as they resounded in the bedroom's darkened interior.

"Morgan didn't say when I should leave, but I'm hoping I won't be gone longer than a week. Morgan made it sound like it's a routine check, but I have some misgivings about that. I know how long it took us to get the station up and running when we first began, and if there are problems, they may take even longer to rectify."

"Well, a week is not so bad. Perhaps it will give me time to get this place kind of sorted out too. This may be a good thing," Lauren said then, trying to look at it from a different perspective. She hadn't wanted to appear ruffled in any way, but Michael's words resonated throughout her mind, casting a chill over her entire body. She shuddered then and Michael looked at her, wondering if they would, indeed, make it through this stage of being newlyweds.

"I leave in a couple of days. Come here, you must be cold," he said drawing her closer to him. "Let's get some shut eye. I have to be in the office tomorrow morning at seven-thirty to bring Duke up to speed on everything."

"Okay. Would you like me to help you pack at some point?"

"Sure. You're a pro at that aren't you? I'll just need one lightweight suit, a dark blazer, some khaki pants, and a few shirts, you know? I'll wear jeans on the plane."

"It reminds me of when we met. You were on your way to L.A. then too," Lauren said, wondering if he had any misgivings about being away from her, possibly for an extended period of time. She was unable to bring herself to ask.

"Yeah, that flight changed my life." He wrapped her in his arms then, marveling at how her body fit with his as if by design. He wanted to make love to her, wanted to say that of all the things he thought they would be discussing on this night in the third week of their marriage, separation had not been even a remote possibility, even if it was only for one week.

He continued to hold her to him, intimately curving his body around hers. They each fell asleep with unspoken words on their lips and a nagging sense of uncertainty in their minds.

Chapter Seven

Morgan punched the intercom button, glaring at it as if an automatic response was what he anticipated. Noelle's voice came through the speaker softly.

"Yes, was there something you needed?" she asked.

He wondered if she was being a smart aleck. Morgan wanted to give the answer that was on the tip of his tongue, but knew that in the current environment of sexual-harassment suits, he could be facing definitive charges if he did.

Since their return from Barbados, Noelle behaved as if their vacation had never occurred. And that ticked him off. But he had other things that were far more important to handle than his temporary interest in his secretary.

On Tuesday morning, Morgan received a report from the board of directors which highlighted third-quarter results. Cityscape Broadcast Network was in the black; its affiliates and sister stations in the Northeast and related markets were all operating at a plus factor. Although the news was absolutely fantastic, something about its delivery was in direct contrast with the statistics he'd received only six weeks before. Either the WJZZ accountants had prejudged on the side of conservatism, or there had been a flood of cash going into the station during the last month of the quarter. Either way, the projections were off by more than three hundred percent.

He'd already ordered a full-scale discovery by Taylor, Rooney and Bent, LLC, the accounting firm Gino Sorrentino had relied on for more than a decade. They would either give the go-ahead or the red flag to Cityscape Broadcast Network's attempt to go public in the next six months. The results of their in depth probe would determine everything.

Morgan remembered Gino once saying, *Kid, never look a gift horse in the mouth.* He knew that with the acquisition of WJZZ and the change to smooth jazz, his new partners had successfully entrenched themselves in the CBN family of networks. This was something that Gino and the other board members had fought in the very beginning. It was only through Morgan's persistence that they'd changed their minds. Because of a prosecutorial investigation, it had taken seven years to acquire the station, and CBN had lost Gino, their most powerful component during that time. Gino Sorrentino was an irreplaceable element, but his death meant that Morgan had no choice but to move into the vacancy created by his step-father's untimely passing.

As uneasy thoughts of his business venture threatened to ruin his day, Morgan adjusted his mind to a more pleasant topic: Noelle.

He'd wanted her to be easy in Barbados, to enjoy his company. But she wasn't having any of it; Morgan discovered he was waging a losing battle when she'd left the wedding reception early. She had not shown her face again until the following morning on the beach. By then, it was eight o'clock, the sun was blazing, and Morgan was hungover as he sat on a beach chair with a towel draped around his shoulders. He'd sweated out most of the rum he'd consumed the night before, and he really didn't give a damn what she did.

"You don't look so good," she'd whispered as she set her beach bag on the chaise lounge beside his.

Morgan looked up at her with one eye glinting against the glare of the sun and wondered why he'd even brought her. He wanted to laugh, if only to show her that her behavior the day before had not fazed him one bit, but the pain in his head prevented him from doing so. Instead, he smiled without showing a single tooth.

"You must be from New York. Not only are you observant, but you're damned rude," he barked. In his mind, he wondered just who the hell she thought she was anyway, running out on him like that. After she disappeared, he'd gone into the bar, ordered a few rum punches and made a night of it. Around three in the morning, he'd made it up to his room, sprawled himself across the king-sized bed fully clothed and passed out.

"Sorry if the truth hurts, but it still stands. Exactly what did you do to yourself last night?" she asked. Her question hung in the air annoyingly as the ocean rhythmically pounded the shoreline.

"Now that's surely none of your business, but I had a party. If you were so interested, you would have stayed and checked it out for yourself," Morgan answered glibly, waiting for her to retaliate with an equally smooth answer. Moments passed and he could still feel her eyes on him. "What? What is it?" he asked then, suddenly becoming annoyed as he realized that she obviously planned to set up camp right next to him.

"Nothing. Do you mind if I sit here? I thought I'd start off the final day here with a little sun and fun. If you'd rather, I can take my things and set them up on the other side of the beach," she added in total seriousness.

Morgan thought a moment, figured this might be his chance for one additional shot and spoke. "No, don't be silly. Why should you move to another zip code just because I'm here, miserable with a terrific hangover. Sorry I took it out on you—it's my own fault."

Noelle nodded, not at all sure of his intentions, but put her things down anyway.

"Exactly how did you accomplish that?" she asked bravely.

Morgan almost ignored her then thought better of it. "Rum punch, made with overproof rum. It's a drink that should be limited to no more than two at the very most," he added as he reached an unsteady hand toward a large bottle of water which sat in a container filled with ice.

"I see. I take it that you went over quota?"

"Yeah, I guess you could say that. Listen, do you mind if we change the subject?"

Noelle smiled as she pulled her shades over her eyes. This assignment was becoming more of a challenge every day, but she wasn't quite ready to throw in the towel. The Bureau had not yet specified exactly what it was they were looking for. This mission might take more than the allocated time, but Noelle's commitment to producing a successful outcome was still one hundred percent intact.

The morning passed quickly and Morgan gallantly ordered a light lunch for them at noon. By that time, he was feeling almost human, and Noelle had made him laugh at least twice.

"You got a great tan," Morgan commented as she prepared to gather her things.

"Thanks. You got some sun too. Dad was Italian and my Mom is black, so it doesn't take much for me to tan."

"Really. That's an interesting combination." He wanted to ask her more but was afraid she would clam up on him. He changed the subject, hoping to keep her talking.

"I definitely needed to get rid of some of the demons from last night. I feel almost human again, especially after that lobster salad," he added.

"Yes, that was delicious. Thanks for taking such great care of your staff." Almost as an afterthought, she turned and said quickly, "And thank you for inviting me. It was a lovely weekend."

"Yeah, but the three days went by too quickly. Maybe we can do it again sometime," he said and waited for her response.

Noelle looked up at Morgan then, smiled, and didn't say a word. What she wanted to say could have gotten her fired.

Morgan smiled too, coming out of his daydream. He hadn't figured Noelle out, but he was determined to do so. Shaking off his thoughts of Barbados, he resumed the business of operating a thriving multimedia operation.

He was determined to find out if he was on to something or if he was simply misinterpreting the numbers. If what he had suspected had even the tiniest inkling of truth to it, there would be hell to pay.

Any tampering with the numbers would be just the indication that would give the FBI, or the "lettermen" as he'd come to think of them, the prosecutorial ammunition they had been seeking for eight long years. During that time, the FBI, NYPD, and ATF had collaborated in an effort to bring Gino to his knees. He'd averted their success by suffering a fatal heart attack. Morgan realized that the agencies would probably never stop investigating if they suspected there was a way to bring down CBN. This was why he had done everything in his power to keep the company legitimate since he'd taken it over.

Morgan massaged his temples, realizing he had a pounding headache. His thoughts once again returned to the words he'd exchanged with Gino eleven months ago while his stepfather lay in a hospital bed at St. Francis Medical Center. In the moments before his death—as Morgan's mother Cora Sorrentino wept in the arms of her stepdaughter—her son and husband had come to a final resolution with each other.

Promises were made, vows exchanged, and a silent oath taken.

Deep in thought, Morgan looked over at the Native American totem pole that had been a gift from Gino when he'd first joined the staff at CBN. *Not worth a plugged nickel* was printed on the back of the six-foot statue, which filled one entire corner of his massive office. Morgan could almost hear Gino's laughter as he recognized its implication.

Morgan's eyes clouded for a moment, and his powerful hands went back to massaging his temples. His headache had only just begun.

Pushing the intercom button on his phone, he alerted his assistant of his needs. "Noelle, I need you to pull every file you can on the second-quarter results and then get my partners on the phone. Either Duke or Michael, I don't care which," he said quickly, hanging up before she could ask any questions.

In his mind, a plan was being formulated, and he needed time and the requisite information to pull all the fragments together. If his prior thinking was correct, there could be serious trouble on the horizon—the kind of trouble that Gino would have avoided like the plague.

It took Noelle all of fifteen minutes to pull the files Morgan demanded. She knocked softly at the door, waited for his response, and walked in with a cart filled with more than twenty manila folders.

"Is that all of them?" Morgan asked.

"Yes, I also made sure to include the financials of the merged companies, too. Will that be all?"

He looked up and shook his head. "No, have a seat. I think I want to dictate some notes while I go through these."

"Excuse me for a minute. I didn't bring my notepad." She turned and walked quickly back to her desk.

Morgan wondered if he'd be able to accomplish all the things he wanted to at CBN. Flipping open the first batch of files, he looked through them, made a couple of notes on his notepad, and continued to read. Noelle came back and sat down, pen in hand, waiting for him to recite whatever it was he'd want her to transcribe.

"Okay, here is the first part of what I'd like you to take down. It's a list of all stations in the metropolitan area that are part of our original network of stations."

"You mean before the acquisition of WJZZ?" she asked.

"Yeah, I want to do a comparison of our numbers in terms of advertisers before the acquisition and after. Then you can prepare a spreadsheet that will track the numbers for the past six months."

"That doesn't sound too bad. When would you like this to be completed?"

"As quickly as possible. If you can compile all the data by tomorrow sometime and then cross-reference it to make sure we cover each entity, that'll be great," he added.

Noelle smiled and nodded. "No problem," she answered, rising from her seat and gathering the scattered files from his desk.

If there was one thing the FBI prided itself on, it would have to be the assembling and dissemination of information. Every agent was a thoroughly trained professional in each aspect of his or her expertise. Morgan's request was like offering clichéd candy to a baby for Noelle. It activated her curiosity as to exactly what aspect of the information had Morgan Pryor so fired up. It also alerted her to the fact that there was probably more to the recent acquisition than the Bureau had originally thought. Noelle's instincts told her that the information she would soon assemble could be crucial to the investigation.

She prepared the spreadsheet quickly. As she entered the final pieces of information, two very important things became apparent. One, her boss was obviously on to something if what she was reading was correct. And two, at least four of the revenue entries had been made by someone who was no longer part of the staff. That fact alone meant there was no accountability. Her liaison back at the Bureau would have to be notified immediately.

Chapter Eight

Michael looked around his office without noticing its contemporary design. His mind was on neither the paperwork which lay on his desk, nor the replacement he'd recently hired for the radio show so that he could devote more time to management duties.

He sat back in the black executive chair, his hands behind his head and wondered how he could have fallen in love so deeply without seeing any of the warning signs. He knew he was in trouble when they made love for the first time on his boat and he discovered Lauren had been a virgin.

Instead of being angry that she hadn't told him she'd never been with a man before, or wanting to put distance between them, that night had served to bring them closer together. Michael realized that her actions, and her reactions to him, were probably more than she was capable of handling, which he found intriguing. He'd vowed to see Lauren a few more times, even if it was only to reassure her that all men were not alike. By the time he realized that he genuinely enjoyed her company, he was hooked.

Michael smiled then, shook his head at his days as a

player, and picked up the phone. Lauren answered on the second ring, sounding breathless, but happy.

"Hello, Townsend residence," she sang into the phone line.

"Oh, is it now?" he responded, wondering if she answered that way on every ring.

"Yes, it most certainly is, Mr. Townsend. What can I do for you today?"

"Well, since you ask—I find myself in need of a luncheon date. Are you free?"

" 'Free,' well, that is a relative term. If you mean will I charge you, no. If you'd like me to come downtown and meet you, well the answer is yes," she responded, holding back laughter.

"You're real sassy today, huh? But that's okay, cause I like smart women and can't think of anything more important than having an intelligent wife. Yes, woman, I'd love to see you for lunch. How about one-thirty?"

"Okay, sure, I'd love to," she responded. She wondered if anything was wrong, then dismissed it.

"Okay, great. I was just sitting here thinking about the time we spent on the *Megahertz* and I realized I miss you."

She blushed at the memory of the first time they'd made love. "Michael, you just saw me this morning. I slept beside you last night, if I remember correctly," Lauren responded, wondering if Michael was teasing her.

"I know, and you'll be there tonight too. Lunch is just foreplay for what I really want." His voice had softened, becoming intimately seductive, and Lauren felt her body respond despite the distance between them.

"Are you trying to seduce me?"

"Absolutely. Is it working?"

"Yes, but I should warn you that lately I seem to have no control over myself when I'm in the company of a certain tall, dark gentleman who also happens to be a radio person-

ality for one of the fastest-growing stations in the Northeast."
Lauren laughed, knowing that her wrap up of CBN's status
in the marketplace would surely crack her husband up.

"Wow, are you sure you're not one of those marketers?
'Cause your spin on the station is an entrepreneur's dream. I
love it when you talk marketing to me, sweetheart. Listen,
come as soon as you can. I want to see you."

"Okay, Michael. I'll be there. See you at one-thirty."

"Love you, Lauren," Michael added as he hung up.

Lauren walked into his office two hours later wearing an
off-white suit, an orange tank, and beige lizard pumps. The
skirt was short, which enhanced the length of her legs.
Michael stood and walked around the desk to embrace her.
Lauren had worn Mark Cross, his favorite fragrance, and he
breathed in the scent for a long moment. Then he reached
down tipping her chin up and kissed her gently.

Their kiss quickly deepened as a volcano of desire threatened to erupt. Michael held Lauren to him tightly, feeling
her body against the length of his as passion overtook them
both. When they broke apart, both were breathing rapidly.
Lauren looked at him and smiled a knowing smile.

"Are you sure lunch is what you wanted?" she asked suggestively.

"No, but I'll take whatever is offered," he responded with
an arched eyebrow.

Lauren laughed and stepped back. "I'm really hungry.
Didn't have time for breakfast. I was unpacking my clothes.
Now it feels as if all my strength is waning. I think you
should feed me before you suggest anything more vigorous,"
she retorted, a smile playing about the corners of her mouth.

"Food, the woman wants food, and all I can think of is
love," he said, teasing her. "Okay, if practicality is what will
do it, then so be it. Come on, I have a great place I want to
take you to," Michael said as he led her to the door. "By the

way, you look scrumptious. Almost good enough to eat," he added giving her a lingering glance. Shaking his head, he closed his eyes, put his hands together, and said a mock prayer, "Thank you Lord," then looked at Lauren for her reaction.

Lauren laughed, knowing that he was happy that she'd been able to join him for lunch. Dressed in charcoal-gray trousers and a black sweater with the collar opened at the throat, he appeared corporate but relaxed. He reached for a black tweed jacket and they headed for the elevator.

"I warn you that if you don't feed this hungry beast, it will be your overwhelming responsibility for whatever happens," he warned as they entered the elevator.

"Michael, we're on our way to lunch now. You surely can survive the next few minutes," Lauren said.

"Not really," Michael responded as he instinctively reached up to her shoulders and turned her to face him. Their lips met in a kiss that was tentative in its beginnings. Lauren wound her arms around his neck, and Michael felt her body against his full length and groaned. Michael slowly circled her waist with his hands, then put them under her shirt, exploring the planes of her back.

Lauren sighed and felt her knees grow weak. She leaned against the wall of the elevator, no longer able to support her own weight. They felt the elevator slow and pulled apart reluctantly.

Michael looked at her, passion etched into her face, and almost canceled lunch. Lauren reached out and with the back of her thumb, dabbed lightly at the corner of Michael's mouth. Her lipstick had left a small stain there.

"Serves you right. That's what you get for being irresistible," Michael said as he succumbed to her clean-up work. Lauren watched him, her eyes smoldering with passion, and knew she would never be unaffected by his kisses.

Michael reached for her hand, leading her out of the ele-

vator as it stopped. "Come on, Mrs. Townsend, you're dangerous. A man could die of starvation with you around. I don't
know how you expect me to focus on anything other than
making love when you're in the same room," he charged,
shaking his head.

Lauren laughed. "Sure, blame it all on me. I practically undressed you in the elevator, right?" she asked as they walked
in the direction of Madison Avenue.

"No, but that wouldn't have been a bad idea. Look, let's
change the subject. I can only take so much," he added, a
look of absolute torture on his face.

"Fine," Lauren answered, wondering how she too was expected to turn off the passion his mouth had ignited.

"How's the station holding up with you not being on the
regular air schedule?" she asked, knowing the impact of that
one change could cause a significant decrease in the number
of listeners.

"So far, so good. The guy who replaced me had been an
intern forever. We figured it wouldn't hurt to give him a
chance to try his on-air skills, and it worked."

"That's a relief. Now what?"

"Well, we still have to fine-tune everything. I'll be recording my segments for awhile, until we can come to some
agreement as to what portion of my duties are irreplaceable."

"So you're saying that you may return to the air at some
point and in the same capacity as before?" she asked.

They had just reached the restaurant and stepped inside,
the darkened interior offering intimacy. The aroma of exotic
spices reached them, intensifying their hunger. Negril, a
popular eatery on West Twenty-third Street, was crowded,
but they were shown to a table immediately.

"To answer your question, yes, I may be back on the air
full-time as soon as we're able to straighten things out,"
Michael said, pulling out a chair for Lauren. "Morgan and

Duke both realize the listening audience can be fickle, so we have to temper whatever we do. The reality of it is 'the listener is king.' " His statement was issued with a knowledge that came from years of experience. None of the decision makers at CBN wanted to alter the station's basic formula for success, even though they had changed the type of music played. As soon as possible, the plan was to return to business as usual and get Michael back on the air.

The happy couple scanned the menu, selected an appetizer to share, then ordered their lunch entrees. Pepper shrimp was served at the beginning of the meal. After, Michael had brown chicken stew that was tender, flavorful, and served with a healthy portion of rice and peas, and steamed vegetables. Lauren's baked red snapper was delectably arranged, with a healthy helping of bok choy and several slices of sweet plantains. Lauren had enjoyed the combination of fish and vegetables while they were in Barbados, and was delighted that the New York restaurant's rendition was every bit as spicy.

By the time they were finished dining and chatting, Michael was tempted not to return to work. "Why don't we just take a cab home? I can pick up the car tomorrow morning," he proposed.

"Michael Townsend, you need to go back to work. I will not be labeled a 'distraction' because you have things on your mind other than CBN," Lauren stated, a playfully stern look on her face.

"Okay—guilty as charged. But I'll just tell you this: When I do get home tonight, I expect you to make this up to me. It's hard being the only breadwinner," he said, laughing.

After Lauren's miscarriage, he'd insisted that she take a leave of absence. Since then, he had talked her out of returning to work.

They returned to the office, and Michael called Lauren a cab. Remembering Lauren's words, he diligently plowed through the paperwork that had been on his desk since that morning, and left the office at 7:25 P.M. Heading uptown, he noticed a small shop at the corner of Eighty-first Street and Columbus Avenue which carried women's clothing, jewelry, and lingerie. The windows were decorated with mannequins dressed in shades of orange, yellow, and white, bringing to mind Lauren's outfit. On an impulse, he pulled over and parked. Walking into the boutique, he realized it sold the kind of clothing he'd seen Lauren wear, and knew she would like almost anything he chose.

When he walked into the house some forty-five minutes later, he thought he detected the smell of apples and was mildly surprised.

"Lauren," he called out, as he picked up the mail which lay on the marble-topped table in the foyer. He glanced through it, recognizing nothing of particular importance, and headed for the stairs.

"Lauren," he called again, heading for the bedroom, which turned out to be empty. He looked into the master bathroom, then placed the small shopping bag on the bed and headed back downstairs to the kitchen.

Lauren was bending over the open oven door as he walked in. She'd changed her clothes from earlier and now wore khaki shorts and a skimpy, pale green top, which was tied under her breasts, revealing the expanse of skin between her midriff and the top of her shorts. Her hair was pulled back into the ponytail she usually wore and she had oven mitts on both hands. She looked adorable.

Michael thought of his purchase and smiled. She didn't need it. She was thoroughly enticing in anything, and even more so in absolutely nothing. He walked toward her, pulled her into his arms. "Hi," he said, before lowering his lips to hers.

Lauren received his kisses hungrily, forgetting for the moment that she'd ever had any second thoughts or misgiv-

ings about their marriage. The heat of their kisses fueled
their desires slowly, deliciously. Michael placed soft kisses
on Lauren's neck. His hands caressed her bare back below
the rim of her blouse and came around to her rib cage.
Lauren moaned. He needed no further encouragement, and
slowly began to untie the blouse, his kisses now focused on
her neck and the tops of her breasts, which stood firm and
high as Michael untied the blouse. He realized that she had
not bothered to put on a braissiere, which triggered another
level of response in him.

They were standing in the kitchen, Lauren's back against
the center island. Michael seemed unaware of that, though,
and was thoroughly intent on making love to Lauren right
there. She took both of his hands, kissed him on the lips and
then both cheeks, and led him into the living room.

"Don't you want to go upstairs?" he asked, as he realized
that she'd responded to his urgency.

"I don't think we can make it that far," Lauren answered,
reaching for the band of his trousers. She unbuckled his belt,
and looked at him meaningfully. Michael then lowered his
zipper, stepping out of his pants, and they both fell back-
wards onto the leather sofa that dominated the room.

Dusk had fallen and the one lamp in the corner of the
room had not been turned on. The darkness was punctuated
by the occasional glare of headlights from a passing car or
truck, the sounds of jazz coming from the CD player providing ample atmosphere.

Michael took his time making love to his wife. They lay
lengthwise for a long time, each savoring the power and the
strength of the passion they were experiencing. Michael removed Lauren's blouse, nuzzling her breasts repeatedly, softly
until she cried out in pleasure. She closed her eyes and blocked
out all thought. She only felt. Putting the back of her hand
over her mouth, Lauren moaned in ecstasy.

Michael teased her breasts with his lips, his tongue, as

Lauren arched her back to bring him even closer to her. Each tug of his mouth sent shivers of excitement through her body as she felt need overtake all rational thought.

He pulled her on top of him then, and Lauren smiled down into his face. "Dangerous, isn't this, Mr. Townsend?" she asked as she wiggled out of her shorts, tossing them to the floor as he struggled out of his shirt.

"Not as dangerous as it's going to be," Michael replied, as Lauren lowered her head to kiss him deeply. Michael rested his hands on her hips as Lauren raised up and guided him into her. The heat, the fit, the fire that ignited them both was searing. Michael no longer controlled any of it as Lauren set the pace, the depth, the speed of their union.

Lauren felt as if she'd entered another dimension of time with no recognition of anything past or present having a meaning, as she reached a level of sensual abandonment that took her over the top. Michael felt the tremors of her body, held her tightly to him and waited. He then gently lowered her to the side, kissed her lips softly and continued to trail kisses from the top of her head to the tips of each breast.

Michael's caresses never ceased and in moments, Lauren felt herself respond as he brought them both to a fevered pitch. Afterwards, they lay tangled in one another's arms, exhausted but happily fulfilled.

"That's what happens when you make me wait all afternoon."

"Michael, I don't even want to think about what would happen if you had to wait for a longer period of time. And you're also making me into some kind of sex-starved wife. I could barely concentrate on the things I wanted to complete after I got home today. I wanted you all afternoon," she admitted, looking at him boldly.

"Baby, I want you all the time, which can be a huge problem. I have to try to concentrate on other things just so I can get some work done," Michael said then. "Speaking of concentrating on other things, what's that? It smells delicious," he asked as the aroma of something baking hit him for the second time.

"Oh, it's a surprise. Dessert. Or, after dessert," Lauren replied as she smiled, pulled on her shorts and stood to put on her shirt. In the dimly lit room, Michael could just make out her profile and knew that he would never go unaffected by the sight of Lauren Trayner-Townsend, either clothed or not.

She headed into the kitchen, and Michael pulled on his slacks, ran his hand through his hair and sat back against the sofa. *So, this is what it feels like to be in love and to be married to a woman you desire over and over again,* he thought to himself.

Lauren brought in a tray filled with apple turnovers and two cups of coffee. "Dessert is served," she laughed as she sat beside him after putting the tray on top of the two square ottomans that anchored the sofa.

"Baby, you were here baking for me? Isn't that the sweetest thing," he said kissing her quickly on the tip of her nose.

"Mm-hm, I thought that after that wonderful lunch we had, dessert would be the only thing to follow it up with. Try this," she said as she offered him a forkful of warm apple turnover. It was delicious, filled with raisins, and cinnamon-flavored apples, the crust flaky and light.

"Honey, it's wonderful. Did you really make this?" he asked incredulously.

"No, Pepperidge Farm did," Lauren said laughing. But I did make the coffee. Have some," she offered as she reached for one of the large brown coffee mugs.

They finished dessert, cleaned up the kitchen and listened to jazz from Michael's extensive CD collection for the next hour before deciding to call it a night. As soon as Lauren walked into the bedroom, she spotted the bag marked UPTOWN GIRL, and squealed.

"Michael, you didn't. How'd you know that's one of my favorite boutiques?" she asked, surprise written on her face. She held the bag up, turned it around to different angles, but did not attempt to retrieve whatever was inside.

"Honey, open it up. Shake it out. I want to see you in it," he said.

Lauren reached in, took out the tangerine-colored teddy and smiled slowly. "Was I supposed to put this on before or after what just happened?" she asked, placing one hand on her hip.

"Baby, you can put it on right now if you want to. I'm willing if you are," Michael said. They both laughed.

Neither of them got much sleep that night. Or the next. Or the next. It seemed the honeymoon was on and in full effect.

Chapter Nine

"Good morning, New York. Welcome to the wake-up show that's your ticket to an unforgettable day. I'm your host, Michael Townsend. And this is WJZZ—the best in contemporary jazz. We're just coming off a long set which featured Wayman Tisdale, David Sanborn, Al Jarreau, and England's finest export of late—Down to the Bone."

Michael reached over to queue up the next four singles that would be played. The micophone hung directly in front of him, and he gauged his next words carefully.

"Don't forget to fax us your lunchtime suggestions. One lucky winner will receive complimentary dinner for two at Portofino's on Manhattan's West Side. Just send us a list of at least six of your favorite artists and we'll do the rest! Okay—sit back and relax or sit up and take notice—here's the latest from Four Play—Bob James, Nathan East, Harvey Mason, and Larry Carlton—four guys who are recognized worldwide as incredible talents in their own rights. The combination is a powerful element. This one is from their new CD entitled *To Thine Own Self Be True*." He hit the PLAY button, and the sounds of smooth jazz reached the tri-state listening audience.

Michael removed his headset and sat back in the chair, his body filled with tension. Under normal circumstances, this was the time of day he loved the most when there was time to sort out what the remaining hours would hold—when he could do whatever it was he needed to and still have the opportunity to sample the best in contemporary jazz. On this day, however, he was faced with the very real possibility that perhaps, he'd gone a little too far.

He'd been totally honest when he'd outlined the reasons for his upcoming trip to the West Coast, but he had neglected to mention to Lauren that the decision of who actually went to L.A. had been left up to himself and Duke. In fact, he had volunteered to handle the long-distance assignment.

Duke had looked at him with amazement, shook his head, and then looked away. The two had been best friends since college; there wasn't much between them that went over either of their heads. If Michael was volunteering for a business trip three-thousand-miles away from his new bride, then things were not what they should be. Duke wanted to ask why, but he remained silent. Experience and friendship quieted his tongue; respect suppressed his curiosity.

"Okay, man," Duke agreed. "I'll hold down the operational end of the company. Morgan really hasn't left us any choice. We need to turn in a report that shows WJZZ's performance to be as solid as we initially said it was."

With less than twenty-four hours before he was scheduled to leave for California, Michael had gathered as much preliminary information as possible and was still working with the accounting department on the additional numbers. So far, he still hadn't found anything that would peak Morgan's interest. "Do you have any idea what may have contributed to his initiating this in the first place? The last time I checked the quarterlies, everything was in the black. Either that has changed or he is questioning something that should be a good thing," Michael stated, a puzzled look creasing his brow.

"Hey, you know these corporate types. Don't forget, Morgan is probably a frustrated 'suit' dressed in a venture-capitalist outer layer. Now that the old man is gone, he's probably trying to prove his self-worth by dotting every "i" and crossing every "t.""

Duke's explanation for their new partner's motivation was a plausible one, but Michael wasn't buying it. After all, Morgan had been the chief reason the deal had even been put on the table. It was his energy and enthusiasm which had made it happen. Why would he suddenly begin to have second thoughts, especially after some of the most difficult obstacles had been overcome? *Maybe I'm overreacting,* Michael thought.

"Since we met this dude, things that are totally unexplainable have been the norm. So why should this be any different?" Michael asked. "I'm going out to the coast, get a handle on the situation and compile a full report. And I'm asking you to be just as diligent on the operational side. Something is up, we just don't know what it is."

"Now you know I'll hold up my end of the deal here in the city. That's no problem. In fact, I have a couple of ideas of my own for getting a little further insight into what it is that Morgan is up to. So when are you leaving?" Duke wanted to move the subject along as quickly as possible to get to the topic that was really on his mind. The more they talked about the pending trip, the more Duke felt certain that Michael was behaving suspiciously too, but for totally different reasons.

He was certain that whatever it was, it had everything to do with his recently forged marriage. The fact that there might already be trouble in paradise did not bode well. And although Duke himself had been the first to caution Michael in the early stages of his relationship with Lauren, he now felt a great deal of affection for her.

"I'm headed out tomorrow night. Just rearrange the schedule so that the coverage for my morning show is in place, and be sure that the weekend spots are recorded in enough time to air for the upcoming week. Everything else is in place. If you really think that Morgan needs to be 'Robinsoned,' then handle it."

Duke laughed, realizing that the term they had made up in college was still effective some seven years later. They both loved old movies, with James Cagney and Edward G. Robinson holding a tie for their two favorite actors from an era that had long since passed. When they'd come upon the James Cagney classic "G Man" wherein his character joins a federal agent, they talked about the film for days, arguing that Robinson would have been more effective in the part. After that, whenever they needed to research a paper, get more information on a particular topic, or find out the specifics on a beautiful girl, they'd refer to the 1935 film star and crack up. Duke's use of the familiar term meant he would be doing his own brand of research into Morgan's request for the WJZZ financials.

Michael continued to prepare the studio for his absence while he and Duke firmed up their respective assignments for the coming week. Unbeknownst to them, plans were being put into effect that could change the entire scope of their current business relationship with Morgan Pryor and Cityscape Broadcast Network.

As Duke prepared to return to his own office, which was directly across the corridor from Michael's, he turned toward his friend. "Do you want me to look in on Lauren while you're away? I mean, I know she's an adult and all that, but you know women, they can get pretty upset when we have to leave the landscape. I figure if she has at least one of us around, it might cut down on the reaction you're sure to receive when you leave." Duke's face showed signs of real concern.

He remained silent, resolving to say nothing further if Michael showed the least resistance to discussing his situation.

"Actually, she will probably be busy decorating at the house. I think she wants to show me that she has some of the same talent her mother possesses. You know Eva works for an architecture and design firm in Maryland."

"No, I didn't know. I mean, I only met her briefly at the wedding. We were introduced at the reception, and then I was too busy to notice much else."

Michael laughed hard then. "Man, what are you talking about? If you mean the chick that showed up with Morgan as his assistant, I think you can forget it. And if you're talking about who I think you're talking about, you had *really* better forget about it." The look of seriousness on Michael's face only enhanced the message behind his statement.

Duke hesitated before responding. It wasn't that he was afraid to speak his mind on the subject, it was more that he had decided early on that if he were to come to a decision to pursue Gloria in any serious manner, it should be done with extreme caution.

"You know, you're trespassing on very sacred ground here. You and I both know that Gloria Sorrentino would be one huge challenge, not to mention all the possible dangers which could very well be in place. I never said I was going to *marry* her, so don't start reading me the riot act just yet," he said, conviction and a large degree of annoyance recognizable just under the surface.

Duke's emphasis on the word "marry" caught Michael totally off guard. He and Lauren had discussed the possibility of a minor flirtation between the two, but nothing as serious as a relationship had ever been considered. Michael decided to change the subject then. Duke was a grown man and it was not Michael's place to shelter him from anything.

"We were talking about your possibly doing a minor baby-sit of my most precious possession. How did we make the transition to the daughter of a deceased media mogul, a man who to this day can evoke or reduce most men to a shadow of their mere selves at the mention of his name? I think you're being a tad defensive." Michael issued the last statement with a rueful smile, letting Duke know he was off the hook.

"Look, I know you have been holding a torch for Gloria ever since you couldn't attend that dinner party Morgan threw over a year ago. I ran into Lauren again at that party, and the rest is life-changing history. That night actually became the catalyst for every major change that has occurred in my life between then and now. And don't forget, this is not over until it's over."

"In the meantime, thanks for the advice you were going to dispense, but I don't need it." Duke's statement was final. He'd come too far to back away from anything that spelled "challenge." And that was exactly what Gloria represented to him. In Duke's mind, her father was dead. Gino Sorrentino was no longer part of the picture or of the CBN business empire. He no longer existed. There was no effective way that his memory, no matter how vivid, could hold anything over his daughter's head that would affect her ability to forge ahead in her life. There was another nagging thought, but he pushed it even farther into the recesses of his mind.

"So, man, what do you want me to do? Should I at least call Lauren to check on her? I just know that your having to leave is not cool. Man, you know women keep track of stuff like that. They chart it in a little book, wait until they get enough marks to clobber us, and then hit us with it when we're least expecting it. That's what my ex-wife did. It only took six months for me to accumulate enough marks to be put in 'annihilation' mode. Then it took another six months for her to file for divorce, and another year for it to really happen. Two years down the drain." He stroked his prematurely grey and black beard as if it might provide insight into his past, then looked Michael directly in the eye. "I'm trying to spare you, man."

Michael laughed nervously then cleared his throat. He hadn't realized that Duke's words would affect him, hadn't known that his inner feelings were that easily tapped, but the sudden heaviness in his chest told him that he had been reached.

"Don't I know it. And by the way, thanks for the offer of checking in on Lauren, and thanks especially for the kernels of knowledge about women and all that. It's a wonder that we get any work done around here at all, what with our discussions of nonwork topics."

Michael's retort was an effort to quell the rise in his emotional vulnerability. He refused to allow his friend and partner to witness the turmoil he was already experiencing. He'd always given Duke a hard time about the short span of his own run at marital bliss, now he had very little to say. He almost felt as if he and Lauren would be lucky to survive to the one year mark. In the last few days, things had been going well between them, but with his pending departure, the assurances he'd given her since their wedding day now seemed almost ludicrous. He'd told her he'd only be gone about a week, but he had a sneaking suspicion he'd be in L.A. much longer. When he'd volunteered to go, he thought giving Lauren time to herself, time to adjust to the idea of marriage, would be wise. But now he had second thoughts about this decision.

"Look, man, I appreciate what you're trying to do—I really do—but I don't think it's necessary. Maybe if I back off a little, Lauren will come to her senses. In the past, distance has always served to bring us back together somehow. This trip may be more of a godsend than either of us imagines," Michael said with a distinct lack of conviction. His voice was heavy with emotion. Duke listened intently, wondering if there was anything at all that he could do to eliminate some of the pressure and pain his best friend was obviously experiencing.

"Look, why don't I just give Lauren a call. If there's anything she needs, she can always ask. She doesn't even have to know that we spoke on this." He'd just inadvertently given Michael an out too.

"Sure, that's exactly what I was thinking anyway. Don't worry—it's hard for Lauren to admit that she might need anybody. The only way she'll pick up that phone and call you is if there is a dire emergency, one that she cannot handle any other way."

"I get you: the self-sufficient woman. I've experienced it before in my own household. Clariza would also never admit to needing assistance either. I'll bet she has rethought that one by now," Duke added, his smile doing nothing to detract from the totally ruthless look on his otherwise handsome face.

"Sounds like you two were a match made in heaven. Anyway, I have to get home and get ready for my flight. It leaves pretty early in the morning."

"Okay, don't worry. I'll hold down the fort while you're out scouting the bad guys. You don't have to thank me either. It's part of my promise to myself to uphold my end of the partnership." Duke chuckled as he headed toward the door. Michael was such an easy person to read. He thought Duke was clueless about the state of his marriage, but he'd exhibited all the telltale signs of stress. Duke had experienced all the same emotions during his own short marriage.

"Go on home, dude, you look beat—as beat as I feel," Michael said. "The only saving grace for me is that I get to go home to a woman who is the love of my life." Michael swept up the program notes he'd been working on, added them to his briefcase and continued to clear his desk. He wasn't looking forward to the L.A. trip, but was hopeful that it might give him and Lauren the space they sometimes seemed to need.

"Yeah, I'm headed that way too. Home sounds good right about now. But there's one thing I have to do before I make the day part of history. And don't even think of asking me what that is. I too have a personal agenda you know." Duke lumbered toward the door, swung it open, and turned within its frame. "Have a good trip. Don't worry about anything here. When I finish looking under the rocks, I'll let you know what I find. Call me in a couple of days though, just in case I forget to reach out. You know how research and development can rob you of your good intentions. Don't forget," he stated, closing the door softly.

Michael muttered, "I won't," and went back to clearing his desk of the important documents he'd need during his extended stay on the West Coast. Twenty minutes later, he pushed the intercom signal for the building's garage, and waited for a response. When none came, he noted the hour. It was six forty-five. The parking garage closed at eight p.m. on weeknights, so the attendant had to still be there.

Michael turned out the lights in the recording studio and his office, headed into the garage, and spotted the attendant talking with another customer.

"Hey, Benjamin, could you pull out my car? You have the keys," Michael added, his mind already on the drive home.

"Sure Mr. T., I'll do just that." The attendant, a longtime employee of CBN, made his way across the rows of vehicles, some hidden by dustcovers, and pulled out Michael's dark blue Jaguar XJ6. It shone brilliantly even in the darkened interior of the garage, and Michael slid into the tan leather seat exhaling a brief sigh of relief. He started the engine and drove toward FDR Drive North. He exited at Ninety-sixth Street, heading downtown on Lexington Avenue. Then he stopped at the corner of Eighty-third Street, where he purchased a bouquet of pink roses from a local florist, who swore his flowers were flown in from Miami on a daily basis.

Parking the car down the street from the townhouse, Michael breathed a sigh of relief. He whistled a few bars from a song on the CD he'd been listening to on his drive home—the newest release by a multitalented musician named Brian Culbertson—and smiled for the first time that day.

It was a perfect ending to a hectic day. That is, until Lauren told him she was going back to work.

Chapter Ten

Lauren's announcement that she would be returning to Worldwide Airlines bothered him. It wasn't that Michael didn't want her to work, it was the reason he suspected was behind it. If she sincerely wanted more to do with her time besides decorate the house, he understood, and even would have been supportive. But if her reasoning was to simply spend time away from home, away from the marriage, away from him, their problems went even deeper than he suspected.

He'd come to recognize a distinct pattern of response in Lauren's behavior. Her modus operandi had been to use her job as a flight attendant to fly all over the world and avoid the problems that were staring her in the face. Before they'd married, before they'd moved in together, and even before she'd become pregnant, she'd used her job to remove herself from his life. He suspected that her intention this time would be the same.

Michael knew the scheduling issues that would arise as soon as she was back on active duty with the airline. They would hardly ever see each other. He also knew that Lauren was aware of this. This not only saddened him, but also angered him too. They had been doing so well. She'd seemed content to transform his bachelorlike townhouse into a home for them and he'd been happy to see the changes.

The evening had begun like any other, except he'd picked up roses on his way in from work. Lauren shrieked when she saw them.

"Michael, oh, they're wonderful. Thank you, sweetheart. You're so good to me," she added, kissing him quickly.

She'd put them in a vase, added water, and then checked on dinner. Michael glanced at the mail tray and noticed an open envelope from Worldwide Airlines. He held it up as he followed her into the kitchen.

"Honey, what's this?" he asked. He respected her privacy, and would not open or read anything which had not been addressed to him directly.

Several days earlier, Lauren had called her former supervisor at Worldwide Airlines and asked to be reinstated. Lauren was one of their best employees and the airline had been waiting eagerly for her to come back. She was scheduled to begin working again around the first of the month.

That afternoon, Lauren tried on her Worldwide Airlines uniform. After putting on the navy blue skirt and matching blazer, the crisp white and gray striped blouse, and the navy pumps, she looked in the mirror. She'd expected the uniform to need some alterations, but to her amazement, it still fit perfectly. Somehow she had remained exactly the same size. It seemed the pregnancy and subsequent miscarriage had had very little effect on her weight.

She'd felt nervous, but she was ready to assume her position as senior flight attendant. Still, Lauren wondered if she was doing the right thing. Her marriage to Michael was barely off the ground. Already, he was deeply involved in the affairs of WJZZ, but Lauren knew it would be smart for her to also have something to keep her mind engaged as well.

Plus, she'd never planned to be a stay-at-home wife. After the miscarriage, taking some time off work seemed like the right thing to do. Michael had encouraged her to take all the time she needed, and she had. Now, it felt right to be part of something larger than herself, and Worldwide certainly fit that description.

Lauren reasoned that Michael wouldn't be affected by her schedule, not on most days anyway. She'd purposely chosen lines which would minimize the likelihood of overnight stays and she took a flight schedule which spanned three days per week with each day ending in her home city. Lauren wanted to become acclimated to traveling again before she jumped in with both feet. She also wanted to be fair to the marriage.

For now, Lauren controlled her scheduled time out of state, though she realized she could only do that for a short period. At some point, she would have to seriously think about finding a different career if she couldn't convince Michael to get used to having his wife sleeping in another city for a living.

"Oh, I was going to talk to you about it over dinner. I've asked to be reinstated at work," she answered without turning around.

Michael realized that she was avoiding looking at him. "Lauren, we never discussed this. You could at least brought it up before you went ahead and put the wheels in motion," he said, curbing the anger becoming apparent in his voice.

"Michael, you act as if I've done this behind your back. You knew that at some point I would go back to work. What's the big deal? You work too. At least I'll still be based here in New York, in this house." With that, she felt she had said too much. She quieted, but it was too late.

Michael sighed, took a step closer to her and circled her waist with his hands. "Honey, is that what this is all about—the trip to California? Tell me that you didn't get reinstated just because I have to go away on a business trip. Lauren, that doesn't make any sense," he said, disbelief and disappointment seeping into his tone.

He turned her in his arms, and stepped back. It was important to him that he see her clearly, read her correctly, and he wanted to look into her eyes as they had this important exchange.

"It doesn't make sense to you. I can understand that. You have to admit, though, that it is pretty awful for us to be apart so soon in our marriage, especially when you don't really know how long you'll be gone. I just figured that if we were going to be apart, we might as well both be doing something we enjoy," she added.

Her matter-of-fact delivery did not fool him for one moment, and he dropped his arms to his sides in defeat. The airline had reinstated her and her return to work was a moot point as far as she was concerned.

Michael was overcome by anger and frustration. He'd done his best to avoid this kind of regression, done everything in his power to assure and then reassure her that the love he had for her was genuine. He did not believe, for one moment, that her going back to work was simply in order to having something to do. He knew Lauren better than that.

Michael's flight was scheduled to leave late the following evening and he had a full day's work ahead of him. Lauren lay beside him, her breathing irregular and shallow, and he knew that she too was unable to sleep.

Finally, after tossing and turning for hours, Lauren reached for him blindly, seeking refuge from the misery she knew she'd caused. She came to him willingly, with a need that was more than sexual. He responded, knowing it would be the last time they would make love for a while, based on his projections for his trip.

Their lovemaking was tender, gentle, and tentative. Michael caressed her as if he were committing each curve of her body to memory, and Lauren responded despite the sadness which filled her.

The torrent of passion which overtook them came in waves, building slowly and reaching a powerful crescendo as the emotions that filled their hearts and minds converted to a desire that neither of them could repress. As strains of early morning light filled their bedroom, they finally fell asleep, exhausted from holding back the many things they wanted to share.

When Michael left for the office that morning, Lauren walked him to the door, her eyes rimmed with red from unshed tears, her voice filled with emotion. "I want you to understand that I signed up for work not to hurt you, but to help me," she said quietly.

"I'm trying, Lauren. I'm trying to understand a lot of things right now, so bear with me. I thought we were over these hurdles, but they keep coming up."

She hung her head then, clearly holding back tears, and swallowing hard. "Give me time, Michael. You promised you'd do that. I never said this would be easy and you never said it had to be," she responded.

"You're right. But I didn't think you'd make it any harder than it had to be, either. Lauren, you're not playing fair right now. I need to know that you're at least on our side. Notice I said 'our,'" he repeated.

"Yes, I did hear that," she said, the faint beginnings of a smile on her face.

He pulled her into a loose embrace, not wanting them to part without clearing the air.

"Look, we'll talk about this some more, okay," he said.

"Sure. It's not as if I go back to work tomorrow. It doesn't become effective until the first of the month," she said, telling him more than he really wanted to know.

"Good, then we have some time to work out a schedule."

"Absolutely. See, it's not so bad," she teased, wanting him to approve of her decision.

"Lady, what you are doing to me is not really fair, but I have a feeling that you're still testing me so I'm going to handle myself and you at the same time," Michael said then. He pulled her closer, kissed her for a long moment, and then released her. The suitcase Lauren had packed stood by the entrance to the townhouse. He carried it to the car with him.

Lauren continued to stand in the doorway, clad in white silk pajamas, her hair still tousled from sleep, her face full of love. Michael committed the scene to memory, knowing he'd miss her the moment he left New York City.

Later that morning, at the offices of CBN, Noelle was working on a report that would be delivered to the board of directors of Cityscape Broadcast Network at their next monthly meeting. The meeting would focus on data that had been compiled from Arbitron ratings covering radio markets throughout the United States. Each market survey comprised feedback from thousands of homes in which radio was a major component: Telephone surveys documented the listening habits, station preferences, and most regularly chosen formats of listeners. It was a standard industry poll that had been established decades earlier. This research played a pivotal role in marketing, and Noelle took note of the published statistics.

Noelle wondered if Morgan was aware of her inner turmoil and prayed that he was not.

That thought was at the forefront of Noelle's mind as she began to transcribe some remaining notes from Morgan's dictated items. She was hoping to finish before he arrived, knowing he probably had even more work with him. Noelle glanced at the clock atop her desk and realized it was noon.

Morgan had not arrived at the office, though he'd called earlier to say he was on the way back from a meeting. Her brow furrowed as she hurried to complete the final document.

The phone rang, breaking the silence which existed in the otherwise empty offices of CBN. Many of the staff members had taken the day off in order to get an early start on the upcoming holiday weekend. Noelle picked it up even before glancing at the caller-identification panel. "Good morning, Cityscape Broadcast Network."

Static and background noise that indicated a noisy, urban environment greeted her. Then Morgan's voice boomed into her ear and she could not hold back a smile.

"Hey. Are you holding down the fort?" he asked with authority.

"Yes. I've actually almost completed the board meeting report you dictated. Where are you?" she asked, but didn't wait for him to answer. "Are you still coming in?"

"Yeah, I'm on my way. Got caught up in a little traffic and some other business I had to take care of," he said quickly. "I'll be there in about twenty minutes. Did anyone important call?"

"No, the phones have been pretty quiet. Mail was just delivered, but I haven't gotten to it yet," she added. It was stacked neatly alongside her desk.

"Okay, great. Listen, I've been running around all morning and didn't even stop to get breakfast. I'm going to pick up some lunch. Would you like something?"

Noelle hesitated, her mind instantly alert. She hadn't had anything but coffee for breakfast and realized that she was hungry. He wasn't asking her to lunch, just if she wanted food. *What harm could there be in eating?*

"Actually, I'm starving, thank you for asking." She wondered if she was doing the right thing.

"Okay, I'll have Rodney stop somewhere, and we'll pick up something. Anything you want in particular?" he asked, which almost made her giggle into the phone. She felt like they were on a first date, where first impressions were still being made.

That realization put her guard back into position, causing her to almost decline his invitation. "Look, it sounds like it might be a hassle. You know I can always order out from one of the menus I have here in the desk drawer," she added quickly.

"Don't be silly. You can't order the stuff Rodney can find down here. We're in Little Italy. See you in about half an hour." He hung up.

Just that quickly, he'd turned the tables, taken control, and was in full charge. Noelle felt weak. She was uncomfortable having lunch with someone whom she was investigating— probably an investigation that would lead to prosecution by the United States District Attorney's office.

Despite those thoughts, she found herself only moments later in the restroom reapplying her lipstick, checking to see if her hair was in place. The face that looked back at her in the mirror was one of a young woman who was confused. Acknowledging her plight did nothing to settle the uneasiness in her stomach, so she returned to her desk.

Morgan arrived exactly a half hour later, laden with two shopping bags, looking as if he'd enjoyed whatever it was he had been doing earlier that day. He put the food in the conference room, went into his office, and closed the door. Noelle was unsure of his intent, but hunger motivated her to find plates, napkins, and cutlery while she waited.

"Noelle, can you come in here for a minute?" he called to her. She wanted to tell him that the food was getting cold, but felt it would be rude—especially since he was the one who had brought it in the first place—so she simply walked into his office.

From the looks of the disheveled desk and the mahogany credenza which sat directly behind it, he was searching for something.

"Have you seen the file marked ONYX dated either November 2000 or 2001? It should have been right here, but now I can't seem to find it."

"No, not at all. I just finished the correspondence you dictated a couple of days ago. The files I worked on for your board meeting report are all back in place now," she answered with equal certainty. In the back of her mind, she frantically retraced her steps and located each of the files she had copied and hopefully returned to its original place. Noelle silently prayed that she hadn't misplaced the file in question. It could be her undoing if that was the case, the smoking gun that would alert Morgan that there was more to her existence in his life that met the eye.

Morgan continued to dig through the manila folders in his lap. Finally, he pulled one out and held it up. "Sorry to bother you, Noelle. I just found what I was looking for. The meeting I had this morning has me convinced that there are a couple of loose ends that need to be tied. That file has all the pertinent information to do just that."

Noelle breathed an inaudible sigh of relief. Only a tiny element of guilt over her purpose for being at CBN lingered in her mind; it was immediately brushed away by the presence of integrity. She was getting a job done—a job that had been initiated by the Federal Bureau of Investigation. Noelle recognized it was a tough job, but she was one hundred percent comfortable in completing it. Even if she had to dupe her very handsome boss to do it. The nagging knowledge that thus far none of the information they'd recovered suggested wrongdoing by the man seated across from her was a moot point. He had yet to be exonerated.

Moments later, Morgan invited Noelle to join him in the conference room. He dug into the various take-out containers he'd brought from Il Pestorino's. Linguine Bolognese, sautéed calamari, broccoli rabe in olive oil and veal scallopini filled the room with the pungent aromas of fresh garlic and oregano. There was also peasant bread, herb-filled extra-virgin olive oil, and a bottle of Merlot he'd picked up on the way.

"My God, this is a feast. I can't eat like this. I'll never be able to do any more work this afternoon," Noelle exclaimed, obviously impressed as she surveyed the assortment of dishes.

"You're not expected to work directly after experiencing a meal like this. Talk to me for a while, then we'll go back to work. In Sicily, we'd both take a two-hour nap before working again," he offered with a single wink of an eye. He was flirting with her, and Noelle knew that whatever the outcome, she'd probably regret having agreed to have lunch with him. It was too late to back out now. So she did the next best thing and began serving them both.

"I thought you'd probably pick up a pizza, or maybe a little antipasto. This is unbelievable," Noelle said.

"No pizza for me, thanks. I rarely eat the stuff. After you've been exposed to really good Italian food, nothing less will do. My mom is a great cook and my stepdad made sure he taught her a few of his specialties. They made a great couple, and cooked lots of good food together."

It was the first time Morgan had talked openly about his family to her and his statement caught her off guard. She wondered if the death of his stepfather had affected him greatly at the time it happened, or if he was simply caught up in reminiscing. Then she chastised herself. Clearly, the man was not a monster. Then, she wondered if she was selling out for an expensive Italian take-out lunch.

"My parents were married for a short time before they divorced," she found herself saying. "I never got the chance to see them together, happy, laughing, or even in the same room. I grew up spending summers with my dad and winters with my mom." The statement had come out before Noelle realized it. Afterward she became silent, feeling as if she'd exposed more of herself than she'd meant to.

Morgan picked up on her reservation and changed the subject. "So, how do you like the calamari?" He noticed that she'd cleaned her plate and was helping herself to seconds.

"Love it. It's so tender and the garlic is delicious," she exclaimed.

"Good, but don't fill up on that only. Have some of the veal and the pasta too." He continued to watch her silently for awhile, his mind on the morning's task as well as the woman who sat before him. He still hadn't come to any concrete conclusion concerning Noelle. He'd admitted to himself that he liked her, but there were too many unanswered questions about her. She was confident, intelligent, and something else that he couldn't quite put his finger on. She was also extremely attractive. At that moment, he was enjoying lunch with her, although he knew that if he'd asked her to leave the office for the meal, she probably would have turned him down. He wasn't sure of the reason, but she'd put a barrier between them, and it was solidly in place. At least for now.

The intercom sounded, interrupting their meal, and Noelle picked it up. "Yes, actually he's right here. Sure, hold on," she responded, hitting the hold button and replacing the receiver. "It's Michael Townsend," she told Morgan. "He needs to speak with you before he leaves for L.A."

"Sure." Morgan pulled the phone over to his side of the conference table and picked up the receiver.

"Hey, Michael, what's doing?" he asked quickly. "Okay, okay. Listen, if you'd like, you can come over to the conference room. I stopped in Little Italy and picked up lunch. I think I might have overdone it. There's enough food for an army here," he added, laughing.

"Okay, good. See you in a few," Morgan said, and then hung up. He looked at Noelle. "I don't think you've met Michael Townsend outside of the wedding, and that didn't count, 'cause he was preoccupied," he added, a grin on his face.

"I've seen him coming into the building, but I always think he won't recognize me, so I've never spoken to him," Noelle admitted.

"Well, even though he's married, I don't think he would have forgotten you. At least I know I wouldn't have," Morgan said candidly. Noelle looked at him and continued eating, unable to tell if he was joking or serious.

There was a knock on the door and Michael entered, wearing a brown knit shirt, gray corduroy pants, and brown cordovan loafers. He looked slightly distracted but handsome, and Noelle wondered if he realized how attractive he was.

Morgan immediately stood, introduced Noelle, and told Michael to dig in.

"I appreciate your invitation. I've been working on some loose ends all morning. I'm trying to get them taken care of before I leave for California tonight," he added.

"Listen, if you don't finish them before that, just work on them while you're out there." Morgan's suggestion sounded nonchalant, like a pragmatic approach, and for the first time since being asked to review the WJZZ books, Michael felt it could be easily resolved.

"Thanks, that's a good piece of advice. If I can't resolve the issues quickly, that is exactly what I'll have to do."

Michael served himself from the various containers and cartons that were lined up in the middle of the conference table.

"Try the calamari. It's so good," Noelle advised, her mouth still full of the garlic-spiced appetizer.

"Thanks," Michael answered politely.

Morgan, realizing that Michael did not recognize her, stepped in. "Oh man, please forgive me. This is my new assistant, Noelle Stephenson. I brought her out to the wedding also. You may remember her from that weekend," he offered.

Michael looked at Noelle, took in the expensive cut of

her clothing, the unwavering direct look she gave and shook his head. "No, but I usually remember a beautiful woman. Please forgive me, I've had stars in my eyes since I got married," he admitted.

"No, don't apologize. That's a wonderful thing to hear coming from a newlywed. Congratulations, by the way. It was a lovely wedding," Noelle added.

"Thanks, we thought so. I can't believe it's only been a month."

"Time flies when you're having fun," Morgan said.

"That's the truth," Michael chimed in as he sat down with his plate.

As they ate, the two principals of CBN discussed a few of the key points which Michael would investigate during his trip. Half an hour passed before Michael wondered if Morgan always invited his assistant to lunch in the company conference room. He wasn't sure there was anything going on between them, but he thought it odd. Then he chastised himself for being a frustrated matchmaker, and dismissed the thought altogether. Morgan was dedicated to CBN and to getting the job done.

Though he was full, Michael forced himself to eat some more of the good food on his plate, and then explained that he needed to get back to his desk to finish the work Morgan had requested.

Before leaving, he thanked Noelle for attending the wedding, and laughed when she smiled and said, "I had no choice. He told me I'd be fired."

Morgan laughed and confirmed it. "She's telling the truth. I did," he said, unashamed of the fact that he'd exerted playful force to get her to go, none of which made up for the fact that nothing at all had occurred.

Michael closed the door, wondering if Morgan always exhibited that kind of odd charm in his personal pursuits. It could explain a lot.

The phone rang just as he walked into his office. Duke's voice was barely audible over the rumble of the train.

"Man, where are you?" Michael asked.

"I'm on my way to the office. I know I should just stay out of there, but I have some things I want to talk to you about before you leave for California. What's your day like?"

"It's almost over. I'm just putting some last-minute touches on everything before I head out."

"I'll be there in about a half an hour," Duke said. "If you're there, fine. If not, I have my work to do anyway, and I'll talk with you in a day or so."

"Sure thing. I'll talk to you. Bye," Michael said absently, already preoccupied with the papers on his desk.

They hung up.

Chapter Eleven

Michael sat back in his leather desk chair, closed his eyes and allowed his mind to go blank for a moment. He'd finished everything, packed all the necessary items he would need and was only hours away from a trip he didn't want to take. He knew going to L.A. was necessary, which made it all the more distasteful because there were no alternatives.

He breathed deeply and thought of Lauren, almost picking up the phone to call her. Something stopped him, though, and instead, he sat back and closed his eyes, allowing his mind to wander.

Their month-old marriage was fresh in his mind, the details of their short honeymoon still clear and concise. He thought of the walks on the beach, the Jacuzzi in their suite and the cove they'd found the first day, when they'd walked the entire length of the resort's property and beyond. He remembered the way the sunlight looked in Lauren's hair, turning it different shades of auburn, brown, and red. He'd reached out to touch it, and Lauren had laughed when he commented on its colors.

* * *

"Even when I was a kid, my hair was never one color. Now that I've become an adult, it's even more varied. My mom says it's our Native American heritage coming through," she added, laughing.

"Well, it looks good on you," Michael replied, his hand warm on her neck. They continued walking, sunglasses, sunscreen, and bottles of water their companions in an effort to combat the Barbados heat and sun.

The stretch of pearl-colored sand leading to several other hotels and resorts was well-traveled by guests, locals, and anyone wanting to quickly span the distance between Christ Church and its neighboring township. They walked slowly, holding hands, watching the surf and several bathers who had chosen to jump waves or to swim leisurely along the shoreline.

The cove they'd found completely by accident further down the beach had been nature's handiwork. Made entirely from layers of coral, it rose high on one side and leveled into a flat plane of embedded rock on the other. The opening was large at the beginning, and then tapered off into a small, narrow path, which filled with water at high tide. Small seashells littered the entrance as testimony to their occupants' having visited at one time or another. Unless passerbys were looking from a specific angle, the unique structure was all but invisible to anyone walking along the beach.

Michael and Lauren stopped, spread out their towels just outside the mouth of the cove, and headed for the water.

"Last one in is a newlywed," Michael called over his shoulder as he ran toward the surf. Lauren laughed and joined him only a few steps behind.

"I think I'm guilty," she called out and dove in headfirst.

A good swimmer since childhood, Lauren swam to where Michael was, then turned onto her back and floated. He *watched her, saw that she could handle herself, and added that to the list of her accomplishments.*

"So, you're pretty good, huh?" he called to her.

"I do okay. You look as if you've taken a few lessons yourself," she said turning her head toward him. "Remember, you tested me before, when we visited your family home here," she reminded him.

"Yes, we definitely did test the water that day," he said, laughing. Lauren shook her head, the memory of their lovemaking on that trip sending a flush to her face. "My dad made sure I could swim well. He and Mom were both excellent swimmers, so it was a priority for me." He continued to tread water as he watched his wife closely.

Lauren's yellow-and-white striped bathing suit, a two piece with a pale yellow halter top and bikini-cut shorts, was both fashionable and practical. The colors accentuated the warm brown tones of her skin, and Michael found he had trouble tearing his eyes away from her. She floated effortlessly, appearing peaceful, calm, and relaxed. Something about that made him think of disturbing that veneer, so he dove underwater, came up right beside her, and flipped her over.

Lauren went under, came up sputtering mad, and headed for Michael. The chase was on. They laughed, teased, and played like dolphins for close to an hour, then realized they were both getting too much sun. They headed for their towels, ready to reapply sunscreen. They positioned themselves close enough to the opening of the cove so that the noon day sun was blocked.

Michael watched Lauren as she poured a quarter-sized portion of sunscreen into the palm of her hand and motioned for him to lay down. He did so, exposing his back to her, and wondered if it was really necessary. He had never burned, but he'd never declined an opportunity to feel Lauren's hands on his body. He sat still while Lauren applied the lotion.

Her hands, firm and cool, relaxed and excited him. He found himself thinking of things which had absolutely nothing to do with sun, sea, or sand and was glad he was laying on his stomach.

Lauren's hands traveled in a circular motion, marveling at the play of muscles on her husband's physique. Michael was tremendously well-built, and Lauren felt herself respond to the feel of him, the nearness of him, as she continued to apply sunscreen lotion to Michael's back, his arms, and the backs of his legs. He lay sprawled on a giant beach towel, his eyes closed, his breathing coming in slow, short bursts.

Her hands traveled the length of his body and felt the strength of it, felt the power he possessed. Michael was so relaxed that sleep would have been the next logical option. Instead, he sat up, motioned for the bottle, and poured a healthy dose into one hand. He gestured for Lauren to lie down, and moved her hair over to one side.

He rubbed the lotion between both hands, then began to apply it in even strokes and measures against the skin of her back, sliding up to her arms and back down again, against the waistline of her bikini bottoms and the tops of her thighs. His touch was gentle, yet firm, and Lauren felt herself becoming aroused.

Michael marveled at the supple texture of her skin and the way she felt in his hands. He wanted to plant kisses along her back, up and down her thighs, and then turn her over and repeat the process.

Lauren's breathing changed as his caresses became more detailed. He moved to the center of her back, unhooking the back of her bathing suit, then made his way to her bottom. Lauren felt as if she were slowly being set on fire and wondered how much more she could take.

Michael's voice seemed to come from far away. "Turn over, honey, let me do this right." Lauren did as she'd been told, thankful that the sunglasses she wore hid the look of pure lust which surely must have been present in her eyes.

Michael carefully poured additional sunscreen into his hands, his eyes feasting on the sight before him. Through her sunglasses, he could see Lauren's eyes were closed. She appeared to be asleep, but Michael knew that was not the case. He smiled as he began to rub the lotion onto her exposed belly. He also applied the lotion to the area of exposed cleavage above the bikini top and to the tops of her arms as well. The area of the bathing suit that he'd unhooked hung loosely and Michael's hands circled the area slowly.

Lauren's breathing changed suddenly, passion overtaking her as she did her best to remain calm. She reached up, removed her sunglasses, and watched Michael's face. He remained involved in what he had been doing, then looked at his bride.

"You have beautiful skin, Lauren," he whispered, looking down at her intently.

"And you have wonderful hands," she said looking into his eyes.

Michael lowered his lips to hers, and the kiss inflamed the desire which had been smoldering since his first touch. One of his hands found its way beneath her swimsuit top, and began circling the tip of one breast slowly. Lauren's sharp intake of breath signaled a level of desire that had been simmering for the past moments. Now, she felt as if her entire body was on fire. She cradled his head in her hands as their kisses became more intense.

Michael pulled her to him then and whispered into her ear. "I can't wait any longer," he said, his plea echoing her own need.

He helped her to her feet, and they moved their beach towels farther into the cove.

Lauren immediately felt the change in temperature and marveled at the difference. It was definitely cooler, with the sunlight being cut off by the coral buildup, which created a roof over them. Michael laid the towels together, then sat down and reached for Lauren's hand. She bit her lip for a moment, then stepped forward holding the top of her bathing suit with one hand.

"Let me," Michael said simply as he took the garment from her. Lauren looked at him boldly and smiled. He had always been able to affect her this way, even when she hadn't wanted him to. She wondered if that would always be the case, and then the thought was gone, replaced by the feel of his strong hands as she welcomed his embrace.

They lay on the towels, facing one another, and kissed slowly. Michael's lips drank from her mouth, creating a haven for her, a place of refuge for them both.

Lauren ran her hands over his body, still hot from the sun. Michael leaned over her, looked into her eyes, and whispered, "I love you, Lauren."

"I love you too," she responded. He lowered his mouth to hers, playing tentatively with her tongue. Lauren wound her arms around his neck and gently pulled him down to her. This time, the kiss was not at all tentative. Michael was no longer surprised at the depth of Lauren's passion. He'd witnessed it on their wedding night, but the lovemaking they experienced on this day was different from any time before.

Michael placed kisses along the length of her body. "Do you want me to stop?" he asked softly, knowing they were still in public although the cove was practically hidden.

"No, please, no," she moaned, need filling every nuance of her voice, as Michael helped remove her bikini bottom.

He looked at the beauty of her and shook his head in wonder.

"You're the most wonderful thing that's ever happened to me," he said, placing tiny kisses along her belly. His tongue darted into her navel slowly and Lauren arched her back. She'd closed her eyes, blocking out the vision of whatever *was to come. However, she was unable to block out her sensory perception, as Michael continued sampling the delights of her body.*

Lauren moaned, one hand thrown across her mouth, as Michael continued to explore her body knowingly. He brought Lauren to the pinnacle of her desire time and time again before he finally joined with her. Each time Lauren cried out in ecstasy, Michael covered her mouth with his and began earnestly to make love to his wife. He marveled at the heat she generated, and knew he never wanted to be joined with another the way he was with Lauren. She offered herself to him fully then, and he reached the depth of her, marveling at the fit, the feel, the response she was able to provide.

He took his time, loving her slowly at first, then as she urged him through the thrusts of her body, he quickened the pace, knowing he too was reaching the end.

Lauren felt as if her body were not her own as she responded to Michael's lovemaking. She felt him fill her, felt the power and the pride that was her husband, and knew beyond a shadow of a doubt that she loved this man. Whether or not they would be able to withstand the test of time, at that moment, all else was forgotten. Her body became an instrument of desire in his arms, and each found fulfillment in the next moments.

Lauren was quiet as Michael rolled them onto their sides still joined together. He reached out to touch her face and again whispered "I love you," kissing her softly.

"I love you too," she responded, wondering if they would truly make it through the twelve months they'd agreed to. They would always make love, she suspected. The chemistry between them was too strong for it to be any other way. That was not the problem, and had never been.

At that moment, the thoughts running through Lauren's mind mirrored those of her husband. He continued to cradle *his wife in his arms long after their lovemaking had ceased as they napped in the hidden cove. They were awakened later by the sounds of children's voices and the lapping of the ocean at the door of their haven. The tide was rising, and with each successive hour, the Caribbean Sea offered more of itself onto the shoreline, bringing the sand and the sea together as one.*

They smiled at one another, retrieved their discarded garments and donned them without words—they were not needed.

They walked the beach back to their hotel, hand in hand, silently, satiated both mentally and physically.

Michael's memory of that day filled him with hope. He knew the trip to California would offer the big obstacle, the first real challenge that he and Lauren had faced since they walked down the aisle. He hoped that memories such as the one he'd just recalled would sustain and guide them during the upcoming weeks.

The intercom rang then, and his secretary announced Duke's arrival.

"Sure. Hey, Monica, would you please also have a couple of Cokes brought in?" he said quickly, realizing he was thirsty.

"Sure, Michael," she answered.

Duke walked in then, sat in the guest chair opposite Michael's desk and looked at his partner.

"So, you're almost out of here, huh?"

"Yeah—it's almost a done deal. I hope you can hold down the fort until I return."

Duke laughed, smoothed his beard, and sat back into the chair more deeply. "Look, you and I both know I can do that. I'm here more to reassure you on your end of the deal. If there's anything you need, anything at all, Michael, don't hesitate to get on the horn."

"You don't have to worry about that. You know that I'm perfectly capable of reaching out to you, if necessary. I don't even know why you felt you had to say that," Michael responded, suddenly looking at Duke as if he were seeing him for the first time.

Duke looked away. "Man, I'm just a little concerned with the entire layout of this thing. Morgan is no fool. But neither are you and I. So, why does he all of a sudden have this tremendous need to analyze WJZZ again?"

Duke's question went unanswered for a long moment, then Michael looked at his partner and smiled.

"You know, I don't really know or care. We both know that when it's like this, it has to get done. How many times have we witnessed something we didn't like, didn't understand, and hadn't anticipated, but had to respond to anyway? And respond we did, right?"

"Damned right. So, I guess you're saying back off, huh?" Duke asked then.

"Yeah, as much as I appreciate your concern. Man, it's just part of doing business. You and I both felt that Morgan was a straight shooter even after some portions of the original company were involved in that whole big scandal just after Gino Sorrentino passed away. But, that's what gave CBN such a positive prognosis."

"I remember it well. And that's probably why I'm a little concerned about what's going on right now. Morgan came out of that smelling like a rose. Now we join the ranks with him and the next thing you know, he's crying foul, demanding that we both do an in-depth study of our company books and such. I'm sorry, maybe I just don't like the guy," Duke admitted.

"Morgan? What's not to like? The dude keeps to himself, minds his business for the most part, and generates a ton of cash just by being who he is."

"Yeah, but he also tries his best to control the lives of

everyone around him. Mikey, you can't seriously be taking up for him. He just sentenced you to West Coast Purgatory for a week—at least—without blinking an eye. And he was just at your wedding," Duke said, his emotions clearly escalating.

"Whoa, whoa—either of us could have agreed to do the thing on the coast. I stepped up to the plate because I've always been totally involved in that operation. It will be easier and faster for me to examine and analyze whatever is going on out there. You do agree, don't you?" Michael asked, his eyebrows raised.

Duke watched him, and broke into a chuckle. "Yeah, you're right, but I still don't like it."

"Maybe there's something else about Morgan that bothers you," Michael offered, watching Duke carefully.

"Maybe. Maybe I don't like the way he thinks he's so in control of everyone and everything. I don't know, can't explain it. And you know what? I'm not even going to try," he added.

Michael watched him closely and wondered if his partner's attitude had anything to do with Morgan's sister, Gloria. He wanted to ask, but figured Duke might take it as another sign of meddling.

Duke sat back and wondered if he should have come. The things that were really on his mind were far beyond Michael's scheduled trip to Los Angeles and Morgan's meddling, though both tied in together.

"Look, partner, if there is anything you need while you're out there, anything at all, you pick up the phone and you tell me," he repeated. "None of this 'higher moral ground' stuff. I mean it. I'm not one hundred percent sure of Morgan's true intentions, but if there's anything that comes up that seems shaky, I want to know about it. And you can be damned sure that I'll stay in touch with you too," Duke added emphatically.

"Man, you have my word. If there's one thing we both pride ourselves on, it is communication. That's our business, it's our policy, it's our livelihood. Right?" Michael waited for a response as Monica brought in two cans of soda.

"Absolutely. I have some things to do myself, so I may be a little busy, but don't worry about that. If you need me, just call."

Michael looked over at his partner then and wondered what he was referring to. The last time Duke had something to do that he'd neglected to talk about, the guy had wound up buying a 1957 Corvette with no engine, no carburetor, and no battery. The body alone, though, was worth what he paid, so the restoration had been worth it. Michael knew that Duke could be impulsive. The trait often landed him in precarious positions.

"Man, just don't do anything you can't undo with the least amount of effort," he cautioned, pointing a finger in Duke's direction.

Down the hall, Noelle was startled when an FTD deliveryman walked in, asked for her signature, and left a long box filled with roses on her desk.

She opened them cautiously, wondering who would have sent flowers, and was shocked when she read the card. *Happy Birthday. Your brother, Neal,* it read.

Obviously, the bureau wanted to work every angle possible, hoping to get a reaction from anyone who was affected by the gesture. Noelle figured Morgan would rather cut off his own head before he'd show any curiosity. She didn't have long to wait before she had a definitive answer.

Morgan walked in sometime later, said good morning and walked into his office. He never uttered a word about the flowers. Noelle wrote the whole gesture off as another unnecessary bureau expense and continued working. The day passed quickly, with the phones ringing off the hook, messengers delivering documents, including the two reports Morgan had been waiting for, and an even higher volume of incoming calls from each of the CBN satellite offices. Noelle wondered if there had been any change in policy or procedure that prompted them, but realized it was probably simply a knee-jerk reaction to the quarterly results that had been issued two months earlier and had only just been analyzed.

Noelle wanted to see that report, wanted to evaluate its findings and indications. She suspected it would quite possibly contain both clarifying and damaging pieces of information that could make all the difference to her investigation. For several weeks, she watched and waited, hoping to seize an opportunity to access even the most rudimentary portions of good information for the Bureau. As yet, nothing had surfaced, and she realized that it was taking an inordinate amount of time for her to come up with anything.

She completed the report which she'd been asked to do earlier in the week, moved on to Morgan's daily log, and saw the light in his office go out. She braced herself, knowing he hadn't forgotten the brief exchange of the morning or the flowers which still sat on her desk.

He walked past her desk without speaking, then turned around almost as if he'd forgotten his surroundings. "By the way, I was wondering if you'd consider being the assistant on an assignment that's crucial right now," he said, his eyebrow raised.

Noelle looked up, smiled, and said, "Sure—what is it?"

"I'd like you to assist Michael Townsend. He's working on the West Coast on an assignment. We'll fly you out to L.A. for awhile until you guys can get a handle on some data he's been analyzing. It shouldn't be more than three or four business days," he added calmly.

"So, when would you want me to join him?" Noelle's

heart beat rapidly, she knew this could possibly be the break she'd need to wrap up the investigation.

Morgan's demeanor was in direct opposition to his inner feelings. The flowers on her desk had both surprised and unnerved him. He wanted to bring them up, but couldn't bring himself to utter the words.

"I haven't decided yet. Let's give Michael a chance to investigate first. I'll let you know when you'll head out."

Noelle watched him closely, grinning broadly. *This is what I've been waiting for,* she thought. She quickly recovered her demeanor. "You know, not that it's any of your business, but those flowers are from my brother. Today is my birthday," she lied.

The look on Morgan's face was strained. Finally, he smiled and said, "Why didn't you tell me it was your birthday? I would have acknowledged it in some way for sure."

"I really don't like to make a big deal of it." Noelle continued to look directly at him when she spoke, wondering how quickly she could get to Los Angeles. She suspected the answers to many of the questions the Bureau had could be found in the records she'd just been assigned to scrutinize. She couldn't believe her luck.

Meanwhile, Morgan watched her with curiosity, wondering if she knew he'd just exiled her, even if it was only for a few days.

"Anyway, when you make reservations, put it on the corporate account. The information is in the Cityscape Corporate Travel folder" he added.

An hour later, Noelle finished the assignment she'd been working on. The smile that had appeared on her face, after Morgan told her she'd be going to L.A. was still there. She'd get to see what the West Coast operation of WJZZ was up to. In her mind, Michael Townsend could also be useful to her investigation. Just because he'd only recently joined CBN didn't absolve him of all possible culpability. It wouldn't have been the first time a major corporation had made an acquisition simply to mask its dirty books. She has seen her share of corporate malfeasance and knew that Cityscape Broadcast Network certainly fit the profile, at least on paper. Now would be her opportunity to see the books—not just the reports.

Noelle made contact with her supervisor that evening, eager to get the okay for the change of locale. He gave the okay, then confirmed a new contact number. The division would do everything necessary to support Noelle's efforts to bring down Cityscape Broadcast Network.

Chapter Twelve

Lauren hadn't bargained on being abandoned, at least not in the first month of her marriage. She knew she was being dramatic and silly, knew she was quite possibly overreacting, but the memories she still carried of her father leaving her mother were reawakened now that Michael was gone. These emotions resurfaced constantly making her daily routine difficult. Her thoughts frequently returned to events from the past, like the time she'd been invited to the "Father-Daughter Dance" at her school. She'd torn up the invitation, cried for a day, and vowed to never become a wife or mother. She'd wished she could change her status as a daughter but realized that was impossible. Now, she wondered if her marriage to Michael had been a bigger mistake than even she had bargained for.

Like any true survivor, Lauren resolved to think back on the formula she used to get through those difficult times during her youth. She remembered it well. Concentration on school work, detachment from those around her, and a strict discipline to keep her mind off her father had been key. It had worked before, and she prayed that it would work again with Michael. This time, there was even more riding on her ability to handle whatever came her way.

Until Michael returned and her job began, she busied herself integrating the prized possessions she'd brought from the apartment she'd shared with Gloria into Michael's townhouse. Each day she tackled a different room, and by the middle of the first week that he was gone, the finished product was ready for scrutiny.

Michael's two-story townhouse had been furnished in a rudimentary way: Sparse, masculine, and noticeably absent of the pieces that defined a space. His taste was still both elegant and expensive. Lauren added several coral and peach accessories throughout the house, including vases, artwork, and a few suede pillows, adding warmth and texture to the rooms. She also added several kitchen utensils, wondering how Michael had managed beforehand. There was not a single spatula in the house, nor did he own a large mixing spoon. She laughed when she realized that he probably cooked with difficulty, especially when trying to remove or stir anything larger than fork-sized.

The bathroom that connected with Michael's bedroom was beige, beige, and more beige. Lauren added large black towels, purchased a dark brown oval rug with black accents, and filled a shiny wood bowl with black marbles. She also hung a series of black-and-white prints on one wall and a small mirror framed in oak on the other. A single square black ceramic vase placed on the pedestal sink now held an oversized spray of baby's breath. The change was dramatic. She wondered if Michael would like it.

Lauren cautioned herself not to make the decór too feminine. She didn't want Michael to feel as if she'd taken over, but she did want him to recognize that she'd moved in.

He called her at least once each day, usually in the evenings when he returned to his hotel room, and often at some point during the course of the day. Lauren waited for his call each evening, savoring the time they spent, the things they said, and, more importantly, the things that were left unsaid. She purposely refrained from sounding lonely, and tried her best to make him believe everything was running smoothly. Truth be told, she missed him so much that she had entertained thoughts of flying out to L.A. to see him. But reason over-ruled anxiety. She knew he was working, knew it was impor-tant for her to show some backbone. She pretended his absence didn't matter.

"Are you sure you're keeping yourself busy?" he asked her each time he called, recognizing an element in her voice that signaled something was not quite right. He knew she'd never tell him outright that she missed him, knew she'd keep that to herself, afraid it would make her appear vulnerable.

"Listen, there's so much to be done here that I'm never bored. Today I tackled the bedroom. Wait until you see it. I know you're going to love it and I didn't even have to do much, just a coat of paint and a new comforter."

"Wait, are you telling me you painted the bedroom? The whole thing by yourself?" he asked, his disbelief evident.

"Michael, please. I'm fine and I know what I'm doing. I'd only intended to do one wall today, but I finished the whole thing. Once I started, it was easy. Duke has been calling every day and offered to come over and help, but I wanted to tackle this myself. It's a new shade called 'asparagus,'" she ended breathlessly. It seemed that whenever she talked to him, there was not enough time to say all the things she thought of, so she rushed as if there were a time limit.

Michael liked hearing the excitement in her voice, and knew that she was rushing so she would not leave anything out. He was also relieved to know that she was occupied with the house. He didn't care what color she used. Hell, she could paint the room in multiple colors if she wanted, just as long as she was in it when he got back.

"Hey, Duke is only trying to be helpful. And by the way,

asparagus is my favorite color. How did you know?" He laughed then, and Lauren joined in.

"Okay, I know you're making fun of me. And I know that Duke is only trying to be a surrogate for you. You guys don't fool me for one minute."

"Honey, we're not in some kind of conspiracy. He told me before I left that he would call you and check up on you while I was out of town."

"Well, I appreciate it, and I'm going to tell him that. As for you, don't make fun of me because Mom's decorating sense rubbed off. Asparagus is all the rage right now. It's different from sage, kelly, or fern green. You'll like it, though, because it's subtle yet strong. I paired it with black and white. That's all I'm telling you, Mr. Townsend. You'll have to see it when you get back. By the way, just when are you getting back?" She hated herself for asking, hated the fact that whenever she spoke to him her insides turned to mush. She also hated to admit that she had absolutely no control over any of these things.

Unfortunately, her question was unanswerable at that point. Michael had yet to tie up all the loose ends. Each time he thought he had solved all the problems, answered all the questions, and found the right solution to the problems he'd uncovered, there seemed to be another issue to address. He'd hoped that he'd be able to stick to his one-week plan, but it was becoming evident he could not.

"Honey, you know that as soon as I have the answer to that question, so will you. I am practically dying here, thinking of you every night and day, wanting to be there with you, but knowing that I can't. Please be patient. It's not easy for me either."

"Michael, I know that, but can't you trade places now with your partner? Duke would probably love to be in the warm L.A. sunshine, in the midst of all the blondes he could ever even think of counting. It is quite the haven for a single male. And not a good place for a married one," she added, her voice clouding over with repressed emotion.

"With what I have at home, I dare not look at a blonde, a redhead, a brunette, or an albino. I had better warn you, though, that when I get there, there will be no coming up for air, food, or water for at least forty-eight hours," he teased.

"Just like on the honeymoon when we managed to remain in our suite for almost two days?" she asked wistfully. "It was fun. I miss you and that funny noise you make when you first wake up," she said remembering her husband's sinus problem.

"I know, I miss you too. I miss everything about you. Look, let's just get some rest and maybe in the next couple of days, I'll be able to wrap things up here and get my butt home where it belongs."

"You really should," Lauren added, unable to verbalize the feelings she frequently had about their future. The longer Michael was gone, the more deeply she was reminded of the way she felt when her father had left her mother. She'd hoped that in a very short time, Michael would resolve all that he was working on and return home. In doing so, she felt it would be easier for them to both face whatever there was to come. "Bring all of you, I miss you one hundred percent," she said through clenched teeth into the phone, winding the cord around her hand. It was an uncommon admission for Lauren.

"You're actually starting to sound like you miss me. Baby, you don't know what it does to me to hear you talk that way. If you don't tone it down, I'm gonna hop the next flight to New York just to make love to my wife. It'll cost the company a bundle, and will probably cost me a serious brownie point with the board of directors when I tell them that I don't have the results because I had to get home." He smiled thinking of the absurdity of it.

Michael took a deep breath and hesitated for a moment.

"Look, I'm promising you that I'll do everything in my power to get the job done here. I'm sorry all this came up and believe me, I plan to make it up to you." He sat back in his hotel room desk chair, closed his eyes, and imagined her standing before him. His heart beat rapidly in response to the visual image. Michael sighed, letting out some of the tension which had been building in his mind and body.

"You had *better* make it up to me. I plan to hold you to that. Don't worry, I've been making myself acquainted with all the vendors on Columbus Avenue. I've developed a fondness for all the wonderful fresh flowers and great ethnic foods available too. And Gloria is supposed to stop by one day this week, so I'm keeping busy."

"Good; that's what I want to hear. You're taking care of yourself just like you had all the years before we met. That's one of the things I love about you, you know."

She paused, hesitant to admit what she was thinking. "Listen, I have one more thing to tell you, then I'm going. Do you know that I've dreamt about you each night since you've left? Vivid, memorable dreams . . . ," Lauren added suggestively.

"Really? That's incredible. I'm sure I dream about you too, but I usually forget whatever I've dreamt. How do you remember them?" Michael asked naively, not getting her meaning.

"Because sometimes they wake me up. I'm warm all over and I'm all tangled up in the bedclothes. The sheet and bedcovers are halfway thrown off the bed and it generally looks like I've been tossing and turning the entire night. Then I look over for you and realize that I'm alone."

The admission told him more than he wanted to know, and he vowed to wrap up his work in California even more quickly. "Honey, I feel awful. I know that was not your intention in telling me that. Just know that I'm being tortured too." His voice deepened with the realization that Lauren needed him as much as he needed her. He stood up, pacing back and forth in his hotel room.

"Michael do think we did the right thing?" she asked quietly. Lauren's voice was filled with genuine concern.

Although the question had come unexpectedly, he was not caught off guard. He shared her torture, and knew they both wanted to end the pain, but not the marriage. "Not only do I know we did the right thing, I'm going to make a believer out of you, just as soon as I can hold you in my arms again. Don't start to second guess our love, Lauren. Just because we lost the baby doesn't discount all the very real things that had developed between us. That's why I insisted we marry anyway. If I hadn't you would have bought into thinking that I asked you for the sake of the child. I asked you to be my wife because I love you. The miscarriage was unfortunate, but we're young, we'll have other opportunities to build the Townsend clan." With that statement, he reassured her that he was looking forward to them both growing old together, with a passel of children to call their own.

"I know what you're saying is true, even if my mind sometimes tells me different. I'm sorry if I seem insecure, but, honestly, I've never been in this situation before," she admitted. She wanted to add that the closest she'd ever come was with the divorce of her parents, but cautioned herself against that.

"You don't have to apologize, Lauren. I love you and I know you. That's what's important. We have a lifetime to lean on one another. I'm here for the good times, the bad times, and all times. Now, go to sleep, woman, and let me get some rest too!"

She laughed, blew kisses into the phone, and hung up. Preparing for bed, Lauren realized that the house was more quiet than she'd ever remembered. She crawled into bed and wondered if Michael was having the same difficulties she had. She was tempted to call him and say good night again, but knew it would only make things worse. She ached for him. Wrapping her arms around a pillow, she fell asleep with his name on her mind.

Michael lay awake three thousand miles away, unable to sleep, dream, or relax. His mind refused to stop churning, refused to stop trying to discern all that he was confronted with concerning CBN. Pushing his thoughts of business aside, he focused on one thing as he lay alone amid crumpled sheets. That focus was on the woman who was his wife, his love, his mate.

Their conversation was still with him, stuck uncomfortably in the middle of his chest much like an undigested meal. No matter what he told himself, the fact of the matter remained that his new bride was now on the opposite side of the country. Top that with the fact that their marriage was one which he'd had to insist upon, convince her of, and practically coerce her in participating in. That he felt a fiercely strong commitment to the longevity of their union was evident. The skepticism she'd expressed during the phone call worried him. In the days leading up to his departure, he'd made progress in their relationship. But her doubts tonight let him know there was still a long way to go.

He realized that it would take more time, more patience, and more than a little diligence in getting her to believe as strongly as he did that they were meant to be together. He was committed to keeping her as his wife.

He didn't want to believe that it was a task, much like the one which faced him with CBN. The company was in trouble, and he couldn't seem to figure out what caused the problem. Since his arrival in L.A. only one week before, he'd assessed the past nine months of accounting records, project expenditures, and the monthly credit analyses. The numbers didn't add up. In fact, there was an overflow of cash but

Michael couldn't figure out where the extra funds were coming from. Undoubtedly, the extra money was what had set off an alarm in Morgan's mind.

Morgan had instructed him on what to look for, and had indicated that there would be hell to pay if things were not straightened out. Although it hadn't been confirmed, there was a rumor that CBN was going public in a few months. All discrepancies in financial reporting needed to be rectified by that time. This pressure made Michael's work even more crucial and time sensitive.

He'd spoken to Duke earlier. He said things were fairly straightforward on his end. Michael suspected that possibly Duke hadn't dug deep enough.

Michael looked up at the ceiling, one arm behind his head, wondering just how long it would take before he would be able to uncover why the numbers were skewed. What he'd found out was unusual, but he was not yet ready to disclose his findings with either Duke or Morgan.

In the past, whenever he and Duke had been faced with company issues, the dilemma would be discussed thoroughly, pertinent actions explored, and then a final decision arrived at jointly. In this case, cautionary bells were sounding in his head on a daily basis. Until he had each piece of the proverbial puzzle in place, Michael thought it would be prudent to keep the most sensitive information under his hat.

Most of the employees in the West Coast office were young graduate students except a skeletal management team which had been put in place under the direction of the CBN corporate offices. Michael's instincts told him to investigate each of these individuals first, then figure out who was responsible for the various operations in the company. He also made a personal vow to reach a conclusion in no more than an additional week. WJZZ called for a monumental commitment, one that nearly paralleled the importance of his obligation and responsibility to his marriage. He didn't feel comfortable allocating a time frame for wrapping up such an important business issue, especially one which could make all the difference in the success or failure of his company. But his bride needed him.

Lying there in the dark, knowing that Lauren was probably still thinking of him, Michael realized that she'd become more important to him than he had ever thought possible, which made him even more determined to straighten out the situation within the company. Their future quite possibly depended on it.

Chapter Thirteen

All of Lauren's things had been unpacked. She'd redecorated most of the house, painted two more rooms, and rearranged the contents of the kitchen cabinets so that everything was in its proper place. Now Lauren was not only bored out of her mind, she was lonely.

She would begin working soon, but not soon enough. In a week, she had an overnight trip to Atlanta; then she was off to Florida before she returned to New York. But until then, she had nothing to do.

Lauren plopped herself onto the living room couch with her cordless phone in hand and dialed Gloria's number. If her best friend was home, maybe they could amuse themselves with a shopping spree on Fifth Avenue.

The phone rang five times before Gloria's answering machine picked up. *Great, she's probably working,* Lauren thought miserably, her mouth in a pout as she clicked off the phone. She stared at the black and chrome instrument for a moment and thought about dialing Michael. She hadn't seen him in a week and the distance was driving her insane. *Was this what my mother felt like?* she wondered. Lauren constantly reminded herself that Michael had not abandoned her the way Colin had abandoned Eva, but whether that was the case or not, her heart still ached the same way.

She needed someone to talk to about her loneliness and could think of no one who would understand more than Eva. Pressing the ON button, Lauren dialed her mother's number, hoping she would pick up. Eva picked up on the fourth ring.

"Hi, honey. Just got in from work. How are you and Michael doing?"

"We're okay. I think I have the post-honeymoon blues. Is that possible?" Lauren asked, immediately hating herself for letting her doubts take precedence over the mostly pleasant memories she and Michael had shared together.

Eva sensed something was wrong. "Lauren, I guess it's possible. I'd be a little more encouraged if you told me you were in ecstasy, but then you've never been one to exaggerate. Is anything wrong?" she asked, concern filling her voice.

"Well, Michael's out of town on a business trip and I'm lonely here by myself." Lauren reached up, twisted a curl of her auburn hair around her finger, and pulled. "And I've been thinking about the miscarriage too. It just seems as if that still has a hold on me. Everything that happens now seems to be tied in to it and leaves a bit of a cloud."

Eva's heart went out to her daughter. Lauren often put up a hard front, but she was a very sensitive soul and easily troubled. "Michael will be home as soon as he can, honey. I'm sure he doesn't want to be away from you any more than you want to be apart from him. It's not like he volunteered to go out there," Eva said, trying to elicit a laugh from her daughter.

When Lauren remained silent, she continued. "You can't let yourself get bogged down by the events of the past, Lauren. I know you loved the child that you lost, but you have to make peace with that and move forward somehow."

Lauren heard her mother's words, but she still couldn't

see the promised light at the end of the tunnel. "I think it would be easier to deal with if Michael were here, you know? I'm just so bored, so lonely with him gone, All I do is think about how much I miss him, and then I think about our baby."

"That's natural, but you have to be strong, Lauren. If I let all that I went through with your father weigh on me, I'd be an old, broken-down woman. Have you talked to Michael about any of this? Honey, if there's no communication, there's no marriage."

Lauren's body slumped with the heaviness of the conversation. "He doesn't get it, Mom. Every time we talk about the baby, he's just so optimistic. He keeps telling me that we can just have more children someday. I know he was affected by the loss, but he doesn't feel it the way I do." Lauren paused, giving herself a moment to regain her composure. "Plus, he's got his hands full with Cityscape problems. I'd feel as if I were a burden to him, and I don't want to do that. I'm trying so hard to stand on my own until he returns. Only I have no idea when he'll be back. I don't think either of us should have to live this way." Tears streamed down her face and she let them fall freely.

Eva was taken aback by her daughter's anguish. She had no idea that Lauren had been suffering through so much. She knew her daughter well enough to know that Lauren's reactions to tough situations could sometimes be drastic. Though Lauren had never told her so, Eva also knew her daughter had married Michael with some reluctance. Lauren had tried hard to mask her fear at the wedding, but her attempts to hide her feelings were no match for Eva's keen eye when it came to her only child. If what she was hearing was a repeat of the uncertainty she'd seen, there was trouble on the horizon for Michael and Lauren. She hated to think in those terms, but Lauren's conversation, as well as her tone of voice, triggered every guard she had.

"I don't think Michael sees it that way at all," she said in a soothing voice meant to ease her daughter's pain. "In fact, you'd probably be surprised at his reaction if you told him how you were feeling. You're overreacting to his absence—probably because you love him very much. It's natural. And the fact that you two are separated so early in your marriage and after the loss of the baby does not bode well. Please promise me that you will discuss how you're feeling with him tonight. Don't wait another day, because it sounds like you are misinterpreting a lot of what's going on."

Lauren released a huge sigh, but said nothing.

"Why don't you fly out and join him for a couple of days?" Eva pushed. "That way, you two will be together. Distance is not good for a new relationship, and especially a new marriage."

"Mom, I appreciate your wanting to help, but you don't understand. These are what you might call 'special circumstances.' Michael is out there to oversee a very intensive project. I don't think he'd appreciate his wife showing up to rekindle the marital fires, if you will." She'd delivered the last line with total cynicism.

Eva realized that Lauren was on the verge of a deep depression. She decided to try another tactic. "Okay then, why don't you come down here for a couple of days? It'll do you good. Can you take some time off from work now?"

"I don't have any vacation time, and it's too early to begin setting aside personal days. Maybe I can string together a couple of my off days when I pick up my schedule. Let me work it out."

"It would be great if you could come down and help me decorate the guest bathroom. I know you love shopping for design elements just as much as I do, and they've just built a Design Expo center here." She waited for her enthusiasm to catch hold, waited for Lauren to buy into her suggestion of mother-daughter time, but realized it wasn't happening when Lauren's only response was another sigh of resignation.

"Honestly, I will never know why you went back to work in the first place. It's only been a couple of months, not even a full quarter. Lauren, I really do think you're behaving a bit drastically. Have you spoken to Michael about this? Does he even know?" Her question remained unanswered for a moment. The thought crossed her mind that Lauren had possibly never even discussed the decision to reinstate her Worldwide Airlines tenure with Michael, but she didn't say that.

"I'm glad I'm going back to work," Lauren said defensively. "It's difficult to sit in the house day after day, racking my brain for things to keep me occupied. Michael of all people should understand that, and if he doesn't, so be it. Look, Mom, I've got to make my own decisions. I'm a grown woman, a married lady, all of the above. I almost brought a child into the world. I think I'm capable of making major decisions when it comes to my work and my marriage. Don't take this the wrong way, but it's my life." With that statement, Lauren put her head back against the pillows, her body listless from the surge of emotions she'd expressed.

"Honey, I know it's your life and believe me, I would be the last person to try to tell you how to live it, but I think you may be making a huge mistake. Now I know you're not willing to make any changes based on anything I have to say, but will you promise me one thing?"

"I can't really say yes to that, Mom. You're probably trying to get me to talk to Michael about this, and I don't think that's the right way to go about it. Please don't ask me to promise anything. There have been too many promises, too many vows, and way too much of a commitment on the table already. That's part of the problem."

"Honey, please stop sounding so final, you're scaring me. With Michael more than three thousand miles away, my biggest fear is that you'll take matters into your own hands and destroy the marriage. And don't tell me that you don't love him, either." Eva's voice had risen then, anger just below the surface. She recognized Lauren's ability to throw away things that were not necessarily rubbish, and feared that she was indeed witnessing such an act.

"Mom, listen, don't worry. I promise I will not disappoint you. That's the only promise I can make right now. I have to go because I have a terrific headache. I'm sorry to run off like this—I'll call you tomorrow night. And maybe in a few weeks or so, we can get together and pick out some new stuff for your bathroom. That does sound like fun. Mom, I love you. Talk to you soon." She hung up quickly before she fell apart.

Lauren continued to hold the receiver in one hand, while the other held down the button. She turned off the ringer and lay across the couch, tears slipping down the sides of her cheeks as she lay unmoving, unable to confront the life she faced.

Chapter Fourteen

Duke walked toward the front of the platform, whistling as he looked over his shoulder for the train. He mind was not on work, nor on the project he'd been asked to complete for CBN. His mind and the smile he wore were both caused by his memories: He'd spent the morning having breakfast with Gloria.

He'd waited at the restaurant for more than twenty minutes, then spotted her immediately as she walked through the door. From the way she looked around the room, he could tell that she was nervous, but he'd stood and waved to her anyway.

She was wearing a dark green pantsuit, with an olive green blouse that seemed to enhance the green of her eyes. To him, she was breathtaking, and he wondered if she affected other people in the same way. He was nervous, shy, and excited all at the same time. He was also eager to spend the time with her, willing to forgo his former hesitancy, and definitely willing to endure any minor physical discomfort associated with the experience.

Gloria smiled and headed toward the table, wondering

why she'd agreed to meet with him. Duke seemed nice enough and his premature, salt-and-pepper beard somehow intrigued her. But it was his ponytail, which was comprised of thick, sleek graying hair that really made him stand out in her mind.

"Hi," she said, sticking her hand out in a combination handshake and less formal greeting.

"Hi yourself," he returned, taking her hand quickly, unable to think of anything else to say. He let it go just as fast, but not before he'd felt its warmth, and noted its firm grip.

Duke and Gloria sat down, suddenly nervous and not at all sure of what was next. They both started to speak at once, and laughed for a quick moment. Then Gloria held up a hand.

"Let me say this first. I'm not used to meeting people at our-of-the way places, so please forgive me for being late. The cab driver almost couldn't find it, and I wasn't able to be very helpful," she offered, looking around at the modern restaurant whose West Street address had thrown her off slightly.

"I apologize but I thought you would be more familiar with Manhattan than anywhere else. I should have set it up in Brooklyn, but I didn't want it to be uncomfortable for you so close to your place," Duke said, remembering that he'd thought of Morgan the entire time he was putting their date together. He'd wanted to avoid him at all costs.

"It's okay. It was something of an adventure. I'm glad I came. You always seem so quiet, but nice. Are you?"

Her question caught Duke off guard. She looked up at him, and his heart hammered in his chest. He reminded himself who she was, then remembered she was also an adult, capable of making her own decisions and leading her own life.

"No, not at all," he said, looking directly into her eyes. They were an incredible shade of green, and Duke wondered if he would ever get used to looking into them. He cleared his throat and offered her a menu which had been left by the waitress only moments before.

"I hear the waffles are great." he said.

"Really? I love waffles," Gloria responded. She questioned what Morgan would do if he knew she was having breakfast with one of his partners, then she dismissed her concern as extremely immature. She was grown, capable of handling her own life and fully in charge of her own actions. What Morgan thought or did not think should have no consequence whatsoever on her choices was what she told herself.

Duke ordered the same, with a side order of turkey bacon and a carafe of coffee. They made small talk until the food arrived, then dug in, grateful for something else to focus on.

"I understand you folks are pretty busy. Morgan mentioned that you and Michael have to prepare a bunch of reports. Sounds like something I wouldn't wish on my worst enemy," she said without smiling.

Duke watched her and laughed out loud. "Well, I don't think Morgan would like to hear you say that," he said, wondering how the two had gotten along when they were young and both living under the same roof. Then he remembered that Morgan had been part of a second-marriage package. Gloria had been the biological daughter of Gino Sorrentino. With that thought, Duke once again cautioned himself. It was too late, though. Gloria was sitting across from him, sharing a breakfast of waffles, bacon, and company gossip.

"What's so funny? I don't give much credence to what Morgan thinks or doesn't think. He's my brother, but he's not in control of anything, other than CBN. Gino made sure he got to run that, but that's about all he's running. He likes to try to strong-arm me when it comes to my personal life. I've already told him to back off, but every once in a while I have to reinforce it. I'm almost thirty-two years old, and he's still trying to play the Boy Scout with me. At this point, if I don't know to come prepared, it's a lost cause," she ended, looking down at her plate.

Duke wanted to remain silent, but found he could not. "I think you have excellent instincts. You don't have to worry about me, just in case you were concerned. I mean, I have wanted to spend some quality time with you since the first time I met you, but the timing sucked. Your father had just passed away. I figured your mind was definitely not on socializing," he added.

Gloria watched him closely, her hands clenched at the mention of that time in her life. The pain she'd experienced washed over her briefly. "My father and I never got along. His sudden death was a shock to everyone, but especially to me. I felt as if I had never really had an opportunity to understand him. I still feel that way," she admitted.

Duke watched her, saw the tremendous energy she was expending in an effort to control her feelings, and was moved. Gloria Sorrentino was nobody's fool, nor was she to be taken for granted. She obviously had regrets, and for those he admired her. The fact that she'd butted heads with one of New York City's most powerful men was not unusual. The fact that she was his daughter was daunting. With Gino's blood running through her veins, Duke figured they shared many similarities, a fact which often created conflicts with people of strong mind-sets. He wondered if that was one of the things that attracted him to her, and smiled.

"Private joke?" Gloria asked. Her observant nature picked up on most things. At the moment, Duke Hayes was being scrutinized with a microscopic lens.

"Pleasant thoughts," he responded easily, then wondered

if he was doomed to repeat the same mistakes with women over and over again. The thought made him acknowledge that whatever he and Gloria shared, it would not be insignificant. He looked away then, not wanting to risk exposing the fleeting thoughts which went through his mind.

An Important Message From The ARABESQUE Publisher

Dear Arabesque Reader,

I invite you to join the club! The Arabesque book club delivers four novels each month right to your front door! It's easy, and you will never miss a romance by one of our award-winning authors!

With upcoming novels featuring strong, sexy women, and African-American heroes that are charming, loving and true… you won't want to miss a single release! Our authors fill each page with exceptional dialogue, exciting plot twists, and enough sizzling romance to keep you riveted until the satisfying end! To receive novels by bestselling authors such as Gwynne Forster, Janice Sims, Angela Winters and others, I encourage you to join now!

Read about the men we love… in the pages of Arabesque!

Linda Gill
PUBLISHER, ARABESQUE ROMANCE NOVELS

*P.S. Watch out for the next Summer Series **"Ports Of Call"** that will take you to the exotic locales of Venice, Fiji, the Caribbean and Ghana! You won't need a passport to travel, just collect all four novels to enjoy romance around the world! For more details, visit us at www.BET.com.*

ARABESQUE

SPECIAL OFFER!
4 BOOKS FREE!

BET BOOKS

www.BET.com

A SPECIAL "THANK YOU" FROM ARABESQUE JUST FOR YOU!

Send this card back and you'll receive 4 FREE Arabesque Novels—a $25.96 value—absolutely FREE!

The introductory 4 Arabesque Romance books are yours FREE (plus $1.99 shipping & handling). If you wish to continue to receive 4 books every month, do nothing. Each month, we will send you 4 New Arabesque Romance Novels for your free examination. If you wish to keep them, pay just $18* (plus, $1.99 shipping & handling). If you decide not to continue, you owe nothing!

- Send no money now.
- Never an obligation.
- Books delivered to your door!

We hope that after receiving your FREE books you'll want to remain an Arabesque subscriber, but the choice is yours! So why not take advantage of this Arabesque offer, with no risk of any kind. You'll be glad you did!

In fact, we're so sure you will love your Arabesque novels, that we will send you an Arabesque Tote Bag FREE with your first paid shipment.

* PRICES SUBJECT TO CHANGE.

YOU'LL GET 4 SELECT ROMANCES PLUS THIS FABULOUS TOTE BAG!

Visit us at: www.BET.com

ARABESQUE

THE "THANK YOU" GIFT INCLUDES:

- 4 books absolutely FREE (plus $1.99 for shipping and handling).
- A FREE newsletter, *Arabesque Romance News*, filled with author interviews, book previews, special offers, and more!
- No risks or obligations. You're free to cancel whenever you wish with no questions asked.

INTRODUCTORY OFFER CERTIFICATE

Yes! Please send me 4 FREE Arabesque novels (plus $1.99 for shipping & handling). I understand I am under no obligation to purchase any books, as explained on the back of this card. Send my free tote bag after my first regular paid shipment.

NAME _____

ADDRESS _____ APT. _____

CITY _____ STATE _____ ZIP _____

TELEPHONE ( ) _____

E-MAIL _____

SIGNATURE _____

Offer limited to one per household and not valid to current subscribers. All orders subject to approval. Terms, offer, & price subject to change. Tote bags available while supplies last.

Thank You!

AN015A

ARABESQUE

Accepting the four introductory books for FREE (plus $1.99 to offset the cost of shipping & handling) places you under no obligation to buy anything. You may keep the books and return the shipping statement marked "cancelled". If you do not cancel, about a month later we will send 4 additional Arabesque novels, and you will be billed the preferred subscriber's price of just $4.50 per title. That's $18.00* for all 4 books for a savings of almost 30% off the cover price (Plus $1.99 for shipping and handling). You may cancel at any time, but if you choose to continue, every month we'll send you 4 more books, which you may either purchase at the preferred discount price. . . or return to us and cancel your subscription.

THE ARABESQUE ROMANCE CLUB: HERE'S HOW IT WORKS

THE ARABESQUE ROMANCE BOOK CLUB
P.O. BOX 5214
CLIFTON NJ 07015-5214

PLACE
STAMP
HERE

Chapter Fifteen

Almost six weeks after Michael and Lauren's wedding in Barbados, Morgan initiated a conference call between the three principal partners of Cityscape Broadcast Network. Michael had been in L.A. for eight days and so far he'd made no progress figuring out where the extra revenue had come from. He still hadn't told Morgan or Duke about the discrepancy.

"First, let me tell you that CBN is fortunate to have you on board. As I explained when we first negotiated this merger, the talent you guys bring to the table is recognized and respected. The industry needs more people like you, but as it stands now, I'm just glad you're on our team." Morgan rarely gave compliments, and when he did, they usually preceded something big. At the moment, the new partners were unsure of his real intentions, though they suspected the rumors of CBN's going public might be one of his reasons for the call.

"Thanks, Morgan. I think I can speak for Duke as well as myself when I say that we wouldn't want to be anywhere else," Michael said from his hotel room in California.

"Good, I'm glad—and actually that brings me to the reason for the call. The board of directors has put through a motion for CBN to issue publicly held shares of the company. We're going public!"

There was a moment of silence, and then all three men began speaking.

Duke chimed in first. "When is the expected launch date?"

"Has the due diligence been confirmed already?" Michael, almost at the same time. His entrepreneurial instincts told him that although the announcement was a business owner's dream come true, it would also carry substantial fiscal responsibility.

Morgan smiled and sat back. "Whoa, guys. Listen, we've taken all aspects of going public into consideration. The other reason that I've gathered us together this morning is to request something from you both. For the last couple weeks, I've had you just looking over the books to make sure everything is generally in order. So far, no one's reported anything suspicious, but if you see anything at all, it should be brought to my attention. I can't explain how very important this is."

Where only moments before there had been excitement on the phone, it was now replaced by silence and anticipating. Something in Morgan's tone elicited caution.

"Go ahead," Michael said, he figured Morgan knew about the additional revenues, but he didn't know why they were there. There was so sense in telling Morgan about the problem if he couldn't find the solution.

Morgan cleared his throat. "There are two sides of the company that have to be examined internally. Operations needs to be examined in terms of efficiency, productivity, and the day-to-day structure." He hesitated then, and both Duke and Michael listened even more intently. "I've been advised that we'll also need a *comprehensive* report on WJZZ's revenues for the past year. The suits are playing hardball. It's required when you're asking John Q. Public to buy shares of the company you own," Morgan added. He neglected to mention his suspicions about the California-based company and hoped neither man would pick up on his thoughts.

"I've already been working on the operations end. I should be able to tie my side up pretty quickly," Duke offered.

"I know WJZZ's internal structure like the back of my hand," Michael interjected. "It shouldn't take me too long to be able to provide you with any additional data you'd need," Michael said optimistically. He didn't want to give Morgan or Duke the idea that he'd discovered something wrong on his end.

"Sounds like we're all on the same page. Thanks guys, in advance. I already know you'll do a great job."

"Hey Morgan, thank you too. With CBN going public, we all stand to win," Duke said.

"That's right, we do," Morgan added, his mood suddenly lightened by Michael and Duke's receptiveness. An hour ago, he hadn't been at all sure how they would take the news. Going public was one thing, but the work involved in getting to that point was another issue altogether, especially coupled with the time frame and the discrepancies in revenue. Though they were unaware, Morgan had just handed Michael and Duke assignments in Purgatory, uncovering and detecting any and everything they could to substantiate his suspicions about the third quarter surge.

Michael hung up the phone and leaned back in his chair. He knew that to delve deeply into WJZZ's books and figure out where the revenues were coming from would mean being hands-on for a long time. Very possibly beyond the deadline he'd set for himself. Los Angeles had always annoyed him, and he did not look forward to spending time there.

He decided to fly home for the weekend to see Lauren and then come back. Michael picked up the phone and made reservations to return to New York early Saturday morning with a flight back to L.A. on Sunday evening.

Michael picked up the phone again and dialed. He ordered two tickets, paid for them with his American Express Platinum card, and then called home.

"Hi, kitten, what's doing?" he asked, his mood light with good news when Lauren answered.

"I'm packing. My first overnight trip is scheduled for tonight," Lauren informed him.

His disappointment mounted before he'd even thought about it. Michael took a deep breath, then exhaled. It wasn't Lauren's fault he wanted to surprise her with a weekend of spending time together.

"When will you return?" he asked, his voice sounding controlled.

"Actually, I get back in tomorrow evening. It's just an overnight in Atlanta. The I fly to Florida and return to New York. I'll be back home around five o'clock. Why, what's up?" she asked, noting that he'd remained silent.

"Nothing. I'm coming in for the weekend. I thought we could spend some time together," he added. He smiled then, thinking of the tickets he'd just purchased, hoping the surprise would help him score points with this wife.

"Oh, Michael, that's wonderful! When do you get in?"

"My flight comes in around four, so I should be home by five or so. Guess we couldn't have coordinated it better if we'd tried," he added. What he didn't say was that it had worked out *this time*.

"That's great. Wow, my husband will be here for the weekend. I can't wait!" All the second thoughts, and reservations she'd had were put aside, for the moment and she wondered if he knew how unhappy she'd been, missing him.

"Good, I can't either. Okay, I'm going to finish tying up loose ends here. See you when I get there. Oh, honey, be careful and have a safe trip. Call me when you get to Atlanta. Don't forget," he added.

"I won't. Love you."

"You too."

They hung up, looking forward to the weekend, unsure of what was next in their complicated lives.

Lauren's first flight had gone almost too smoothly. A nonstop flight from LaGuardia Airport to Atlanta's Hartsfield, then on to Miami International, and back to LaGuardia.

Nothing out of the ordinary occurred, and Lauren marveled at how easily she'd been able to make the transition. She'd attended the mandatory orientation which accompanied each beginning leg of a flight crew's trip and then boarded the aircraft. The Boeing 727, which had a capacity of two-hundred-plus seating, was only half full and only beverages were served. Many passengers now brought their own meals on board, and Lauren smiled when one teenage boy traveling with his mother asked for a knife and fork.

"I'm sorry young man. We don't supply cutlery anymore. That's definitely against the security rules. I think you may be able to manage that without it though," Lauren offered, pointing to a bag that held a large container of chili and another one which held the largest serving of French fries she'd ever seen. "Let me see if I can find a spoon for you. I think I brought one for my yogurt," she'd added with a wink. The boy's mother smiled and went back to reading her novel.

She was home in less than ten hours, though she was exhausted by the time she arrived. Her excitement over seeing her husband that evening kept her adrenaline running.

Later that evening, she smiled thinking about her first flight as she placed a diamond earring into her lobe.

Michael stood in the full-length mirror in his asparagus-colored bedroom, wearing a conservative black tuxedo and struggling with his bow tie. He and Lauren were getting dressed for a gala at the Museum of Modern Art, the event he'd bought tickets to.

"Here, let me," Lauren offered.

He watched her intently as she expertly tied the black and white fabric into a bow. Lauren wore a pale green chiffon wrap dress, which hugged her body tightly, the strapless bodice offering an alluring view that made it difficult for Michael to focus on anything but her.

When she finished, he leaned forward and pulled her into an embrace. "So who taught you to do that?" he challenged playfully.

"Dad. I used to watch him closely when I was a little kid. He showed me how to do it, saying it would come in handy. I laughed at the time. Now look at me," she added, smiling.

An overwhelming desire to make love to his wife filled Michael as Lauren looked at him. He would have acted on his impulse, but they had an event to attend. He was sure there would be time to fill his desires later. Michael kissed Lauren on her forehead, and they continued to get ready, leaving the townhouse soon afterward.

The Museum of Modern Art had been outfitted with hundreds of yards of pastel tulle hanging from the forty-foot ceilings. The effect was ethereal and magnificently offset the powerful pieces of art. Champagne, hors d'oeuvres, and a carving station were set up in two rooms, and hundreds of patrons of the arts milled about.

They entered the museum and began touring the assigned rooms. Many of the art pieces were the works of modern masters. Michael and Lauren were discussing a sculpture, a starburst of blown glass by Dale Chihuly, when Michael spotted Morgan across the room. He was alone and heading straight toward them.

"Well, I had no idea you were back in town," Morgan said as he approached, extending his hand to Michael.

Michael shook Morgan's hand and looked at his wife,

pride and happiness beaming from his eyes. "Couldn't stay away," he replied, a smile creeping across his face. "I did as much work as I could before I left. I'm headed back on Sunday afternoon."

"No problem. I figured you'd be back and forth. If I were a newlywed, I'd do the same thing, I imagine."

They all shared a quick laugh.

"I had no idea you were a philanthropist," Morgan offered, making small talk.

Michael and Lauren laughed, sharing an inside joke. She knew her husband was not a big fan of art, much less of sculpture. He'd only bought the tickets because he knew how much she would enjoy the gala.

Lauren responded first. "Michael surprised me. He knows I love art, design, and anything to do with architecture."

Michael put his arm around Lauren, looked at her again, and smiled in appreciation.

"That's right. I knew she'd love the glass sculptures in particular. This guy's phenomenal," he commented, honestly impressed.

Morgan nodded in agreement. "I agree. I've thought many times that I should own something of his. Maybe this is the year," he added, giving the work an appreciative glance.

"Congratulations on your marriage by the way—the ceremony was beautiful," he said for Lauren's benefit.

Lauren looked at Michael. "Yes, we thought it went off without a hitch," she said, a curious smile playing about her lips that only Michael noticed.

By now, the gala was in full swing, with hundreds of people from Manhattan's high society, minor celebrities, and many of the movers and shakers of New York City in attendance. Michael watched the manner in which Lauren carried herself, noting her response to the throngs of socialites and saw how relaxed she was when she interacted with Morgan. He was pleased.

"I've always loved museums and fine art. I think it's wonderful that this event will raise money for juvenile diabetes too. I'm sure they will make a bundle with all the folks who are here," Lauren added looking around the room, doing a quick calculation. There had to be more than five hundred people in attendance, which would drum up a pretty penny.

Morgan watched Michael and his wife and was somewhat envious. He'd never had what Lauren and Michael so obviously shared. He wondered if he ever would. As head of CBN, he'd given up most of his social life to run the business. Gino's death had cost everyone something, but most of all, it cost Morgan the freedom to make mistakes.

He's tried to walk away from the responsibility, tried to avoid the involvement, but to no avail. And even though portions of the companies had been under investigation by the FBI when he took over, Gino's death had made it possible for him to run the company without too much trouble from the authorities. Now if he could only figure out what happened to WJZZ's revenues, he could sleep better at night.

"Let's all have a drink together. We can toast to CBN's coming-out party," Morgan offered, signaling one of the waiters circulating with trays. There was a moment of uncomfortable silence, then Michael cleared his throat.

Lauren looked on in surprise as Michael's gaze reached her. "I was going to tell you later. The company is going public." His grin was enigmatic; it made her want to hug him, then scold him for keeping such important news from her.

The three then lifted their glasses, drank to the successful future of CBN and WJZZ and continued their small talk.

After several minutes, Michael looked at Lauren, smiled, and signaled the waiter for another round of champagne. They toasted again, this time to "longevity, health, and success," then Michael and Lauren said their good-byes to Morgan and walked away to continue viewing the exhibition. Moving through a room filled with Picassos, Michael pointed out one work in particular that he found interesting. Taking her hand, he led Lauren toward it.

"Notice his use of color to delineate style and form," Lauren said, making a sweeping motion with her hand. The colors are so bold, they're bright, they're intense. Just like the emotions they evoke. He was a definitely a genius."

Michael was impressed—not by her words, but by her sensitivity. She possessed more of the qualities he admired in a person than he'd remembered. Even now, as they stood side by side, moving through the gallery of works by modern masters, champagne flutes in hand, commenting to one another in barely audible tones, he recognized that she was a fabulous companion, a beautiful woman, and a wife worthy of the title.

"Why didn't you tell me about the company going public? I mean, even if it was a surprise, you could have given me some hint that this was coming," Lauren said. She wondered if this was part of the reason that he'd been sent to L.A.

"I didn't discuss it with you right away because it entails a full-scope audit, SEC filings, and lots of other reporting mechanisms that will determine when and if it's able to go through. Morgan has no clue if and when we can do this, yet he announced it prematurely, if you will," Michael admitted, his annoyance clear.

"Well, you still could have told *me*. Who would I tell? Lauren responded evenly. She knew it was silly, knew that Michael had come back to New York just to take her out for the evening, but it bothered her that he hadn't included her.

"You'll have to forgive me on that one," Michael said sincerely.

Chapter Sixteen

On the other side of the museum, Morgan watched as a man and woman made their way through the thinning crowd, approaching him with smiles on their faces. The man looked vaguely familiar, but he couldn't put his finger on how or why he knew him. Finally, when they were only a few feet away, it dawned on him. It was Gino's Godson, Duane Capparelli, and his wife.

Kellyn Capparelli, a former model, looked like she'd stepped right out of the pages of *Vogue* magazine. The white floor-length matte jersey dress she wore clung to every curve, her blond hair completing the look of flawless vanilla ice cream. Duane, a large man who was given to adult acne, hadn't changed at all. His suit jacket, though ill-fitting, was expensive.

Morgan stiffened, becoming instantly wary of the two and all that they represented. He would never forget the tangled web of deceit that Sorrentino Waste Management fostered. He'd also never forgotten the promise Gino had pressured him into on his deathbed, the words still as fresh in his mind this night as they had been on that chilling day. He'd promised to stay as far away from that side of the business as possible.

"Hey, long time no hear. What's up?" The larger man pulled Morgan into a bear hug while his wife looked on.

"You must be his wife," Morgan asked, a look of amusement on his face.

"Yes, Kellyn Capparelli." The blonde, who was taller than her husband, gave Morgan an icy glare. Her husband was busy grinning and doing his best to convince Morgan that their bumping into each other was a total coincidence.

"Honey, can you see if you can scare up something to drink. My throat is about to close up," she added, giving him a look of consternation.

"Sure, babe, just a minute. The waiters come by all the time until you want one. It figures," he added looking around the room.

The fact that her husband, a fairly powerful man, had come to grovel at Morgan's feet, annoyed her immensely.

"Duane, I'm surprised to see you here. I had no idea you supported the arts," Morgan said, an unspoken question present just below the statement.

"Oh, come on. You know the old man was serious about us being involved in anything that could be labeled 'blue ribbon' in this town." He elbowed Morgan conspicuously in the ribs, a gesture which was noticed by two women who were walking by, although they appeared to be deep in conversation. It appeared the gala had been attended by all sorts of people, the passing pair wondered how that could be prevented in the future.

Morgan wondered exactly why Duane had shown up. If Duane was ever in need of fine art, then he was the type to attend the next P. Diddy concert. Morgan knew that wherever Duane went, Anthony Sorrentino was not far behind, a fact which inched his curiosity up another notch.

Morgan was uncertain if either of them could mean anything detrimental to the future plans of CBN. It had been two years since several law-enforcement agencies had brought Duane and Anthony to justice. Obviously, someone had managed to pull a few very important strings for the man standing next to him to be on the streets so soon.

Morgan wondered just how much it cost to get such a short sentence. He shrugged his shoulders as Duane tried his best to convince him of Gino's intentions before his death.

"Look Morgan, you've got to do this for me. Can't you see we need your help? This is not the way Gino would have wanted things—not the Gino I knew. Not the Gino who did everything in his power to make it right for all of us."

Morgan wanted to deck him. The first rule of family business was never to talk business in public. There had to be more than three hundred people still milling about, admiring the beautiful pieces of art around them.

He watched Kellyn smile coldly—doing her best to give the impression of a living, breathing woman—and found it laughable. Nothing could be farther from the truth. They were both bloodsucking vampires, and he was their intended victim. He wanted to get rid of them both.

Duane was still trying his best to convince Morgan that they should realign themselves in a business venture, although both already had all the money they would ever need. Gino had seen to it that all the midrange business owners were properly taken care of, right down to their children's college educations.

"Look, why don't we set up something for tomorrow night? Just you, me, and Anthony. We can talk about old times, discuss what's happening now, and plan for the future. You know Gino would want that. I don't know why you're being so stubborn, Morgan. This is the way it was supposed to be. Gino just checked out earlier than any of us ever expected. But that don't mean we shouldn't still try and keep the company together. Sorrentino Construction and Sorrentino Waste

Management have a right to be legitimized too! You're not the only one who needs to be able to live the good life, you know," he added, his voice rising slightly in volume from both the champagne he'd consumed and the enthusiasm he held for his conviction.

Morgan realized the potential for an escalation in the situation and wanted to bring an end to it. He never expected he'd run into any of the "family" at this event. If he had, he never would have purchased a ticket. The last thing he needed was to have Duane become any more passionate about what he obviously felt was his mission in life.

Morgan put one hand on Duane's shoulder, looked him straight in the eye and let him have it. The large man, contrary to his size, was no match for Morgan's steadfast mindset. "Bull. Everything you've said in the past ten minutes is complete bull. Gino didn't want us to consolidate anything. Nor did he ever expect Sorrentino Waste Management or Sorrentino Construction to ever become fully legitimized. That's why he always kept the communications company separate. He knew that one element could possibly taint the others, bringing the wrath of the Feds down on all involved. Look, man, this is not the time or the place to discuss any of this. And I've got news for you: Tomorrow night or the night after that ain't, either. I have absolutely no interest whatsoever in talking to you, or your cousin, about this stuff. Cityscape Broadcast Network is just where it should be. No restructuring, no reorganization, no realignments. Capice?"

The volume of his voice had risen in increments with each word, and at this point, others in close proximity were casting furtive glazes in their direction. Kellyn looked uneasy, but was afraid to say or do anything. She realized she was witnessing her first display of Morgan's notorious temper.

Morgan stepped away from Duane, took Kellyn's hand politely, and smiled through clenched teeth as he said good night and left them standing with their mouths agape. Her husband mumbled under his breath. "Damned hardhead. I told Anthony this wouldn't work," he said as they walked away.

"Looks like you two are going to have to go back to the drawing board. Morgan is as pigheaded as his stepfather was," Kellyn responded, relieved that the exchange was over.

He quickly took her arm and steered her further into the museum to escape the stares of those nearby. "Yeah, one down, two to go," he said meaningfully.

Later, as the evening was coming to an end, Morgan ran into Michael and Lauren again. "You two are still here. Admirable. You must really love this," he added.

"Yeah, she's a museum junkie. Comes from exposure to European art, I suspect," Michael added, his arm comfortably thrown around Lauren's shoulders.

"You know, you're a smart guy. Stay that way," she said, a loving look in her eyes. "I need to find the ladies' room. Be back in a sec," she called over her shoulder as she headed for the lavatory.

Michael and Morgan watched her walk away. Morgan then remembered that he hadn't asked Michael anything about the reports he'd been working on, and although it was neither the time nor the place, brought the subject up anyway.

"Does it look as if we have a major or a minor problem?" Morgan asked, dreading the answer.

"It's too early to tell," he lied. "Don't worry, it'll turn out okay," he said reassuringly.

"I'm hoping," Morgan said, his voice deep with unspoken resentment.

"I noticed that couple you were talking to. Any of that have something to do with your mood now?" Michael asked.

"You know, my stepfather was quite the businessman. Sometimes I wonder if I can ever get away from his legacy.

God knows I've tried." The last words were issued with a controlled degree of frustration. Apparently, Morgan had been fighting against this for a very long time. It explained many things to Michael, and answered questions he'd never have the right or the authority to ask.

"I see. Do you think it was an accident that they showed up here? I mean, is this something they would have attended under normal circumstances?" he probed, unsure of how the question would seem. He'd taken the chance because he really wanted to know if Morgan was being set up for something. Why else would someone *add* money to the bottom line? The answer he got surprised and intrigued him.

"He would have to be a lot smarter than he is to have known I was coming to this event. When Gino was alive, we made it a point to never socialize with any of those guys in public." He paused, seemingly deep in thought, and then continued. "No, I doubt that Duane or Anthony have the brains or the resources to do that," he said, immediately chastising himself for using their names. His troubled mind caused the slip.

At that moment, Lauren returned, and Michael indicated they would be leaving.

"It was a surprise seeing you both," Morgan said. "A pleasant one," he added as they headed for the front entrance.

Something in Morgan's demeanor had signaled immediate disdain for the man and the woman he'd been talking to, Michael thought. He had no intention of getting involved in anything which might lead to disfavor or complications. He had his own set of issues already, and was not looking forward to leaving New York again, but knew he had no choice. The weekend was speeding by quickly. It was almost time for him to leave again.

As they left the museum, Lauren linked her arm with Michael's, her eyes glowing with excitement. "That was wonderful. Thank you so much for taking me. I haven't been to a museum in a long time. Next time, we should check out the works of Romare Bearden. I love his stuff too," she added.

Michael watched her silently, his mind still filled with the images of Morgan arguing with the man at the museum. When the deal had been inked with CBN, both he and Duke had been aware of rumors and innuendoes that concerned the reputation of the company and its founder, Gino Sorrentino. When he died, they'd reconsidered their initial hesitancy, hoping the suspicions of Mafia involvement would finally be laid to rest.

Morgan had helped restructure Sorrentino Waste Management and Sorrentino Construction Supply soon after merging WJZZ into the CBN web of radio stations across the country. Thinking back, Michael wondered just how tightly the doors to the former subsidiary companies had been closed.

"Is everything okay?" Lauren asked suddenly, sensing Michael's pensive mood.

"Sure, I was just thinking about a few things. You're right too. We should get out more often," he added smiling. "See, I was listening to you."

"I wasn't complaining. I know your job is demanding. You probably like to take it easy in the off hours."

"For sure. With all the reports that have been requested, it's as if we have to interpret the entire reason for the company's existence."

"Morgan seems to have a lot on his mind."

"Yeah, he's always all business. I don't think I've seen him with a date." Michael wasn't sure whether Morgan's lunch with his assistant would be classified as a date.

Lauren laughed. "I know. Gloria would be proud of him for just getting out of the office. She's always said he needed to relax a little."

"Probably. Okay, enough of that. Where to for dinner?" he asked, wanting to change the subject.

Lauren thought for a moment. "How about Cleopatra's Needle?"

"Good choice. You're amazing. I was thinking about going there before I left L.A. I wanted to take you there when I got back," he added. Michael handed a ticket to the valet attendant at the museum and they waited for him to bring their car to them. They drove off.

"Well, I'm glad we think alike," Lauren said, kissing him quickly at a red light.

"Hey, not so fast. Come here," he murmured, leaning toward her. Lauren lifted her lips to his, kissed him thoroughly, and placed on hand on the front of his thigh. In the seconds that passed, their kiss deepened.

Michael inhaled sharply as Lauren's palm wandered further up his leg. She smiled in the darkness.

"I think you'd better cut that out if you still want to make the restaurant," he cautioned playfully.

Lauren laughed, giving him a lingering caress between his legs. "I'm thinking that dessert might be better than dinner," she suggested.

Michael needed no further encouragement, and headed home.

"How about a midnight picnic?" Lauren called over her shoulder, heading into the kitchen.

"Sure, I'll get some wine," Michael answered as he headed toward the wet bar. He poured one glass of Cabernet Sauvignon and headed for the kitchen, where Lauren was putting fruit and cheese on a large plate. Michael laughed.

"I'm hungry. I can't help it. Hey, where's my wine?" she asked noting Michael only held one glass.

"Right here. Now come and get it like a good girl," he added, a knowing look in his eyes.

Lauren's smile confirmed to Michael that he'd hit home with his remark. "Sure thing—I'm right behind you," she said following him to the staircase.

"After you, madam," Michael said gallantly, allowing her to pass him.

He watched the graceful swing of her hips in her silk gown, and his heart beat rapidly in his chest.

"Honey, you have no idea what this view is doing to me," he said, tension in his voice.

"Well, darling, in just about a minute you'll have full access to any and everything you want. I'm just trying to provide a midnight snack for us to munch on."

They reached the bedroom, and Lauren put the plate down as Michael walked toward her, offering the wine glass. She drank and so did he, each looking into the other's eyes as passion threatened to overtake them both. Without taking her eyes from him, Lauren deliberately began to unzip the gown, stepping out of it and kicking it across the floor in one movement.

Michael's intake of breath was audible. He stepped forward, lowered his lips to hers and captured her mouth as his hands caressed her shoulders smoothly. He reached out and gathered her head in his hands, the loose pins that held her hair fell from their positions.

Lauren leaned into him boldly, her hips meeting his as she held on to his arms and felt the power beneath her fingertips.

"I love you," he whispered, tearing his lips from hers for a moment, kissing her neck slowly.

"I love you too," she answered, looking into his eyes, which were readable in the moonlit room.

Michael offered her another sip of the wine, then took one for himself. He undressed quickly, stopping only to turn down the bed before he lifted Lauren in his arms and placed her on the sheets.

The cheese and fruit remained untouched as one hunger was overtaken by another.

* * *

Lauren slept fitfully during the night with images of Michael's departure interrupting her rest. When morning finally came, she was exhausted from her lack of sleep.

Michael had tossed and turned too. Lauren's murmurs had awakened him at least once. He'd watched her for a few moments, noting how her brow furrowed with worry. He could see the tension present on her face. It seemed they each had concerns that became more pronounced without the light of day. Michael felt guilty for having to leave again; Lauren felt guilty for not wanting him to go. Neither of them wanted to express their thoughts, thinking it would only make their situation more difficult.

Michael rose first, entered the bathroom and did his best to shower quietly. He wanted to spend time with Lauren before he returned to L.A., but was hesitant to wake her because of her lack of a restful sleep. When he re-entered the bedroom fifteen minutes later with a towel wrapped around his waist, he was surprised to find Lauren gone and the smell of toast and coffee in the air.

Michael's somber mood lifted. After dressing in gray trousers and a white shirt with the collar open, he actually whistled as he made his way down the stairs. During his most recent trip, he'd realized that no one in L.A. wore a tie unless they were attending an extremely important business meeting or a formal event.

He walked into the kitchen just as Lauren was putting two glasses of orange juice on the table. She was wearing a pale green baby-doll nightgown made of silk, which ended near the top of each thigh. Hearing his footsteps, she looked up, smiled, and walked into his arms. Michael held her tightly, feeling the rapid beating of her heart and the heat from her body.

"You're making me breakfast?" he asked, planting a kiss on her forehead.

The question went unanswered for several seconds as

Lauren held back the emotions which threatened to overtake her. Throughout the night, she'd dreamed of Michael's absence even as she lay in his arms. She wondered how she would get through the coming week, or even weeks, without him by her side. The previous week had been hell for her, and she wondered how much more she could withstand without breaking.

Lauren was determined to keep her misgivings to herself, fearing that if she shared her thoughts with Michael, it would only make matters worse. She smiled up at him then, wanting to cherish her last moments with her husband.

"Yes, I'm making you breakfast. It's the least I can do before you go back to the West Coast to save the company. Can I make you some eggs? And, do you want bacon or ham? We have both," she stated quickly, wanting something to focus on besides the fact that he would soon be leaving her again.

"Honey, please slow down. No, I don't want any bacon, ham, or eggs. All I want right now is to know that you're all right. You didn't sleep very well. I know because I didn't either," he admitted, looking at her intently.

Lauren looked away, then returned his gaze. "I know. I'm sorry. I mean, I'm sorry I kept you awake. I didn't mean to. I just kept dreaming all kinds of crazy stuff," she confessed.

"Honey, you put up a terrific front, but I can tell this trip is bothering you a little more than you're letting on. Don't put on a brave face for my sake. We've only been married for such a short while. Now I have to go and handle company problems and leave you behind. I'm sorry. You don't know how sorry I am, but it cannot be helped." He took her left hand into his, lifting it to kiss the palm.

The gesture, one of innocence and reverence, signaled his sincerity. So why did she still feel so betrayed? Why, after the time they'd spent together the past weekend, making love, exchanging ideas, enjoying the small idiosyncratic things that lovers do, did she still feel so uncertain? Those questions plagued Lauren as she sat with Michael that morning in their kitchen watching him have coffee and toast.

The phone rang, interrupting her thoughts. Lauren went to answer it, but was stopped by Michael's' voice.

"Don't answer it honey. I'm spending quality time with my wife. I don't want to interrupt that."

"Are you sure?" Lauren asked quietly.

"Do you really have to ask?" Michael responded, his gaze locked on her. "Come over here," he commanded, moving his cup and saucer aside.

Lauren walked toward him and he smiled, motioning for her to sit on his lap.

"Listen, there's a couple of things we need to get straight before I leave this time," he stated solemnly.

"Go ahead," Lauren said, placing an arm around his shoulder, a serious look spreading over her face.

Michael looked at her, kissed her softly on the lips, and wondered how he'd be able to get through the next few days without her. She wore no makeup, her hair was pulled into a ponytail by the soft hair band he'd seen on the bathroom vanity, and yet she looked absolutely beautiful. He would have liked nothing better than to call the whole trip off, but knew it was out of the question. Instead, he toyed with her fingers on the hand in her lap.

"Okay, rules while I'm away this time are as follows: no worrying, no crying, no sadness. Understood?" Michael felt foolish laying it out that way but knew they both needed to address their feelings. He wanted Lauren to be able to handle his absence but knew she'd have a harder time of it if they avoided the subject. He was miserable without her and knew Lauren had to be falling apart without him, too. If they continued to act like nothing was wrong, it would be harder for both of them.

"I'll do my best to avoid sulking, pouting, and anything remotely close to showing how saddened I am by the fact that my husband will be more than three thousand miles away again. In fact, why don't I do something useful right now like get dressed and take you to the airport," Lauren responded, jumping to her feet with a smile on her face.

Michael laughed, said, "That's my girl," and began gathering up the dishes. He hoped that the enthusiasm she exhibited was not just for his sake and that she actually was comforted by his words.

For the moment, Lauren was glad to have something to occupy her mind, anything to avoid thinking about what was to come. She showered quickly, put on very little makeup and brushed her hair before putting on a pair of pants she hadn't worn since they'd come back from the dry cleaners. She pulled on a shirt, which was a mixture of blue, gray and lilac, and slipped her feet in a pair of black pumps.

Michael double-checked his luggage to make sure he had everything he needed for his return to L.A. He was bending over his suitcase when Lauren came downstairs. He looked up and let out a short, shrill whistle.

"This is just not fair," he said softly, shaking his head.

"Honey, what is not fair?" Lauren replied, wondering if he knew just what was going on inside her head.

"You. You look *sooooo* good. Honey, you make me feel like I'm the luckiest man on the earth. That is what's unfair. That and the fact that I find it difficult to tear myself away from you for even the shortest period of time." His voice deepened then and Lauren sensed that Michael's next words would either leave her with much-needed assurances or a cautionary warning. "Look, you have to promise me something."

"Yes, Michael. Anything," she said, meaning the words she spoke.

"You have to promise me that you will be just as luscious when I return as you are right now," he said, the beginning of a smile at the corners of his mouth.

Lauren laughed then, and so did Michael. She found herself in his arms and had to stop herself from shedding a new batch of tears.

"I'm going to miss you," she said softly.

"You'd better," Michael replied, holding her tightly.

The drive to John F. Kennedy airport went much too quickly. They spent the time making small talk, holding hands, and trying not to think of what was to come.

Chapter Seventeen

Duane Capparelli continued to rhythmically tap his pencil on the edge of the desk, wondering how much longer he'd have to wait. The sun had disappeared from the sky while he waited for his cousin, his coconspirator. He'd expected Anthony to walk through the door more than an hour ago. He'd waited more than long enough.

Three months was a good, long time in jail from his point of view. Institutional green walls, dank smells, and the clanging of metal doors were his most vivid memories of the time he'd spent in lockup. He'd never be able to get those smells or the pictures out of his mind.

He'd breathed a sigh of relief when his conviction had been overturned due to a good, healthy dose of funds placed in the right hands. Now, some twelve weeks after his artfully orchestrated release, both he and Anthony were eager to finish a score which would make them both millionaires. If Morgan wanted to stand in their way, he could try, but they'd already made up their minds. He and anyone connected with him was expendable. This job was simply a matter of principle.

Duane heard Anthony's familiar footsteps and sat back in the chair. He glanced at his watch, realized it was even later than he'd thought, and his anger mounted.

"What's your problem?" he yelled, rising from the chair as Anthony entered the dimly lit room. The lights had been turned down to avoid drawing attention to their presence. The office space had been leased for more than four years, but barely held enough furniture to accommodate even the most meager operation. It was nothing more than a front for the real business, which was handled in forty-foot trailers parked inconspicuously at the Long Island City rail yards.

Despite the tirade, Anthony walked in calmly, smiled, and sauntered over. "Sorry, I know I'm late, but I had some things to take care of that just wouldn't wait." The line was delivered with all the casualness of someone who did not realize the ramifications of an hour and a half time difference between scheduled and actual arrival.

Duane did everything in his power to tightly control his anger. It simmered just below his skin, threatening to overtake both him and his tightrope-walking cousin. Instead, he sat back and simply let his gaze do the talking. He'd been taught that silence was a more powerful medium than idle chatter. Gino had been his mentor, and Duane had learned and done well. That is, until Morgan had become Gino's stepson.

Anthony understood the silent communication, took a seat, and removed his cap. He ran his hands through his hair, assumed a more serious expression, and waited. Duane had never handled lateness, disappointment, or challenge well. This he knew from their history together sharing family chores, duties, and business practices. As a man, Duane had often been given the short end of the stick in the organization, simply because he'd demonstrated the uncanny ability to pull through in the end. For that reason alone, he'd also been the one chosen to take the fall when the feds had come down on the family. The family had decided that Anthony would stay on the outside, responsible for handling any upcoming family interests or concerns.

Now, as the two men eyed one another warily, each trying his best to keep a lid on his true feelings, the reality of the current situation became even more apparent.

"We said we'd meet here at seven o'clock. It's now half past eight and we haven't even addressed the important stuff," Duane bellowed. "Where have you been since seven?" Duane's question hung in the air uncomfortably.

Anthony masked his emotion. He wanted to answer, but his pride told him to do otherwise. After all, he was a grown man, accountable to no one. Not even his partner in crime who sat across from him now, trying his best to control something that had never been within his domain.

"Listen, I'm doing everything in my power to get this stuff done. Sometimes things take longer than expected. We're going to waste more time if we continue to haggle about where we lost twenty minutes today, or half an hour tomorrow. Can we just move on to what needs to be done going forward? I swear, I'm not up for a blow-by-blow—not today anyway."

"Look, smart ass, you can either toe the line like you're supposed to, or you can call it quits. If you think I'm gonna take you smart-mouthing me on top of keeping me waiting all this time, you've got another thing coming. I don't give a damn where you were but just know that this is the last time—I repeat, the last time—that you will have me waiting in this godforsaken hellhole for you." Duane continued to hold Anthony's gaze, unwilling to look anywhere else until his point had been made.

"I know you mean it, and so do I. Nobody else but you and I know the magnitude of what we're working on, so all the loose ends have to be tied up by us. I really hope you understand what we've undertaken. The lockbox operation is incredible. It's working like a charm, and you know it. Tell me that the proceeds are not there, and I'll be the first one to back out. But check the numbers. It's all there like clockwork. And there's not a thing old cousin Morgan can do about it, can he?"

The last statement was issued with both authority and challenge, leaving Duane with little or no comeback. He listened to the words that described the initiative they'd put in place more than two years before. It had taken brains, ingenuity, and guts to even think of doing it, but with the help of one of the most ingenious computer hackers living on the Eastern Seaboard, they'd managed to pull it off. For a price, that is. . . .

Information technology was new to them both. When Gino initiated the first series of conversations, both had sat in, dumbfounded as to why and where this new application would be used. It had taken several lengthy conversations to convince them of its necessity. But it had taken Gino's clout to convince them of its brilliance.

All of this was long before his death. It was before CBN had even debated going public. That didn't matter to the two men facing one another in the poorly lit room as they discussed the next steps in their plans to retrieve almost ten million dollars from WJZZ's, and by extension, CBN's books. Neither of them wanted to think of what would happen if anything went wrong.

The indictments issued two years earlier read more like a who's who of the family business. The Feds, acting in conjunction with NYPD, sought to dismantle both Sorrentino Construction and Sorrentino Waste Management. Each company had been headed by one of the cousins, without whom the companies' continuance would be in serious jeopardy. Reaction had been swift, but not swift enough. Gino's unexpected death had curtailed the extent of the shutdown, but Duane's conviction put a definite strain on their former lifestyles. Anthony assumed full responsibility for the operations of both companies and did his best to assure that life would, indeed, go on.

In the end, it was Anthony's call to implement the computer fire wall they'd first discussed in Gino's presence. Not only would it provide safety in case of infiltration, it would also put in place the capability to "cleanse" funds coming in from several other extremely lucrative avenues of operation, which normally went underreported anyway.

No one expected Gino to die so suddenly or so soon. No one wanted the burden of responsibility that his absence indicated. But in the end, they each rose to the occasion and did what was necessary. Operation Open Sky was launched in the one-room office they now sat in, with one additional person present. That person held the key to the future, the answer to the present, and a direct link to the past. And in the short time it took to type maybe less than one hundred keystrokes, Operation Open Sky had become a living, breathing entity.

"What did you come up with?" Duane asked, no longer interested in pursuing his original conversation. If his cousin wanted to play games, he'd have to do it on his own time.

"Everything is in place. Relax, it's a done deal. Remember when I told you they would be unable to trace any of this stuff?" He didn't wait for an answer. "I was right. The revenue is showing up just where we wanted it, and nobody can link it to waste management or construction. It's beautiful. The plan was so sweet, I'm not sure this kind of stuff isn't done every day. It probably is. But we found an ingenious way to disguise the operation. Did you get to Morgan?"

Duane looked at Anthony for a long moment, choosing his next words carefully. "Not yet—it's more difficult than you think to wear that guy down. He's truly Gino's son, step-or not. They were as close to blood as you can get by the time Gino left this earth." His statement surprised and annoyed Anthony. This was not the time to be sentimental.

"Look, all you have to do is convince him to let you into CBN in the most minute way. You know our people can do the rest. If we can't pull this part off, it will make it harder to pull the revenue out. Those codes had their own firewall protection, put in on instruction by Gino himself. The man was no fool, I'll definitely say that. He just didn't stick around long enough to make sure it wasn't turned around on his own company."

The statement was damning, but no one who could do anything about it would ever know, if they played their cards right.

Anthony's thoughts turned to his uncle in his early years. He remembered the many visits he'd paid to the Sorrentino home before Gino's death. "You know, I kind of miss him. There was never a dull moment with Gino around."

Anthony's mother had been quietly devastated by her only brother's demise. He'd been instrumental in keeping her family close after the death of her husband in a mysterious car accident. He'd also been especially dutiful in helping to raise her only son. Gino wisely involved him in the family business early on, teaching him the ropes from the ground up. The same thing went for Duane, Gino's godson. He taught them everything he knew and had given them the tools to survive. Then Gino had met and married Cora, Morgan's mother. With that event came a new attitude. Now, Gino had a son of his own. His attention had focused more on his newly acquired stepson, who just happened to be a law student at Columbia University.

It didn't take a genius to know that Morgan's future legal expertise could prove to be invaluable to the business. It also didn't take a rocket scientist to realize that Morgan might not be the easiest target to mold. But Gino had an uncanny ability to persuade people to do things and in the end, Morgan was no match for his seasoned talents.

Both Duane and Anthony watched and waited on the sidelines as the attention was focused on the newcomer. Each vowed, for different reasons, to step up to the plate when the time came to get what was owed to them. Neither could have foreseen how quickly that day would arrive, nor could they have predicted the eloquence of their planned retribution.

Now, as they swapped information which would have clearly explained many of the questions CBN's inner circle of executive management was so desperately trying to answer, they sensed it was time to pop the cork. The magnum which they'd cellared was ready to be sampled.

"The one thing to remember is that we have to do it gradually. We'll still do it through the back door. Just be sure to let our guys know all the fine points: increments, dates, and where we want the drop made." Duane issued the statement with authority and finality. He didn't dare leave anything to chance, didn't dare allow Anthony the opportunity to question his authority. He'd be damned if things would be blown due to a lackadaisical attitude.

"I suspect you're right, although my first instinct is to just pull the plug all at once. But that would signal too many things and cause a panic attack." Anthony's statement rang true, and for once during the entire evening, Duane's level of respect for him was reinstated.

"Right. So we're in agreement on this. We take it nice and easy, and have our guy pull it out in steady increments. Make it a couple hundred thousand at a time. We'll pick up and distribute to an offshore account. How's that sound?"

"Beautiful. And you know the best part of it all?"

"No, but I have a feeling you're about to tell me."

"That Morgan and his crew won't even know what hit them," Duane interjected. "I understand they put a guy, Michael Townsend, out on the West Coast to check into things. Check him out and let me know if we need to put him down."

"Sure. You think he could be smart enough to figure this

out? Morgan wasn't, and he's the top guy. I don't think we have to worry," Anthony said.

Duane rubbed his brow. "Listen to me. Check this guy out. I don't like it. If Morgan joined forces with these guys, they must be good. And if he sent this particular one to oversee the Los Angeles books, it's not a good sign. The guy would have to be sharp. Even so, Cityscape Broadcast Network will be trying to figure this one out for the next decade. By that time, we'll both be long gone."

"I'll check," Anthony said. "If there's anything to what you say, we may have to act on it. I see that you're right on one point, but dead wrong on another. Morgan will try to figure it out, but he'll never be able to break through the firewalls put into place by our guy. Where you're wrong is how quickly we can move out of focus. We have to stay around, because otherwise, all roads lead to us. Capice?"

"I don't know if I want to do that. I mean, wasn't that the purpose of this in the first place to get the hell out of New York? I mean if Gino were still alive, don't you think he'd say, 'Take the money and run'?"

"Yeah, but don't forget I'm still on probation and will be for the next three years. Until that's over, I can't even cough on the street without notifying the Feds. The main reason we're moving on this now is because otherwise the numbers will get out of line. There's only so much that we can move into CBN's books without them getting suspicious. Don't worry—once we split up the slush fund, we don't have to move on right away. We live normally for another couple of years, then we do whatever we want to. It takes patience to pull this off, man. Don't blow it by being impatient or greedy."

Duane looked over at him sharply, ready to take offense, then thought better of it. There would be time enough later to assert his growing ego. For now, he'd go along with the program.

"Yeah, okay. I'll contact our expert tomorrow morning.

He knows what to do. In the meantime, is there anything else we need to put in place at CBN? I don't want Morgan to have any idea that there's something going on. You know that guy has become pretty sharp—even Gino would be proud of him."

"Yeah, Gino taught him well. But we're going to teach him a lesson that even Gino never learned. No, I don't think there's anything we need to do to make this happen. Make sure the expert knows we're liquidating it all. But just the overflow. Don't dip into CBN's legitimate revenues. We don't want Morgan or this Townsend guy to pull out all the stops. As it stands now, they still don't realize what's happening. Incredible!" Duane's beefy fist hit the table, illustrating a sudden surge of excitement. He'd really never believed that they'd be able to pull off their scam.

"Well, even Gino said we should cover ourselves. He just didn't know we would do it with a blanket called CBN." Anthony's laughter was infectious, and Duane joined in, his shoulders shrugging with the effort. They were coconspirators once again, joined in a plot which would either deliver them from drudgery, put them in their graves, or deed them to the state for a very long time.

Chapter Eighteen

Lauren had driven Michael to the airport the Sunday afternoon after his weekend visit. She hated to see him leave, although her spirits were much better after the weekend they'd spent together.

For the first time in a long while, Lauren's doubts about her marriage and its ability to endure all that she and her husband would face did not nag her mind. Although Michael was burdened with an excessive workload, he had taken a five-hour flight from L.A. just to be with her for a few days. He never complained about exhaustion, or anything else for that matter. They'd spent a blissful two days together and she was simply giddy with love. *Maybe this marriage can work,* Lauren thought optimistically. She laughed, realizing that Michael's sunny outlook was starting to rub off on her.

Lauren turned her key in the lock and opened the front door of the townhouse. She'd just come from the hardware store with a flesh supply of paint for the living room. She could still smell the lingering scent of cologne that Michael had sprayed on himself two weeks ago during his brief visit. Inhaling his scent, she closed the front door, placed the paint can on the floor, and walked to the kitchen to make herself a cup of tea.

Crossing the room, she saw the blinking light on the answering machine and stopped to play three messages. There was one from Duke who was calling to check on her again and one from Gloria saying they should get together soon. The last one was from the scheduling assistant at Worldwide, asking if Lauren could take over the flights that had been assigned to another flight attendant who was now unable to work.

With Michael gone, she needed to keep herself as busy as possible to keep her spirits up. Lauren jotted down the dates on a notepad by the phone and called back to accept the assignment. A few days ago, her reintroduction to flying had been traumatic at worst. At best, it featured all the ups and downs of a position that had changed drastically since September 11. Airport security now accounted for major delays for both passengers and flight crew. Lauren now had to arrive at check-in a full hour earlier than usual due to new flight boarding procedures.

Leaving the house at five-thirty in the morning to get to LaGuardia Airport wasn't so bad though, and while she was working, Lauren found she'd missed what was once her daily routine. She was happy to take on the extra work.

Lauren returned Duke's call. As usual, he didn't want anything. She invited him to have dinner at the house the following weekend. Then she called Gloria, who, as usual, didn't answer her phone. Lauren left a message telling Gloria to stop by later. Since she was in a better mood, Lauren was ready to tackle the chore of painting another room.

Just as she set the tea kettle on the stove, the phone rang. The number on the caller I.D. let her know it was Michael.

"Hey, babe," she answered enthusiastically, turning on the stove.

"Hey, yourself. You sound mighty happy. What's going on?"

Michael smiled, pleased to hear that Lauren was still in a good mood. Since his visit, she'd seemed much happier, and he was glad to know that his trip had been worthwhile.

Lauren updated him on the travel assignments she'd accepted and waited for his response.

"That's wonderful, kitten. When you first went back to Worldwide, I thought you were trying to get away from me, but you seem to be really happy about working again. It makes me feel bad for doubting your motives," he added sincerely.

"Don't worry about it. I know I'm not the easiest person to deal with sometimes," she said honestly. "But I'm yours, and you'll just have to deal with me, won't you?"

Michael laughed long and hard. It had been a while since Lauren had been this happy for such a length of time, and he knew that what he had to tell her would lift her spirits even higher. "Do you have to work next weekend?"

"Nope. I'm not on the schedule. I have a busy week, though. Why?"

"Well, I have good news. The report will be wrapped up by the end of the week, and I'll be able to come home for good." He smiled, waiting for Lauren's reaction.

A huge grin immediately spread across her face and she squealed in delight. "Oh, Michael that's wonderful. I'm so happy!" A feeling of relief spread throughout her body. She didn't know how tense she had been, waiting to hear those words.

"So am I. I miss you so much out here. You know, I've never been a big fan of L.A. I've always preferred New York."

"I can't wait. Oh, this is perfect timing," she added excitedly. "I just invited Duke to come by for dinner next weekend. This will be great because you'll be here too."

"No offense to Duke, but I'd rather be alone with my wife," Michael added, his voice growing husky with need. It had been entirely too long since he'd made love to his wife.

"There's plenty of time for that. I promise," Lauren said knowingly, feeling a surge of desire rush over her as she remembered the last time they were together.

After chatting for several more minutes, Michael and Lauren hung up the phone with smiles still on their faces as they looked forward to being reunited the following weekend. Their marriage seemed like it was going to work after all.

Duke's Upper East Side apartment was a five-minute ride from Sugar Bar, a cabaret/restaurant owned by legendary songwriters Ashford and Simpson.

He'd gotten up the nerve to ask Gloria out for dinner a few days earlier. After they finished eating and listened to a performance by a talented young singer with a voice made for funky ballads, he invited her over to his place for drinks. He'd held his breath as he'd asked, and was mildly surprised when she accepted.

Their dates had escalated from breakfast to dinner and they were now on their way to his place. The silence in his Range Rover's darkened interior was an emotional breeding ground for both parties.

Duke recognized that this was something he'd wanted to have happen from the first time he'd laid eyes on the woman who sat next to him. He knew that he was now treading on somewhat dangerous ground, then found himself smiling in spite of it all. He was determined to allow the evening to unfold without reservation, knowing they were both adults.

Four twenty-nine East Eighty-first Street consisted of three apartments and a penthouse. Duke owned the entire building but chose, wisely, to live at the top. Gloria stepped into the huge living room and immediately took note of his collection of antique horse sculptures, his lack of frills, and the no-nonsense environment he lived in. She was not at all surprised. The masculine surroundings were a true reflection of the man himself.

"What would you like? Name your undoing," he called out to her from the other side of the room, then laughed.

Gloria smiled uncertainly, wondering why she hadn't noticed his sense of humor before. Then she realized that he probably kept it tightly under wraps on most days, and especially during the course of business. That thought made it abundantly clear to her that *this* was not about business. She faced a major dilemma whenever it came to her personal life, and usually chose to live far beneath Morgan's radar. With this night, she would be stepping directly into it, a thought that both annoyed and challenged her.

Standing in the middle of the huge living room with eighteen-foot ceilings, she took in the wall-to-wall view of the East River. Duke was busy preparing their drinks, and Gloria felt relaxed. She wanted more than anything to finally allow herself the freedom to live. She was tired of being the daughter of a deceased mobster and fed up with being the sister of a powerful media mogul who pulled strings whenever he saw fit. She wanted there to be no recriminations, no second guessing—no matter what happened with Duke or any other man she chose to date.

Duke walked up behind her then, his six-foot two-inch frame a solid backdrop to her petite stature. It was eleven-thirty in the evening, too late for casual conversation and too early for regrets. Gloria sighed, leaned back and allowed her body to relax into his. It felt right, it felt good.

In that moment, Duke knew that after this night, things between them would never be the same. He handed her a champagne flute filled with Cristal.

"So what do you think of the place?"

"I think it's lovely. Everything from the charcoal gray suede sofa to the silver accents on the glass table and the

Oriental touches. It's a magnificent example of texture, fabric, and art. Did you use a decorator?"

"Actually, I did most of it myself. A friend helped me pick out some of the art pieces. It was her idea to put the alpaca rug under the coffee table. Other than that, this is all my doing." He waved his hand to include the expanse of the dining room, which included a rectangular glass and chrome table. Six white leather rollback chairs sat around its expanse and offered a stark contrast to the gray, black, and silver used throughout the rest of the room. The middle of the table held a crystal vase filled with a collection of aluminum fish swimming in an illuminated pond.

Gloria wanted to ask if his "friend" was still in the picture, but refrained. This was only the second time they'd spent time alone in one another's company. It made no sense to ask prying questions about past relationships. Instead she focused on something which seemed to be a safe topic. "What is that?" she asked, pointing to the odd-looking accessory on the dining room table.

"It's my tribute to the seventies. My friend made it for me. I wanted something different for my table, so she concocted a bowl that simulates an aquarium. She accused me of lacking basic parenting skills. The fish don't need any attention, so they're perfect for me . . . or so she said," he added, smiling now at the memory. At the time, it had not seemed so funny and was delivered as a definite put-down. He'd had his share of those, but they had never bothered him. Before Gloria, women had been a commodity to him, and very often nothing more than a necessary nuisance.

Gloria looked closely at the stunning piece. Each of the simulated fish was a work of art in itself, but the fact that they appeared to be swimming—the liquid's movement caused by the heat running through it—made it even more amazing.

"You friend is talented. This is great," she added.

"So are you," he said, quickly moving to close the gap between them.

Duke reached for the champagne flute she held and carefully placed it on the nearest table. Stepping closer, he lowered his mouth to hers in a kiss that was like a long-overdue appointment. His mind was filled with the scent of her perfume reminding him that it was indeed Gloria he held in his embrace. Their bodies fused together without seam or space as their lips met again and again. There were no more words. Talking had been replaced by a higher and more intense form of communication: passion.

Gloria's mind was no longer in control of her body. She knew the danger inherent in her situation and froze. The what-ifs, maybes, and why-nots now spoke to her, cautioning her in clear, practically audible tones. Past actions and present dilemmas all had a field day in her head as Duke took his time making his intentions more than obvious. He found the triangle at the base of her throat and feasted. Kisses trailed down the front of her exposed neckline, causing her to gasp as her hands held his head, relishing in the silky feel of his hair. The halter top she wore offered little hindrance to Duke's hands, and in moments its straps were unhinged.

Gloria gasped as she felt the draft of air on her skin, but Duke had already picked her up and was crossing the threshold to his bedroom. She found her voice, shaky but almost usable; then she managed to utter one word which made him stop in his tracks.

"Duke."

Looking down at her in his arms, his heart beating rapidly, he wanted conversation as much as a drunk on a binge wanted a cup of coffee. But this was Gloria, and he knew that whatever occurred in the next moments, they would wrestle with for a long time to come.

"Yes?" he answered, putting her down beside the king-sized bed. Shards of light came through the vertical blinds, filling the room with moonlight and magic, which only enhanced the strapless lace bra Gloria wore.

He wondered if she knew how long he'd wanted to make love, but before he could risk asking that question, or wait for Gloria's answer, his telephone rang. The sound caught him totally off guard. *Who would be calling at this hour? And more importantly, why?*

He looked at the instrument and shook his head. Muttering, "Sorry," he walked over to the night stand and barked into the phone "What? Oh, okay, sure, man. That's fine."

His reaction was at first rude, then acknowledging, then contrite. Gloria found it immensely funny watching him go through these emotions so quickly, and began laughing. She watched Duke sit on the bed and launch into a conversation he obviously needed to have.

She walked back into the living room, fastened her top back into place, and headed for the bar where she poured a glass of tonic water to clear her head and let out a sigh. Moments later, she walked back into the bedroom and found Duke putting the receiver into the base.

"It was Michael, on West Coast time. Can you tell me why I have been cursed?" His question was not only rhetorical, but also hilarious and Gloria couldn't help but laugh. She knew his frustration well, but felt more than relieved. Michael's timely phone call had served to interrupt a moment that was premature.

"I wouldn't say that you're cursed, just that your life is pretty complex at this point. You obviously have some business decisions that you need to address. They say timing is everything. If you take this evening's chain of events into consideration, they're probably right."

Her matter-of-fact delivery did nothing to soothe Duke's chafed soul. He looked over at her and sighed. Shaking his head, he began to laugh with Gloria joining in.

He held out his hand then, and she walked toward him, taking it.

"Did you have a good time? Please say yes," he added, looking into her eyes.

"Yes, I did. Thanks for inviting me out. It's not often that I actually get to go out on dates," she admitted.

"I don't believe that," Duke said, smiling sadly. "Actually, I do. It must be difficult for you to be who you are," he added.

"Yeah, but you know I wouldn't change it for anything. Even with all our family has been through." Her statement said more than she wanted it to, and Duke watched as she gazed out over the East River.

"Are you sure you don't want to stay over?" he asked quickly.

"No, that will only make it more difficult. I want you to know that I did want to be here, with you, and I still do. Honestly, I'm just not sure that we can pull it off, or that I know exactly how to handle Morgan. It's kind of complicated, you know, especially because CBN is poised to go public. I don't have to explain the tension to you because you're probably living with it every day. I'm sorry. Please forgive me, but I'm just not ready for that kind of complication."

She laid it all out, said it without trying to dress it up, and in the end, Duke understood one hundred percent. That's because he felt exactly the same way.

On the drive to Gloria's apartment in Brooklyn's Cobble Hill, Duke was quiet. He turned to WJZZ, which had a legendary early-morning format. Listening to the sounds of Nina Simone, Duke and Gloria were pensive.

As he pulled onto her tree-lined street, the quiet was peaceful and reassuring. He turned to Gloria.

"Please don't worry about Morgan. Let me handle that. Whatever happens between us is just that: between us," he reassured her.

She was quiet for a moment with her own thoughts, then said in a small voice, "That's a little easier said than done," she said meaningfully.

"Look, let's just take this one day at a time. I had a wonderful evening, and I hope you did too." He held one of her hands and put his head back, but turned to look at her. "I don't want to put a name or number on what we have. I just don't want it to stop tonight," he said then. He leaned forward and kissed her softly on the lips.

"Thanks for a wonderful evening," she murmured.

Duke looked at her and whispered, "No, thank *you*. Thanks for everything." And he meant it.

Chapter Nineteen

Michael was ecstatic. The report was finally filed. The information contained within was both damaging and confusing, but conclusive. He was ready to return home to his bride. He'd already made reservations, and looked forward to boarding a plane bound for New York City in less than nine hours.

The phone rang while he was in the bathroom gathering his toiletries. He almost didn't answer, but figured it might be Lauren, since he had not spoken to her since the morning before. He picked up the receiver and was immediately sorry. It was Morgan.

"Michael, you did a great job. I've got the report right here in front of me."

"Hey, Morgan. It's great to hear from you. Thanks for the kind words. I was just throwing my gear into a suitcase."

"I figured that. It's why I called as soon as I had completed my reading of your report. I wanted to talk with you," Morgan said uneasily.

Morgan's voice took on a serious note and Michael's stomach churned. There had been daily exchanges between himself, Duke, and Morgan in the past week, all culminating in the expectancy of his final filings. And Duke would also be filing a report shortly, if he hadn't already, which made Michael eager to solidify the research he'd compiled during his month-long stay in Los Angeles. But it was only after that period of time that he'd uncovered the data that led him to conclude that someone had intentionally tampered with their bottom line. Michael's instincts were to pull the plug and start over again.

An entirely fresh team of accountants and number-crunching pencil-pushers would be needed if they were to ever get any "real" documentation out of their West Coast operation. He'd stated as much in his report, and more. It had taken someone a lot of time, effort, and energy to massage the documents he'd uncovered. Someone who was firmly entrenched in WJZZ's research and reporting departments, or someone very high up on the Cityscape Broadcast corporate end had to be at the controls. But that research would have to be supervised from New York. Before he made that clear to Morgan, he wanted to hear his initial response to the report. He continued to listen.

"Yeah, I'm sure you're ready to get back here to the East Coast. And I can't blame you. But, unfortunately, there is one thing that worries me a little on the back end of the report. You show that we've accumulated equal revenue status from advertising dollars coming in during the first, second, and third quarters. Can that be correct? It's an industry truism that we always have a soft second quarter—shares of listeners then rise in the third quarter and drop again in the fourth quarter. I just want to be sure the data you analyzed was based on the most accurate sources. Did you double-check the Arbitron ratings, as well as the advertising lineup revenues?"

Michael took a deep breath and sat on the bed, trying to hold his temper back. "Morgan, of course I analyzed those findings. That's not where the discrepancies really showed up, though, if you really want the full skinny on this thing. We're hemorrhaging somewhere else, although the strange thing is that the final numbers are fine. It's almost as though someone is "borrowing" revenue then putting it back with interest to bear, so that we'll turn a blind eye to the discrepancy," he concluded, knowing as he did that he was probably sealing his fate.

"Yeah, that's the thing that bothered me too. The numbers that are showing up here are phenomenal. They're actually higher than one would expect, and nobody should ever question more money than originally slated when it comes in the door. But my stepfather always taught me to look out for the small things. As crummy as this may sound, I have to ask you to stay there until we can get to the bottom of this."

There was a brief silence. Michael's voice was both controlled and steely, his emotions held in check by a compound resolution: He'd signed on for the duration of the investigation, knowing there would be difficult times ahead. But he'd also taken a vow to love, honor and cherish Lauren, and of late, he hadn't been doing such a great job. Although he spoke with her daily, sometimes well into the night, he recognized that with all that they'd brought into the marriage, the last thing either of them needed was even more distance. He could have kicked himself for volunteering to come to L.A.

"Morgan, I'm not entirely sure that another couple of days, or even weeks, will give us the information we're seeking. Have you spoken with Duke? I know operations generally would not have the same window of opportunity for fraud and miscalculation of revenue, but what's his take on all of this?"

"Duke is trying to piece things together also. Hey, man, don't feel that I've chosen you to stay on an odyssey just to make a point. This information is crucial for CBN, as well as you and Duke as partners of CBN going forward. It's extremely important for the board of directors too. These people have put their hard-earned dollars and cents into the company so that it can grow at an exponential rate of return. At some point, we want to be able to go public with no quavering as the normal background checks necessary to reach that rung of the ladder are completed."

Michael took a deep breath and sighed. All of his active business instincts told him that Morgan was dead-on with his assessment of both the situation and the reports. But his heart told him that it was time to get back to home base. Lauren's patience appeared unwavering on the surface. Each day when he spoke with her, she was cheerful, rushing off to catch a flight or busy turning the townhouse into a home. He was looking forward to joining her in New York, and couldn't wait to see what she'd done to the house since his last visit.

Morgan's statement called for his immediate attention. It made no sense to prolong the inevitable. Michael would have to stay and finish uncovering the real source of the discrepancies that continued to show up on WJZZ's quarterly statements and which ultimately, impacted the bottom line of Cityscape Broadcast Network.

"Morgan, you're right on all fronts. There is one other route that I can take, and it'll probably take awhile. It's not the way I want it, but that's the reality of it, I guess." He ended his words abruptly. Although he'd managed to sound firm and committed to the continued project, annoyance filled his being as he thought of a conversation he dreaded.

"Well, Michael, I don't see any other way. I was thinking, Noelle might be a help to you. She's only been here for a few months, but has a real sense of the industry. I put her on a plane to L.A. earlier today. She should be there soon, if she's not already. I gave her all your contact information at the hotel. She can assist you for a short spell and then come on back to New York. She is fast, efficient and very corporate-minded. After all that I've asked of you, it was the least I can do," Morgan added.

"To be honest with you, I hadn't thought of any additional help. I've been so hands-on with this thing that it seems like I've spawned the entire project."

"Nonsense. The discrepancies have nothing to do with you or Duke. What I want to make sure of is that we are able to identify, pinpoint, and stem the flow of revenue coming into our books."

Michael hesitated. He didn't want to offend Morgan, but he sure as hell didn't need an *assistant* looking over his shoulder. Unfortunately, there was no way to get rid of her if she was already en route.

"I wish you had told me she was coming. I would have made sure she was met at the airport by one of our people."

"No problem. I just hope she works out well. It will take some of the pressure off you in terms of analytical stuff too. She's good at interpreting financial data, and I've seen her work wonders."

"Well, that's a relief. As long as she's going to be an asset, I'm all for it," Michael lied.

"You'll thank me for this Michael. I'm looking forward to receiving the final version of this, and I hope to see you soon."

"Sure, Morgan, you too. Say hello to Gloria for me. I know Lauren was planning something that involved her. She was pretty excited about it," he added solemnly.

"I haven't spoken to her lately, 'cause I've been pretty busy with CBN, trying to hold it all together. Hey, I'll talk with you soon. Call me when you discover something, okay?"

"You know I will. And don't expect this thing to take too much longer, either. I miss my woman."

"Take as long or as short a time as is necessary to get the job done. I'm sorry the thing is growing tentacles, but that's business for you. Keep doing what you're doing. It's bound to uncover something we've overlooked."

"I know, that's what I'm afraid of. But don't give it a second thought," Michael said, his trademark optimism returning. "Both Duke and I pride ourselves on follow-through, no matter what the cost. We turned the station around with that attitude as our mantra. In this instance, we're both committed to providing a clear company picture."

"I knew that when we signed the acquisition papers. You guys are the best on the street, and no one ever said otherwise."

"Well, thanks, and don't worry, I'll get back to you as soon as I'm done."

The conversation ended and Morgan hung up, resolved to move forward. Michael placed the phone down with a heavy heart. He had no idea what this extended business trip would do to his marriage.

A minute later, he picked up the phone, called CBN's travel office and cancelled his reservation. Then he called Lauren. The phone rang several times before she answered breathlessly.

"Honey, what were you doing, calisthenics?" he asked, trying his best to set a light tone for a conversation he knew would reverse Lauren's cheerful demeanor.

"No, I was just coming from the salon and the market. I promised to make dinner for your partner tomorrow night, remember?"

In tying up all the loose ends on the report, he'd totally forgotten that Lauren had invited Duke to dinner, and that he'd promised to try to be there as well.

"Guess what? Gloria's coming too," she added, the excitement evident in her voice. "And it wasn't even my idea. Duke called and asked if he could bring her. I had no idea there was any interest between them. Each time we've all been together, she's always been under Morgan's watch, and you and Duke are in conversation about business. How about that?"

"Honey, I'm blown away. But not totally surprised. Duke has been talking about Gloria for awhile now. I suspect he waited until he thought it was the right time." He paused, delaying the inevitable. "Lauren, not to change the subject but I have to."

"Michael, what's wrong? You sound awful." Suddenly, she heard the exasperation in his voice and feared his answer as much as she needed to hear it.

"I don't know any other way to say this. I had to cancel the flight, Lauren. I still have some loose ends to tie up here, although the bulk of the report was filed yesterday. I realize it's not what you want to hear right now," he said softly.

Lauren felt as if all the air in the room had suddenly been consumed. She held the phone to her ear, hoping that he'd add something about it all being a joke—a very bad one. But silence ensued, and she realized that tears were winding their way down her face. A tremendous feeling of sorrow suddenly overwhelmed her. So this is how their marriage would always be—business first, family second, with his commitment to her falling somewhere in between. She held back a sob. His last statement had revealed more truth than he realized and the marriage he'd insisted on held little relevance to her at that moment.

"Michael, you know I'm disappointed. If you think it's important for you to cancel, what can I say? I'll see you whenever you get here," she added, her voice very matter-of-fact so that it hid her pain.

Michael wasn't fooled for a minute. "Baby, I promise to make it up to you. I know you're probably angry. Listen, still have dinner with Duke and Gloria. It'll be good for all of you to get together. Trash me if you want to even, whatever it takes to get you through the evening. Just know that I'd rather be there with you than anywhere else in the world, and I mean that."

"Okay, I will. Trash you, I mean," she said partly joking. She felt as if the wind had been knocked out of her by his words. She'd been waiting for him to come home again for more than three weeks, and realized that she missed him more than she'd thought possible.

"Michael, I'm going to hang up now. I need to put the groceries away. You know, refrigerated stuff," she said, wanting to end the conversation. What more was there left to say? Her husband was staying in L.A. to work and that's all there was to it.

"Honey, are you okay with this? I know it came as a surprise, but I just found out too. Morgan's the senior partner at CBN, not to mention the majority shareholder. I have to follow his lead," he explained. "I promise you that I will make it up to you when I return. Until then, just hold down the Townsend fort, okay?"

Lauren suppressed the sob in her throat once more. "You know I will. Okay, I'm going to let you go now. Call me later if you want to," she added.

"Of course I will. I'll call while the dinner party I'm missing is in progress," he quipped, trying to lighten the conversation again.

"I'm sure Duke and Gloria will like that," she said dryly.

Michael sensed the hurt in her voice, and it pained him to know that he'd caused it. "Yeah, all right, babe. Go on and put the stuff away. I love you," he said, emphasizing his last words.

"I love you too, Michael. I really do." She hung up the phone, unable to hold back her crying.

Michael held the phone in his hands, unwilling to sever the connection. He was filled with emotion and wanted more than anything to erase the pain that Lauren felt. A knock interrupted his thoughts, and he hung up the phone before going to answer the door.

Noelle stood in the hallway, unsure as to her real intentions but determined to find out as much as she could while she was in California. Her standing with the agency was in jeopardy. Her credibility had taken a nose dive with her last reports. Several key pieces of information had been either missed or underreported. The supervisory panel which oversaw her unit now watched and waited. Noelle's next report would either explain or indict. Still, she had something else on her mind that bothered her even more. That something was standing in the way of putting her assignment to bed.

"Hey, sorry to bother you. I just got in," she said when the door opened. "I was reading on the plane and I'm trying to make sense of a couple of the entries for the first quarter." She pointed to her notepad and looked up at Michael, noticing for the first time the look of pure pain on his face. "Did I catch you at a bad time?" she asked quickly.

"Somewhat. Just a minute," he added, stepping back into the room and heading toward the bathroom to blow his nose and splash water on his face.

In that space of time, Lauren dialed his cell phone, not wanting to leave the conversation the way they'd ended it. Noelle picked up the vibrating phone and answered.

"Hello?"

"Hello, Michael?" Lauren uttered, confusion evident in her voice when she heard a female voice.

"No, I'm sorry. He's in the bathroom right now," Noelle answered.

Lauren hung up without saying another word. *So that's why he's staying in L.A.,* she thought, leaning against the kitchen counter with a fresh set of tears streaming down her face. She sobbed harder than she ever had before. She'd never experienced the kind of despair, confusion, and failure she now felt.

Pulling herself together, she went to her purse and pulled out a business card. She picked up the phone and called the offices of Dennison, York, Noble, and Pratt, Attorneys at Law. She made an appointment for the following Monday and hung up.

When Michael came out of the bathroom, Noelle never mentioned the call.

Chapter Twenty

Lauren entered the law offices of Dennison, York, Noble, and Pratt, and took the elevator to the ninth floor. The determined stride she exhibited was totally at odds with her inner turmoil. Reaching suite 9700, she began the process of severing her marriage.

Once she'd arrived at the decision, it had been relatively simple to implement. Apparently, annulment was based on almost any minor infraction of the marriage contract. Refusal to share the marriage domicile was probably the easiest, quickest, and most conclusive element to prove. She didn't mention adultery to her lawyer because she was unable to prove it. Besides, Michael's absence paired with her original misgivings became a damning indictment. Lauren's main intention was to avoid confrontation. There was no way she could listen to Michael tell her that he'd been seeing another woman, that he'd replaced her.

The process would be quick but painful, according to her lawyer. After answering a small battery of questions, Lauren emerged from the offices feeling as if she'd severed ties with a part of herself. The lawyer's questions, though necessary, had seemed intrusive. At one point, Lauren had almost walked out in the middle of completing several necessary forms, but determination held her steady.

Eva called just after she returned home, eager to share the news of her new promotion. Lauren's voice as she answered the phone was filled with emotion.

"My God, Lauren. What on earth is the matter?" Eva asked, her concern unmasked.

"Mom, I can't get into it right now. I'll explain things later. Maybe tomorrow, but not tonight. Just give me that space for now," Lauren replied, her voice seeming to come from elsewhere. "I think I'm just going to take a shower and get into bed. I feel drained."

"Is something physically wrong? Does this have anything to do with Michael? Did you talk to him like I asked you to?"

Lauren couldn't bring herself to tell her mother about the woman who answered Michael's phone, nor could she put into words the feelings of emptiness she felt when Michael was gone. Her head hurt now, but she knew in the long run that her actions would turn out to be for the best. Just thinking of the steps she'd taken to dissolve her marriage made her voice break, and she was unable to stifle a sob that broke through. Tears streamed down her face, and she became silent, unwilling to allow even her mother to comfort her.

"Mom, please don't worry. I have it all figured out. Michael is a survivor no matter what happens. Neither of us has to really worry about him. He'll be just fine," she added, though even she didn't sound totally convinced.

Eva's alert immediately went up. "Honey, what on earth are you talking about? Survive what? Listen to me and you listen to me good, young lady," Eva bellowed, her voice rising with each sentence. "Don't be a fool and cause a man you obviously love to walk away from you. You'll only regret it in the long run."

Unfazed by her mother's warnings, Lauren took a deep breath and swallowed hard. She knew she had made the right decision. She just wondered how long it would take for the annulment to become final.

Her pager went off then and she jumped. She'd practically forgotten about it, since it never rang anymore. It was only used by her former roommate or, if necessary, Worldwide Airlines. The number started with area code 213. Michael probably had attempted to reach her by phone and had paged her when she didn't answer. She took a deep breath and told Eva she would have to call her back.

"Michael just paged me. I have to call him," Lauren said without emotion.

"Good. You need to talk to your husband. Call me back. We need to talk about what's going on with you. You haven't been sounding like yourself lately."

Lauren promised to return the call and hung up the phone. She quickly picked it back up and dialed the number on the screen of her pager.

"Hello?"

"Hi," Lauren said weakly, recognizing Michael's voice.

"Hi yourself. What's up? The phone was ringing off the hook. Did you just walk in?"

"Actually, no. I was asleep," she lied. "I had a horrendous day."

"Honey, I'm sorry to hear that. Anything I can do to cheer you up?"

His voice was full of concern, and his sincerity brought tears to her eyes, but she held fast. No time was a good time to break down. Especially not now.

"No, I'm fine." She forced herself to laugh, to pretend everything was fine. "How did today go?"

"Not too bad, actually. I'm going to try and wrap things up here in the next couple of days. The fact that Morgan wanted me to stay longer to delve into certain inconsistencies was not the vote of confidence I was hoping for. To make a long story short, this thing is becoming more complicated every day that goes by. It also makes me crazy to think of you there all alone. I promise you, Lauren, when I get home I'm going to make all of this up to you."

"Michael, I don't want you to feel guilty about this. It's your work. It wasn't your fault that you were sent on an assignment that has gotten out of hand. You had no choice," she added, wondering if she were trying to convince him or herself.

"So why do I feel so awful? I know it wasn't my fault, you know it wasn't my fault, but that does not detract from the fact that we're apart, and I, for one, am missing the heck out of you." His voice was filled with emotion, unexpressed passion, and something else that Lauren realized she'd never heard before: desperation.

"It's your responsibility though to finish the assignment, isn't it?" she asked, hoping she could complete the conversation without breaking into tears.

"Yeah, but you know where my heart is, where my soul is. Lauren I need you badly. The fact of the matter is that I don't think I can do my job if I don't at least see you again sometime soon. . . ." His voice trailed off, and Lauren's pulse quickened.

She pushed the phone away from her ear, shut her eyes, and tried to think of something else. His voice remained with her, though, filling her with need, wiping out all the indecision and erasing the uncertainties. She didn't want to hear any of it, didn't want to acknowledge that it mattered . . . but it did, and she knew it.

Michael was silent on the other end, his emotions tightly coiled. He knew what he had to do. Some sixth sense told him to keep the details to himself. He ended the conversation with his usual promise of love and a heartfelt, "Missing you," murmured into the receiver.

The end of the line was nearer than either of them imagined.

Chapter Twenty-One

The dinner party was destined to either be a big disaster or a huge hit. At exactly seven o'clock, Duke arrived with a bottle of wine under one arm and a box of gourmet pastries under the other. Lauren put on her best cheerful demeanor, opened the door, took one look, and hugged him fiercely. She couldn't help it. He was the closest thing to Michael that she'd seen in a while.

Duke was surprised but elated. His partner's wife was breathtaking and he had never been one to ignore a woman's beauty. In his mind, this visit was long overdue so he basked in the feeling and hoped he'd get the same response from Gloria when she showed up. An hour and a half later, he got his wish.

Gloria whisked in, still in her Worldwide Airlines uniform, kissed him on the cheek, then hugged her former roommate for a full minute. "I miss you so much, Lauren, you have no idea," she confessed as she removed her coat, shoes, and the pins from her hair. Duke watched, unable to speak as the heavy mass of ebony tresses tumbled to her shoulders. Neither of them mentioned the two dates they'd been on, wanting to preserve the intimacy they felt. They'd decided to keep their friendship to themselves.

Gloria looked directly at Duke as she embraced Lauren, and the effect was immediate. Duke did his best to turn away, not wanting Lauren to see, but he was unable to take his eyes off of Gloria.

"You two visit while I change into something befitting the occasion," Gloria announced as she left the room.

"Sure, why don't you use the only spare bedroom. There's a bathroom in there too," Lauren added. "Just put your things anywhere."

"Okay. Look in that satchel I dropped by the door. There's something from Dallas for you." She took the stairs two at a time. Lauren looked at Duke, who was shaking his head.

"Wow, she's a whirlwind, isn't she?" he said, wondering if his demeanor was giving Lauren any indication of what had occurred between him and Gloria.

"That she is. Remember, I roomed with her for three years, and let me tell you, she is something else. She's also my best friend, so watch it," she warned with a smile.

"You don't have to worry. I'm the one who's probably in danger," he shot back.

Lauren laughed and shook her head. She walked over to where Gloria had left her oversized leather handbag, and picked it up to place it out of the way. A large box with THE TANNERY stamped in large gold and red letters was inside. Several smaller boxes with the same logo lay beside it.

"I'm going to wait for her to open these. Meanwhile I'll check on dinner," Lauren announced as she walked to the kitchen and opened the oven.

The aroma that reached Duke's nose told him that dinner would be enjoyable, and also made his mouth begin to water. He'd looked forward to the evening from a social standpoint for the entire week. Now he realized there would be an additional bonus as well: a good home-cooked meal. He sipped from a glass of wine and enjoyed the blue cheese and crackers Lauren had set out on the table while she continued the last-minute dinner preparations.

Gloria emerged some twenty minutes later, looking as if she'd just come from the beauty parlor, her dark, curly hair meticulously styled. She'd put on jeans and a soft blue sweater, which only served to complement the dark tones of her mane. It also accentuated the pale gray of her eyes. Duke felt the bottom of his stomach take a tumble, and attributed it to the wine.

The two women managed to make small talk related to the airline industry as they went about setting the meal on the table. It was, quite simply, a feast. Pot roast, potatoes and carrots, string beans with mushrooms, crescent rolls, and a huge salad with glazed pecans and gorgonzola cheese sprinkled liberally on top were set on the huge dining room table.

"Girl, you must have been cooking all day—for a couple of days," Gloria teased just before they began the meal.

"Not really, I just started at about one o'clock. I was out taking care of business this morning. Then I stopped at a market on Columbus. All of this is the product of that little visit."

"Well, Lauren, I have to tell you that it all looks and smells wonderful. And I want to thank you in advance, just in case I get so full that I forget my manners," Duke said, smiling at them both because he could not take his eyes off Gloria.

She smiled back, though she was careful to appear to be unfazed by his attention. She wasn't altogether sure she was ready for Lauren to know anything about Duke as he pertained to her personal life. There would be plenty of time to talk about their relationship, if it ever reached that point.

"So, how's the place coming along? Miss me much?" Lauren asked Gloria.

The two women had shared a two-bedroom, two-bathroom

condominium in Brooklyn's Cobble Hill after they'd completed flight attendant school. When Lauren moved out, Gloria had taken the plunge and purchased the place from its owner.

"Immensely, but you know I'm hardly ever there," Gloria said. "I haven't even had the chance to replace the items you took when you moved. We need to go shopping sometime soon. You know how I like to add stuff that winds up being exotic but not practical."

"Hey, don't be so hard on yourself. The apartment was comfortable as a result of your eclectic taste. I think it actually made the place more interesting," Lauren added, as they each took turn filling their plates from the various bowls and platters in the middle of the table.

"Sounds like you women are talented as well as beautiful. I'm in the midst of true grace this evening." Duke laughed, wondering what he'd done to suddenly become so lucky.

Lauren grinned. "You know, I didn't get to thank you for extending that invitation to my buddy here. I think it was a great idea for us all to get together tonight."

"So do I, but I'm only sorry that Michael isn't here with us. He's the missing link. Although I do have to say that he's a trooper for offering to go to California. I think Morgan was hoping I would say that I'd go. I even offered to trade with Mike, but he was adamant. The guy is the consummate professional," Duke added, ending his rambling.

With the mention of Michael's name, the mood somehow changed. Lauren smiled politely and stared down into her plate. Gloria noticed the change immediately and shot Duke a look which he interpreted as *shut up*. They continued to eat in silence before Lauren jumped up, said something about music, and disappeared.

Moments later, light strains of jazz could be heard, and Duke and Gloria breathed a collective sigh of relief. Lauren entered the room, sat down quickly, and behaved as if nothing had occurred.

Duke offered to open the bottle of wine he'd brought. Gloria found the opener and glasses before Lauren could even attempt to get up. "Just sit and relax. You've done enough for one day. You know, the training we receive is a great enabler. I can find my way around anyone's kitchen, the galley of a plane, boat or bus, with my eyes closed," she said, one hand on her hip as both Duke and Lauren laughed.

Just then, the front door opened and Michael walked in laden with a garment bag, a carry-on bag, a briefcase, and a huge smile. Lauren almost choked on her food. Duke stood and walked over to Michael, figuring Lauren was in shock. And Gloria froze, the wine bottle in one hand, the corkscrew in the other, watching her best friend fall apart.

"Looks like I got here just in the nick of time. You three are a sad lot," Michael said. "Come here and act like you missed me," he said, motioning for Lauren to come to him.

She rose from her chair slowly, a million thoughts circling through her mind. What was Michael doing home? And where was that woman who answered his phone when she called? As she crossed the room, her emotions became a ball of confusion. She was happy to see the man she'd loved since the day she first laid eyes on him. But he was also the man who had cheated on her, who'd broken her already fragile heart.

Michael folded Lauren into his arms, his eyes closed while he savored the feel of her. When he opened them, Lauren was laughing and crying at the same time. Duke was grinning from ear to ear, and Gloria still held a wine bottle in mid-air, transfixed by the unexpected change of emotion in the room.

Michael lifted a hand for Duke to join the embrace. The three of them hugged for a long moment, and then Lauren broke into uncontrollable laughter. "You're crushing me Duke. Gloria, please come and relieve me. I can't take the pressure of these two," she shouted.

Gloria laughed, placed the wine on the counter, and did as she'd been told. Duke was only too happy to include her into the mix, and the next moment was one which was felt by all.

Michael cleared his throat. "Okay, enough of this love fest. Where's my dinner, woman?" he asked, looking straight at Lauren.

She was unsure what to do next. Duke's revelation concerning the project had knocked the wind out of her. Michael had volunteered for L.A., he must have been eager to get out there for a reason. *Was that woman who answered his phone the reason?* Lauren had so many questions, but it was not the time to ask them. She put a smile on her face for her guests. She would deal with Michael and his infidelity later.

"Oh my God, Michael, I didn't know you were coming home. Why didn't you tell me when we spoke?" she asked, pretending to be happy. "I would have made something even more special," she added, looking at the spread on the table.

"You're special. That's all I need. And this is a feast. Honey, you didn't need to do all of this for this character," he said pointing to Duke with feigned jealousy.

"Hey, don't discourage her appreciation for the disadvantaged of the world," Duke said, defending his honor.

Michael could not take his eyes off Lauren, noting the fit of her pants, the soft pink sweater she wore, and also the dark half-circles under her eyes. She returned his looks with love and indecision, but he had never been happier to see her.

"Just give me a minute to wash up and I'll join you guys. Don't stop eating. I'll be right back." He started for the stairs, headed for the master bedroom with his bags, and heard Lauren excuse herself. Picking up the briefcase he'd left just inside the kitchen doorway, she joined him.

"I cannot believe you kept this from me," she said, her voice wavering. "You knew even when we said good night last evening that you'd be here tonight, didn't you," she asked, watching him wash his hands. *What else is he keeping from me?* she wondered.

"Sure did. Knew it day before yesterday, but I wasn't going to tell you just in case I had to change my plans. I didn't want to disappoint you again. I need you, woman," he added moving to draw her into his embrace.

Lauren stepped back, moving away from him. She wanted to mention the phone call, but she didn't trust herself to fall apart if he told her he'd been having an affair. She decided to remain silent and make the best of her dinner party. "I think we should join our guests," she said harshly. "They'll think we're ditching them otherwise." She turned and left the room, leaving Michael with a wounded heart and an open mouth.

Duke and Gloria were laughing as Lauren and Michael entered the room. They stopped as the tension between the recently married couple filled the air.

"So can my wife cook, or what?" Michael asked, attempting to break the ice.

"Man, I haven't had food like this since my mom's, and you know that's been a long time," Duke confessed, keeping the mood light, though he sensed something was wrong. "Gloria here has just been bragging about her culinary abilities, so I'm just about to take her up on it," Duke confessed.

"I was not bragging, only stating a fact. Lauren, don't I make a mean spaghetti dinner? I have friends here who can vouch for me," Gloria announced with exaggerated confidence, taking a sip of her wine. She noticed the tension too, but she was playing along with Duke and trying to keep the mood as stress-free as possible.

Michael watched the interplay between them, but could not participate. *What have I done now?* he wondered. *What made Lauren walk away from me?* He dreaded that his greatest fear had just been realized: the business trip to L.A. had cost him Lauren's love.

"Hey, there's no doubt about it. Gloria is a whiz in the

kitchen when she puts her mind to it. Now, getting her to put her mind to it is the trick," Lauren added happily, thinking her friends had not caught on to the rift been her and Michael.

"See, I knew that," Duke teased.

Lauren laughed as Duke joined in, Michael shook his head and Gloria continued to look the part of an injured innocent. "See, I knew I couldn't win. I can't get a fair trial in this town. I move that we have a change of venue. You're all invited to dinner two weeks from tonight. No excuses either. Not from any of you." She delivered the last line with a direct look in Michael's direction. And because she was his wife's best friend, he instantly knew there was more to her look than a meaningless gesture.

He nodded his consent and looked directly at Lauren. "I plan to be there," he added, picking up his fork.

The meal was delicious, with everyone complimenting Lauren over and over again. By the time they sampled the desserts that Duke brought, along with the pot of fresh coffee Lauren brewed, it was well past eleven o'clock.

Gloria insisted they open the boxes she brought in from Dallas. Lauren was so caught off guard by a pair of beige snakeskin cowboy boots that she almost screamed.

"Oh my God, Gloria, how did you ever know? I've wanted a pair of these for so long." Her voice trailed off as she tried them on.

"I know. I had to hear about them every time your trips took you through any part of Houston, Dallas, or Fort Worth. I decided you deserved them, so I picked them up. They were on sale," she added, looking away.

Lauren kissed her, hugged her, and then kissed her again. She doubted they were on sale. Snakeskin hardly ever went on sale. The last time she'd checked, the tag had been somewhere around the three hundred fifty mark. Gloria didn't know the word *discipline* when it came to money. She'd never had to. Still, Lauren didn't feel comfortable having her spend that kind of money on a gift that wasn't even attached to a holiday or a special occasion.

"You really didn't have to do that, but thank you so much. Now, I feel as if I should have had gifts for you all tonight," Lauren said.

"Hey, that meal you just served was the best gift I got all winter. And that includes Christmas," Duke said and everyone, except Michael, who was distracted, laughed.

"Yeah, and speaking of that, what's this?" he asked. Gloria had placed small boxes in front of Duke and Michael. Both men looked puzzled, shrugged their shoulders, and removed the lids.

"Whoa, a snakeskin key chain. Now *that's* nice." Duke laughed, holding up the beige and black object for Lauren to see. The diamondback pattern was immediately recognizable as that of the deadliest type of snake in North America. In Duke's mind, it made the piece even more interesting. He wondered if it was a subliminal message from Gloria, alluding to the danger of their relationship. If so, at least she was aware of the fact that he intended to move forward.

Michael's key chain was flat with a brass ring through it. The skin was all black on one side, dark brown on the other, and held together by a braided trim. The handiwork was exquisite and had obviously been done by very skilled hands.

"This is great!" he said, his spirits lifted for the first time since he'd returned to the dining room. "Gloria, you didn't have to do this. You didn't even know I would be here. Thank you, though," he added, holding it up for Lauren to see.

Lauren looked away. "She's like that, always doing something unexpectedly generous. Didn't I tell you to save your money?" Lauren said, hugging her friend and pretending to scold her simultaneously.

Gloria saw the pained look on Michael's face. "It's okay— really it is," she said soothingly. "The stuff was on sale. Plus, I like helping out our Native American friends. You know, most of the proceeds go to the tribes or to the reservation. So I consider it a double whammy of good intention."

"I'm impressed. Not only are you beautiful and smart, but you're conscientious, too," Duke said then.

Michael watched and wondered if his partner knew what he was doing. Then he realized that he didn't really care at the moment. All he wanted to do was be alone with his wife, so he thanked Gloria and began clearing up the dishes.

"You don't have to do that," Lauren said quickly. "Why don't you and Duke go into the living room, put on something you'd both like to hear, and Gloria and I will straighten up in here? Can I get you some more coffee or anything?"

She was being polite, but he could see the anger simmering beneath the surface. "No, babe, I'm okay," he said softly, looking into her eyes, searching for a meaning to her actions. "Are you sure? I want to help."

Shaking her head, she attempted to push him out of the dining area. She then headed into the kitchen.

Gloria had already begun to load the dishwasher. She looked up when Lauren entered, waiting for her best friend to explain what was going on between her and her husband. When Lauren didn't mention anything, she decided not to bring up the subject. She didn't want to pry.

They made small talk while cleaning up the kitchen, catching up on all the events that had occurred in the past two months, including a promotion for Gloria to head flight attendant with Worldwide. Lauren congratulated her and wondered if any additional company changes were in effect.

In the living room, Michael and Duke's conversation immediately turned to business. Duke revealed that his findings were more or less done, with the main structure of the operation being sound for the most part. Michael disclosed that he was nowhere near being finished and admitted that there was no end in sight. He'd sent in the final reports to

Morgan, waited a day or so, and then received the less-than-welcome news that it would all have to be replicated.

Duke nodded, realizing that this was probably the reason Lauren had seemed so upset earlier.

"What the hell is happening here, man?" Duke said, stroking his beard. "Something is not right. I felt it when I put together my portion of the operations analysis, but there was nothing concrete to dig into. Now, what you're telling me makes more sense. I didn't bring it up with Morgan until I talked to you, because I just sensed some stuff, you know. I even asked him if he wanted me to join you on the West Coast."

"That's not necessary, but I do appreciate your concern. I can handle my business; it's just that the more I dig, the deeper this stuff gets. I'm almost ready to throw in the towel. Morgan is relentless. If I didn't know better, I'd almost say that he knows exactly what it is that he has me digging for. Now, that doesn't make any sense, but you and I both know stranger things have happened."

Duke and Michael were quiet then, each contemplating all that had been said and all that was being considered.

Lauren and Gloria came into the room then and joined them.

"Listen, I think it's time for Gloria and me to get out of here. Can I drop you off?" Duke offered, knowing Gloria had come directly from the airport and realizing Michael and Lauren needed some time alone.

"Sure. I didn't leave my car at the airport this time. I had to take a cab over here," Gloria replied. Turning to Michael and Lauren, she said, "I am so glad you're finally home, Michael. Lauren, thank you for a lovely dinner. The evening was great fun." Gloria hugged them both.

Duke walked over, shook Michael's hand, and then both men embraced one another warmly. "Keep me posted, no matter what. About WJZZ and anything else you need to talk about," he added before walking with Gloria toward the door. "Lauren, dinner was top notch. Thank you so much for thinking you wanted to thank me for whatever. It wasn't necessary but I'm definitely glad you thought so," he added, waving.

"You're more than welcome, both of you. And Gloria, if you need me to do anything for the dinner in a couple of weeks, call me. I'm serious. As it stands now, I'm on board for dessert." Lauren rambled nervously, trying to delay the conversation that would take place as soon as their guests left.

Michael stood next to Lauren, waved goodbye to Duke and Gloria, and closed the door. Alone for the first time in four weeks, he and Lauren were both consumed with tension.

Lauren turned from him and headed toward the kitchen.

"Lauren," Michael called after her as she hurried away.

She ignored him, knowing she was treading on dangerous ground. Lauren wasn't ready to talk to him yet. She was too confused, too angry with him. He'd come home without having resolved the company's issues, which meant that he missed her, that in some way, he was still committed to their relationship, right? *But what about the woman who answered his phone?* Lauren so wanted to ask the question. But once again, she could not bring herself to do so. She knew he'd cheated without having to ask. To hear Michael tell her he was involved with another woman would devastate her.

Lauren finished cleaning the kitchen, turned out the lights, and decided to take a shower. Perhaps it would clear her head of the many thoughts that remained tangled there.

Michael was busy unpacking, checking mail, and sorting through various papers in his office. But his mind wasn't on any of that. Lauren was acting strangely, being more distant than usual, and he had no idea why. He'd never expected their marriage to be a walk in the park, but clearly, he'd underestimated the challenges. Lauren was more than unrealistic when it came to him. She never gave room for error and certainly hadn't cut him any slack. He wondered how long it would take for her to realize just how much he loved her.

He sat back in the leather chair his dad had given him when he'd graduated from college and looked at the degrees and various plaques that lined the walls. An entire history of his accomplishments surrounded him, but it didn't seem as important as what he faced at this moment. None of it mattered if his marriage to Lauren failed.

His life had changed, had become somehow intertwined with a love he could not deny. Folding his hands behind his head, he thought of the first time he'd seen Lauren on the plane, the first night he'd made love to her on his boat, the dinner on Fire Island, the passion, the turmoil, her reluctance, the pregnancy, and finally the wedding. It all flashed before him in seconds, but he realized all that signified was the beginning of a lifetime of love.

Michael knew that without reservation getting Lauren to accept his love was his goal. He turned off the lights in the office and walked toward the bedroom. He could hear the shower running. Silently, he removed his clothes and stepped into the steam-filled bathroom. Lauren did not hear Michael in the room until he entered the shower stall. She gasped in surprise, hating herself for still wanting a man that had betrayed her love, *their* love.

Lauren's soap-slicked body leaned into Michael's, her ability to stand on her own suddenly compromised. He took her weight gladly, folding her into his arms, her wet skin only heightening his passion. Michael held her against him, savoring the feel, the heat, the nearness of the woman he'd come to love and cherish. When their lips met, the desire which threatened to overtake them erupted in tiny fire-tipped flames. Each touch, each caress elevated them to another level of sensitivity.

Wrapping them both in a single bath towel, Michael steered

them from the bathroom to the king-sized bed, tumbling Lauren onto her back, his kisses scorching her everywhere they touched. He pulled the towel from beneath them, dropping it on the floor. The bedside light provided just enough illumination to cast an orange glow in the room, and Lauren's body shimmered. Michael murmured, "beautiful" as he trailed soft, tiny kisses down the length of her body, stopping to tease her breasts, then her navel, then the skin just below her rib cage.

Lauren was breathless as he kissed her passion-swelled lips, sealing them with his own. She wound her arms around his neck and allowed herself to be swept away by the current that threatened to overtake them.

"I love you, I love this, and this," Michael said, kissing and tantalizing her into a new awakening. Lauren responded in spite of her reservations, despite the doubts she held onto in the back of her mind. She had no control of her mind or her body and responded fully to Michael's ministrations.

Michael moved himself inside of her as the light of early morning filled the room with the promise of another day. After they exhausted themselves, still entangled in one another's arms, they fell asleep.

Chapter Twenty-Two

The rain awakened Lauren. That and the warmth of Michael's body. She turned over, felt the length of his leg over hers, heard his breathing, and panic seized her. She still hadn't asked about the woman on the phone. Michael's presence changed things for her, making her decision and the eventuality she'd already put into motion seem premature. Since his return, she'd given a lot of thought to her actions and the only thing she knew for sure was that Michael's presence confused her even more.

Michael awoke, hiding his disappointment with the rain and their not being able to enjoy the outdoors by suggesting they take in a movie.

That afternoon, they wound up at a theater on East Eighty-sixth Street and then had dinner at a local Indian restaurant. Afterward, they walked hand in hand toward the townhouse, window shopping, and occasionally stopping to point out different items of interest.

"Did I tell you how much I liked what you did to the townhouse, especially the bedroom. The color and the changes you made are perfect. I slept better in that bed than I have in a long time."

"I'm glad," Lauren said, clearly distracted by her thoughts.

"Yeah, I almost forgot." He put his arm around her, pulling her close as they continued walking. "I also forgot to tell you how very much I missed you. I was really supposed to try to tie up some loose ends this weekend but I couldn't stand the thought of all the fun you guys would probably have without me. When I knew for sure you had invited Duke to dinner, I knew I had to get here. Not for him, really, but because I knew if you were throwing a dinner party and inviting him, you must have been lonely. It bothered me that I wasn't here for you," he ended, his tone suddenly serious.

Lauren was thrown off by his sincerity and felt guilty for the actions she had put into motion. "Michael, I would have been fine. I don't want you to think that you have to cater to my every need, or come to my rescue each and every time something goes wrong. I knew you were working and trying to get as much of the project completed as you could. By the way, how're things going on that end? Duke sounds very much like he's almost completed his analysis. I overheard him telling Gloria that he thinks everything will be fine. Is that your opinion as well?"

Michael hesitated. The last thing he wanted to do was to discuss CBN or any of the information he'd gathered. Although unfinished, the findings he'd come upon thus far were more damaging than conclusive. He knew that if he passed that knowledge along to Lauren, it would only complicate things. She wanted a time frame to attach to his return, and though he honestly wanted to provide her with that information, or a reasonable estimate, there was no legitimate schedule that he could give. There was still a tremendous amount of information he had to analyze again. Although he would rather die than admit it, things had only gotten more complicated with each additional chunk of information coming forth. He'd taken an assignment from hell. And now he had the additional burden of explaining the nightmare of the century to his bride.

"Lauren, this is not something I wanted to get into this evening—but you asked, and I certainly owe you an explanation." He paused while they crossed the intersection. They were both immersed in a conversation that could either explain or perhaps emancipate them from a commitment that far outweighed anything either could have anticipated.

"It's not what it looks like on the surface. When Morgan initially asked me to cover this, I thought it would be routine. You know, check the reports, pull the accompanying records, and cross-reference everything. But after being there for the first two weeks, I realized something really unusual had taken place. Instead of revenues disappearing from the books, there were incremental increases coming in. None of them match any of the contracts we have in place for either advertising dollars or other accounts receivable. I mean, it's weird, although it should be something we'd applaud. But if you cannot identify the source of something like this, it can be just as dangerous as being unable to stem an unidentified outflow of funds."

He finished, his brow furrowed with concern. "Remember when you were concerned about the merger because Gino Sorrentino's reputation was less than stellar?"

"Yes," she said, remembering all that had transpired with his death and the ensuing arrests of several of his associates.

"Well, I am beginning to wonder if Morgan is somehow connected to something that has spiraled out of his control. I mean, he seems to be trying to get to the bottom of it, but there are a couple of things that don't add up." The discussion he was having with Lauren was a highly sensitive one, but he knew she would give up her life before she would tell anyone what he'd just disclosed.

Lauren could tell by his tone of voice that Michael was genuinely concerned. It made no sense, and yet, in the pit of her stomach, the memory of her early days in New York City came back to her, making her intensely uncomfortable.

Meeting Gloria had been a dream come true. They'd both graduated from flight-attendant training with the eagerness and enthusiasm of two fledglings ready to take on the world. They shared a similar goal, in terms of trying to declare their independence from their families and their separate identities. But Lauren immediately noticed that no matter how Gloria tried to distance herself from her father and her stepbrother, they routinely checked on her. Lauren remembered those visits were always met with mixed feelings by Gloria. She welcomed them with genuine fondness and a strange degree of something else: controlled terror, maybe?

It hadn't taken long for Lauren to realize that her roommate's family was somehow connected to a world she'd only seen portrayed in movies and on television—a world she could never fully visualize even with the advent of films like *Goodfellas* and television shows like *The Sopranos*. Nothing in her reality allowed for the sheer brutality, the privilege, or the callousness that seemed to accompany its existence, so she did her best to ignore much of what she suspected.

Gloria, on the other hand, took it in stride, having grown up with the presence of mobsters in her life, much like an undeclared enemy. She was only fifteen when her mother passed away, leaving behind a legacy of grace, charm, and unrecognized talent. Ilena Sorrentino's existence could be summed up in two words: devotion and sacrifice. Her husband and her marriage provided the perfect breeding ground for an existence devoid of hope. For the most part, she was ignored. The fact that she'd never produced a son only solidified her sub-par status. Gloria suspected, correctly, that her mother's death had been partly due to chronic health problems, but mainly due to a broken heart. And, in light of that fact, she'd never forgiven Gino for his contribution to it.

Now, as Lauren thought back to the days of sharing an apartment with Gloria, she remembered little things which definitely tied in to Michael's words. There had always been an element of indescribable tension present whenever even the name "Gino Sorrentino" had been mentioned. And although Gloria and Morgan had been shocked and sorrowed by his death, Lauren also knew that each had come to accept his death as an inevitability; one which probably unleashed them both from an unhealthy legacy.

CBN had been headed by Morgan Pryor since that time, sealing the merger with Michael and Duke's station the moment that the acquisition had been given the green light by CBN's board of directors and the FCC. Most of the supporting documentation for the merger had been in place prior to Gino's death; only a small number of minor details had been outstanding on the fateful day he died.

As they continued walking along Lexington Avenue, Michael explained the ins and outs of what CBN was currently up against, leaving very little for Lauren to be concerned about. He wanted to reassure her, to let her know how much it meant to him for her to understand his commitment to the project, and, most importantly, wanted her to sanction his being there.

"Michael, I understand what it is that you're telling me. I know how much CBN means to you. This is your baby, what you've dreamed of all your life, I suppose. I know how that feels, although I'm not part of it. Listen, don't worry about me, I'll be fine. Just bring it to a conclusion that the board of directors can live with. Morgan will be proud of you—I'm sure of that, anyway." She ended just as they turned into their street, the houses all lined up majestically.

Michael heard her words, watched her body language, and was filled with a nagging concern. He'd expected more emotion, less support, and had actually anticipated tears and pouting. He chastised himself for being ungrateful. Hell, the average guy would be giddy with relief that his wife was not giving him grief for confirming that he'd be away at least another couple of weeks, on the heels of weeks of absenteeism. Maybe Lauren was really too good to be true, and actually was able to harbor more patience than he'd given her credit for. Either that, or he was losing his touch. He smiled at the thought, then Lauren smiled up at him.

"What's that for? I know you're thinking that I'm probably hiding my true feelings, but Michael, I learned a long time ago, men do what they feel they have to," she lied, trying to appear strong. "Wives are probably always going to be confronted with this kind of stuff. It's part of the territory."

"Wow, honey, you sound like a trooper, and you've only been a wife for a few weeks. Either you were born this way or you've adapted in a very short time," he said.

They entered the foyer and took off their coats. Lauren headed for the kitchen, her head pounding, her heart sinking, her mind spinning. She'd never intended to mislead him, but she realized by the statements she'd made that he would, at some point, interpret it that way. In a little more than twenty-four hours, Michael would board a plane, return to the West Coast, and her life would change as a result. The legal documents in the matter of Townsend vs. Townsend were already underway.

"How about a glass of wine? I'm going to have one," Michael called to her heading toward the wet bar.

Lauren was headed toward the stairs. "Sure. In fact, let's open a bottle of champagne. We're entitled—it's not often I get to spend a Saturday evening in my husband's presence." She wanted to add that it would be the last time, so it was more than appropriate to hold a celebration of sorts, but fear quieted her. She was not at all ready for his reaction, and knew she was being a coward. They would be more than three thousand miles away from one another when he learned of her misgivings. It was ironic really. The distance that had been their undoing, would now offer her some degree of protection.

"Technically, we're still on the honeymoon in my book. Champagne it is," he said, popping the cork on a bottle of Cristal he'd owned since before they even began dating. "I've got the glasses. I'll bring the ice bucket upstairs too."

He was determined to make the most of a night he'd wanted to remember for a long time to come. And he wanted Lauren to savor the moment, knowing it might have to last for some time. He wasn't sure just how long the finalization of the project would take. He never would have believed it would take a month to wrap up, and here it was going on six weeks with no end in sight.

He carried the champagne, the ice and two glasses up the stairs, wondering just how much time it would take for him to get back to the woman he loved.

Lauren washed her face, changed into a lavender negligee, and was rubbing lotion into her hands when he entered the room. The sight of her always affected him in the same way, and he marveled at his inability to become accustomed to her beauty, her presence, and his love for her.

He set the champagne on the dresser and walked up behind her, wrapping his arms around her body, nuzzling her neck. She closed her eyes and savored the warmth of his body, the length and feel of it only added to her pain, although she could already feel desire rising. She turned to face him, reaching up to twine her arms about his shoulders. She lifted her lips to his, and they shared a kiss that was both searing and tender. The champagne was forgotten as passion overtook them, ruling out any need for thought or words.

He lowered her gently to the bed, his lips never leaving

hers. Their kiss deepened and Lauren moved from beneath him, a sudden need for control overtaking her. She climbed over him, her nightgown rising above her thighs, and straddled him boldly. Michael looked up into her face and saw raw passion mixed with something that puzzled him. He was in no position to ask questions, so he simply followed her lead.

Lauren unbuckled his jeans, helped him take off his knit polo shirt, and placed tiny smoldering kisses along his jaw, his chest, and his navel. Michael's deep intake of breath signaled his full attention, and when Lauren continued to place hot kisses below his abdomen, Michael cried out as he fought to keep control. He luxuriated in the feelings her love inspired, yet stopped her, and pulled her beneath him. He held her in his arms for a long moment, each breathing rapidly, each shaking with pure physical need.

Moments later, he entered her slowly, overcome with desire as he merged with her heat. She was on fire, and he marveled at the response he always found with her in his arms.

Michael and Lauren's lovemaking was tender yet frantic, each savoring the moments they shared for entirely different reasons. He was determined to communicate the depth of his feelings, the strength of his commitment, as well as his desire to provide a lasting impression. Lauren was filled with the need to connect one last time with the man she loved. In her mind, theirs was a marriage that never should have taken place. She hadn't anticipated her body's betrayal on this night, hadn't expected the depth of feelings which would surge, overtaking her completely. She had not prepared for any of this and was caught off guard mentally and physically. The one thing which stayed locked in her mind were the papers she'd already initiated.

Michael held her to him as they each recovered from the heights of fulfilled passion. As their bodies cooled and became accustomed to the nighttime temperatures, he pulled the coverlet over them both, wrapping his arms around Lauren again. They fell asleep with different sets of expectations, different mind-sets, and totally diverse plans for the future.

Chapter Twenty-Three

In the week after Michael's departure, Lauren experienced mixed emotions but not enough to make her cancel the plans for the annulment. Although she spoke with Michael often and was encouraged by their conversations, his absence, his return to another woman, was confirmation in her mind that she'd done the right thing.

On the second Monday of May, she walked through the doors of Dennison, York, Noble, and Pratt for the finalization of the annulment. Lauren's hands shook as she signed the document. Her mouth was dry, her eyes misted. The law clerk notarized the signature with his stamp, made a quick copy for the county records office, and it was over. She walked out of the law offices in less than forty minutes a single woman again.

The annulment was final. It left no telltale sign, no lasting marks, and no lingering scent. What it did leave in its wake was a sense of pure emotional devastation that weighed heavily on Lauren's mind. The last weekend she spent with Michael seemed surreal. In her mind, the papers she had signed were dissolution of all they had attempted to overcome. She realized, as she approached the street they lived on, that she no longer belonged there. Tears filled her eyes and made her unable to take the short walk from garage to the foyer. Instead, she sat in the car for more than ten minutes, unable to face further proof that she'd even existed in Michael's world.

Finally, she pulled herself together and entered the townhouse. There were no messages on the answering machine. Lauren pulled out the suitcase she had transported most of her clothing in when she and Michael had moved her things into his home and began packing. She did not include any of the household items she'd so carefully arranged and integrated into the townhouse, knowing they would only serve as a constant reminder of the time she'd spent there. Instead, she gathered only her clothing, books, and the few CDs she'd put in with his massive library.

She tried her best to clear her head of the thoughts that kept clouding her thinking—thoughts of Michael's fury, the disappointment, which she knew would be present when he discovered her absence. Lauren thought about writing a letter, but was afraid she would be unable to put into words all of the complex emotions and opinions she held steadfastly to. In her mind, their future had been doomed from the start, the separation initiated by CBN's most recent problems and finalized by the woman who'd answered his phone.

Suddenly, Lauren realized that although she was almost halfway packed, she really had nowhere to go. She'd neglected to think about that when she realized she no longer belonged where she currently lived. Confused and devastated, Lauren sat on the bed and attempted to collect her thoughts.

She picked up the phone and dialed. An answering machine came on with Gloria's familiar voice giving callers the requisite instruction on leaving messages, and an additional contact number. Lauren dialed her best friend's cell phone, which was picked up almost immediately.

"Hey, how's it going?" Gloria asked, into the phone as she recognized the Townsend name on her caller identification.

"Um, okay. Listen Gloria, I have to ask you a huge favor," Lauren added, stuffing more clothing into the almost half-filled suitcase.

Gloria was immediately filled with dread. She hadn't talked to Lauren since the dinner party and feared the worst. "Lauren, honey, what's the matter? What the heck is going on? Are you all right?"

"Nothing's going on. Nothing and everything. Listen, I can't get into all of this right now, I have to much to do in too short a time. Would it be all right if I used my old room for awhile? I know you finally bought, so if you need me to pitch in on the mortgage, just say the word. Don't ask a lot of questions, please. Just trust me on this. Okay?" Her voice trailed off, and Gloria realized that her best friend had obviously been crying.

That knowledge raised her concern and cautioned her so that she censored anything she normally would have said. "Listen, honey, just know that whenever, wherever, and for however long you want it, your old bedroom is yours for the asking. And it's still intact, although I did change some of the furniture around. You don't have to explain anything, but if you need me, I'm here to talk to. Hey, there's a spare key at the doorman's station."

"Gloria, I want to thank you. You have no idea how off track I am. Right now, I am an emotional wreck," Lauren admitted to Gloria and herself for the first time.

"Lauren, I know it's none of my business, but when we had dinner you guys seemed tense. Is everything okay?" Her question when unanswered for several moments while Lauren tried to come up with a response she could live with. She couldn't go back to the beginning, couldn't illustrate all the feelings and emotions she'd bottled up for so long that she felt as if she were choking on her own fluids. She remained silent.

Finally, Gloria said softly, "It's okay. You're upset and you probably have a darn good reason to be. Listen, just remember that each and every time you go through something traumatic, it makes you that much stronger. I don't know all the ins and outs of the situation, but believe me, you will come to terms with it. I have total faith in you. And in Michael too. You guys are great together, and I mean that."

Lauren wanted to retort, but her voice had left her, along with her breath and her strength. She could not bring herself to disclose the real status of the marriage, and she dreaded having to face Michael once he'd received his copy of the documents.

"Look, I hope it won't be for very long," she said softly, wondering what her next step would be.

"Listen, you stay as long as you like. If you and Michael have issues to iron out, that's normal. After all, you guys are newlyweds, for crying out loud. It's to be expected. I should have known something was wrong when you returned to Worldwide," she said, thinking back.

"Gloria please don't make me feel as if I have to explain what work can mean when everything else in your life has turned upside down," Lauren said in a low voice, unable to speak above a whisper.

"Lauren, calm down. No one said anything about your explaining yourself. Just know that I am here for you. I'll always be here for you, no matter what. Look, I have to run. Take care of yourself and I'll see you in about three days. My trip overnights in Chicago. Page me if you need anything—anything at all," she said, concern in her voice.

"I will, and thanks. I can't tell you what I would have done without you."

"Don't think about that. Just do what you have to."

* * *

After she used the nervous energy that had carried her through the worst day of her life, Lauren could do no more. She looked around at her surroundings, recognized that she'd come three hundred sixty degrees with nothing to show for it—and succumbed to the meltdown that had threatened her all day.

She remained that way, sobbing into the uncovered mattress until she heard the ring of the telephone. The sound startled her, and she recognized it was her cell phone. The last thing she wanted to do was to talk to anyone, so she shut it off.

She looked up and realized it had grown dark outside. Going into the kitchen, she felt drained from the day's ordeal. She was glad that nightfall signaled an end to this day, which had been so uncomfortable for her. Reaching for a glass, she was startled as the wall phone rang abruptly. She looked at it with dread. Lauren listened as the recording picked up the caller's message, and was surprised when the voice she heard was her mother's.

"Lauren, I am so sorry to have to leave his message, but I've been trying to reach you all day with no success. Honey, it's very important that you call me right away." Eva's voice was muffled, as she tried to stifle the tears which kept coming to her eyes.

Lauren heard the distinct tone of desperation in her mother's voice and knew something was wrong. She picked up the phone immediately, dreading what was to come. Added to her already disheveled emotional state was a healthy dose of shame that she had almost made it difficult for her own mother to reach out to her.

"Mom, it's me. What's the matter?" Lauren asked, picking up the phone.

"Lauren, oh my God, I didn't know what to think. I tried calling you all day and got no answer. What on earth is going on?" she asked frantically.

"Mom, I'm fine. Don't worry about me. What's got you so upset?"

There was a distinct pause, then Eva sobbed once. "Lauren, it's your father. I didn't want to upset you, but he hasn't been feeling well. He phoned me this morning to tell me that after several test results came back, he's been diagnosed with cancer." Her voice trailed off and Lauren could hear another muffled sob. Eva had been unable to sugarcoat the news.

Lauren was unable to speak for the next few seconds. She had no words to say, and her stomach churned as her body responded to a new barrage of stress. Finally, she gathered her strength and spoke. "Mom, I am so sorry. Please don't cry. And don't worry, either. We'll both get him through this, I promise," she offered, her voice cracking with emotion as a new set of tears filled her eyes.

"Lauren, I don't know what I should do. He's inconsolable right now." Eva's voice quivered, and Lauren knew that she was facing anyone's worst nightmare. Its impact was a powerful blow to both women.

Lauren's whole world seemed to be in serious jeopardy. She felt as if she were spinning out of control. *Not my father, please God, not the Colonel.* She knew her mother had already gone through what she was now facing. She also knew that Eva needed her to be strong, so Lauren did her best to hide her sorrow over her dissolved marriage.

Her adrenaline kicked in and she knew this was not the time to give up. There were always alternative treatments, always second opinions. "Mom, please don't panic. There may be other opinions that differ. Where's Dad right now?" she asked.

"He called me from Colorado this morning." Her voice trailed off.

"Okay, Mom, listen, pull yourself together, because we're all going to have to be strong. Where are you right now?" She asked questions almost from an automatic mode, never wavering, forgetting for the moment that her own life was in shambles.

"I'm here in Maryland. Lauren, I don't know what to do."

"Don't worry, Mom. I'll be there tomorrow morning. We'll try to decide together. Then we can talk to Dad, and the three of us can figure out how best to handle this. I am so sorry, so sorry," she repeated.

"Lauren, honey, are you sure you are up to the drive? Where were you all day? I called your house, your cell phone—I even called Gloria's place because you two are so close. I almost called Michael in California, but I didn't have his number."

"Mom, forgive me. I was handling some things, personal stuff." As she spoke, she thought of the irony of her mother's words. Twenty-four hours later and Gloria's place would be her home.

"Listen, Mom, I have to do a few things before I can hit the road tomorrow morning. Bear with me, don't make yourself crazy, and I'll be there soon. If you speak with Dad before that, please give him my love. And tell him that we'll both speak with him tomorrow."

"Fine, honey. Drive carefully. I'm going to call your father as soon as I hang up. He doesn't sound so bright-eyed and bushy-tailed right now. I know the military doctors are taking good care of him, but I agree with you: We should secure second and even third opinions."

"Absolutely. No one seeks only one medical opinion anymore."

"You're right. Lauren, thanks for understanding how dreadful this feels. And thanks for coming down. If Michael wants to join you, please let him know that he's welcome. I have a good-sized guest room for you two. When do you think he's due back from California?" she asked, unaware of the current state of her daughter's marriage.

"Mom, we can talk about all of that when I get there.

Right now, the most important thing is for me to figure out how I can research the hospitals, doctors, and medical facilities available to Dad. We can all put our heads together tomorrow when I get there."

"Honey, I trust you. I know you love your father, wouldn't ever think of hurting him, and wouldn't allow anyone else to do that either."

"I love you, Mom."

"I love you too, honey, she said before putting the receiver back onto its cradle.

Lauren felt as if all the air had been let out of her body. She had to sit down. Placing her hands over her eyes in an effort to stem the tears running down her cheeks, she sobbed. Her pain was a great and widening circle within her chest, encompassing sorrow for the times she'd spent holding silent resentments against her father, as well as for the little girl who was no more. Now that little girl had to face the reality of two things. She acknowledged that she might possibly be losing a father who had genuinely loved her. That, coupled with the pain she'd carried since her decision to end her marriage, created an agonizing situation for her.

Lauren dragged herself across the room, threw some things into an overnight case from the pile of clothing which still lay strewn across the bed, and picked up the phone.

In two hours, she had compiled the names of more than twelve specialists who were board-certified in surgery, oncology, radiation, and potential centers that specialized in the follow-up care her father would need. She called the New York chapter of the American Cancer Society to check on the services available across the country, and jotted down the information. She made several more calls before she was overcome with emotion again. Her eyes filled with tears, making it nearly impossible to continue.

Exhausted, Lauren took a shower and waited for the tears to subside. Her head pounding, she lay across the bed and prepared herself for the following day's journey to Maryland. She would drop her things off at Gloria's first and then head south, a woman alone in the world, facing another of life's significant challenges.

Chapter Twenty-Four

Morgan received Michael's call just as he was wrapping up the day's paperwork.

"Hey, just wanted you to know I'm putting the report into overnight courier. It should be on your desk in its complete form by ten o'clock tomorrow morning," Michael said.

"So are you going to give me a hint, or should I guess?"

"Let's just say that with all I've uncovered, CBN should definitely watch its back more carefully going forward. Question: Are you aware of any specific firewall that was built into the computer systems here at CBN?"

"Not really. We employed a team of technicians to do all of that. The mainframe is tied into a company that handles a multitude of corporate clients, so it was never an issue. Are you alluding to what I think you are?"

"Yeah, it has to be that. Now I know that there are some pretty skilled people out there who can do almost anything you need. In this case, someone has deposited an awful lot of money into WJZZ."

Morgan listened silently, his mind calculating and recalculating Michael's words, as he realized that his initial suspicions were being confirmed by a third party who had nothing but the company's best interests at heart. It was unbelievable to him that untraceable sums of money were somehow making their way into the company's accounts on a regular basis and no one could identify the source. He had never seen anything like it.

Almost instantaneously, a light bulb went on. *Yes, I have,* Morgan realized. Gino had once described an alternative way to keep funds out of the limelight if someone or some entity wasn't yet ready to disclose its profit margin. They simply dumped it into another company until they were ready to extract it. If the books weren't being watched carefully, no one would even notice, because the profit would be under the radar of what was actually due in anyway. When it was removed, it would be as if it had never been there.

He thought of the people who would have access to that kind of cash and would know how to do what Gino had described. An uncomfortable feeling swept through him. He remembered several weeks before when he had attended the exhibition at the museum. His clown of a cousin had shown up with his hand-me-down wife. It seemed like an unlikely coincidence then, but in his world, coincidence was suspect, especially if it involved one's enemies. Morgan's brow furrowed in distaste and he sat back in his chair.

"Michael, who else knows about your findings?"

"Just you and I. Duke knows the direction I've been looking at, but in terms of conclusive evidence, he hasn't been informed of my latest findings. Why?"

"I want to keep this under wraps for as along as possible. Obviously, someone is going to come looking for the money sooner or later. We just have to keep an eye on the corporate accounts that have been chosen as the stockpiles for these deposits."

"Not a problem. Look, just so you know, I'm on my way

back to New York again tonight. I have to take care of some personal business. If you need me, try me at the townhouse."

"Sure. Hey, thanks for doing a great job. I didn't expect you to wrap it up so quickly. Is Noelle headed back also?"

"Yeah, actually she is on a flight out in the next hour or so. Thanks for sending her out. She was quite helpful. I didn't expect to wrap things up so quickly and probably wouldn't have without her help. The pieces fell into place in the last few days. Frankly, it happened just in the nick of time." Michael did not elaborate on his statement, but Morgan sensed that with his hastily scheduled return to New York, something was definitely cooking.

"Okay. Thanks for everything, and if there's anything I can do to help, let me know. As it stands, CBN owes you a debt of gratitude. We're excited at the prospect of going forward and making this thing work. Nobody likes it when someone decides to create a slush fund in their own backyard.

"Whoever is behind this is very smart. They chose the WJZZ end as the newest acquisition knowing that those accounts wouldn't send up a red flag. It would be taken as just another spike in earnings based on the acquisition," Michael added, his theory confirming to Morgan that he'd hired the right man.

"Yeah, now we have to put a definite end to it, but we have to do it quickly and without drawing too much attention, Morgan replied.

"You're right."

"Hey Michael, can I ask you another question, off the record?"

"Sure, what's up?"

"Has Duke said anything to you about my sister?"

Michael racked his brain for a quick response. There was

no way he was getting in the middle of this. "Not to my knowledge," he said calmly. "Why do you ask."

"Just asking," Morgan said evenly. "Just asking."

Morgan pushed aside thoughts of Duke and his sister and focused on the issues he faced with CBN. He knew it had to be an inside operation to initiate this kind of tactic. It was ingenious because it was so simple, and it worked because no one ever checked an account that had more funds than was expected. If what he suspected was correct, it meant that Duane and even possibly Anthony were somehow back in business. Their former companies, Sorrenntino Waste Management and Sorrentino Construction had been shut down on more than thirty counts of fraud, racketeering, misrepresentation, and money-laundering at the same time that Gino Sorrentiono had passed away. The Feds had used a plethora of manpower normally reserved for more high-profile clients, and it was obvious by the thoroughness of their investigation that it had been a priority to them.

Now, some two years later, a clear line of connection lay between the funds showing up in CBN's affiliate accounts and the two companies that had been reportedly defunct. Evidently, someone had figured out a way to generate a huge amount of cash, which they were trying desperately to hide.

"Hide, hell," Morgan said out loud. He knew it would only be for so long. Sooner or later, they would come looking for their loot and would extract it either via computer-generated withdrawal or otherwise.

Morgan sat back in his chair thinking. Michael had done a good job. No, he had done a *great* job of identifying the problem. Having no former knowledge of Duane Capparelli or Anthony Sorrentino, he was protected from being able to finger either of them as the point men for this operation, but Morgan knew the family through and through. It smelled like their kind of game. He'd known them since college—not that they had attended, but that's when he'd entered their world as the stepson of Gino Sorrentino.

The intercom rang, and a call from Noelle was announced. He picked up, ready to thank her for the assistance she'd given.

"Hey, I understand you guys are wrapping it up out there," he said lightly. He wanted to keep things professional with Noelle and was committed to treating her like the talented employee she obviously was since she hadn't shown any real interest in him before her departure.

"Yeah, I'm at LAX right now but my flight has been delayed. I'm really ready to leave this place. Have you spoken with Michael?" she asked suddenly.

"He just called. Said everything is taken care of, and by the sound of it, you guys did a thorough job. I'll talk with you more when you get here. Keep me posted on the flights, and if you have to stay over another night, don't worry about it. Room service is on CBN," he said, a hint of laughter in his voice.

"Believe me, I'm not trying to stay over another hour, but I will keep you posted. And thanks for the compliment," she added before hanging up.

Noelle made contact with the Bureau, then tried to find an earlier flight. As she prepared to return to New York, she realized this assignment hadn't been her best work. In fact, the assignment on a whole had become one huge disappointment.

Sitting in his office high above Madison Avenue, in the heart of a city he had come to truly respect, Morgan wondered if there were any other weaknesses in the organization. He picked up the phone and called on a resource he'd only had to use once before in his life. Even Gino himself had done his level best to stay away from these guys, knowing that to be in debt to them could mean certain destruction. Morgan made the call anyway, left a message, and waited.

It only took half an hour to get a call back, confirming Morgan's worst suspicions.

Chapter Twenty-Five

Michael sat back in his chair, stared at the documents on his desk, and couldn't believe his eyes. *Annulment?* What the hell was going on? Was Lauren out of her mind? And secondly, did she have the worst case of bad timing ever?

He'd returned to the West Coast office determined to get to the bottom of the irreconcilable quarterly statements as quickly as possible, recognizing that he had a wife waiting for him on the other side of the country. He had enjoyed his long weekend stay but knew that the pressure of the long-distance relationship was putting an undue strain on the marriage. Lauren had seemed like someone sitting on a powder keg—one that was slated for detonation sometime in the very near future.

Back in L.A., he'd worked almost thirty-six hours without sleep. He'd gathered all the data onto several spreadsheets then he sent it to the analysis department in New York to see what similarities, if any, existed. When he arrived at work two days later, that analysis had been waiting for him. The results were concrete evidence that formed an indisputable case against a formidable opponent.

More than ten million dollars had been moved into the accounts of WJZZ in the past six months. There was no clear line of demarcation pointing to its origin, but one thing was certain: It had most definitely come from a source which was somehow interconnected with CBN. Michael's most recent efforts had been trying to discern that source, without much success.

He was sitting in his office, looking over the results again when the office secretary buzzed the intercom.

"Mr. Townsend, there's a gentlemen here to see you without an appointment."

"From where?"

"He says he's from Dennison, York, Noble, and Pratt in New York."

Michael immediately rose from his chair and headed to the reception area.

Seated in one of the guest chairs was a young man who couldn't have been more than twenty-three years old. He had red hair, freckles, and a bad case of adult acne. Seeing Michael, he rose, swallowed nervously and asked, "Are you Michael Townsend?"

"Yes, I am. What can I do for you?" Michael responded, wondering what this young man could possibly want.

"Actually, this is for you." His answer came in a burst of words and he held out a thick white envelope. Michael took the envelope without hesitation, but with much curiosity. He'd seen the embossed lettering in the right-hand corner and suspected correctly that the documents were from a prominent legal firm.

"Thank you, sir," the young man said, turning to walk out the door.

Michael's curiosity got the better of him and he tore into the envelope. Walking back into his office, the words leaped off the pages at him, toppling his world and crushing his heart.

"Abandonment? I was just with her this past weekend," he said out loud.

He sank heavily into his chair, not knowing what to do first. The pressing issues of an investigation that was quickly striding toward the finish line called to him. At the same time, he felt as if all of his inner organs had been liquefied, felt as if his bones were no longer solid, and that his heart had been turned into stone. He hit the desk then, hard, with his fist. "Damn it to hell, how could she do this?" he shouted, not caring who heard and wondering if all the time they'd spent during the past weekend had meant anything at all to Lauren.

Michael picked up the phone, dialed his home number, and got no answer. He allowed it to ring more than twenty times. The answering machine did not pick up, which worried him somewhat. He felt a rising panic, but told himself that everything would be okay. Lauren was probably out doing God knew what, but she was fine.

He looked at the papers strewn across his desk and wondered if someone had played a cruel joke on him. On the one side lay the documents related to CBN's discrepancy issues, on the other, notification of a court-ordered annulment in the case of *Townsend vs. Townsend*. He didn't know whether to laugh or cry.

The phone rang, and he picked it up immediately. It was his partner.

"Michael, just wanted to touch base with you on the stuff we talked about. What's doing?"

"Well, I just got the final numbers in, and my theory is definitely confirmed. Ten million was pumped into WJZZ over the course of a six months. It looks like the money came from a company-authorized account but it's not clear which one."

"So, your take on it was weird, but right, huh? Now what?"

"Well, we can either wait and see, or we could close all

accounts, freeze the funds, and move from there." He paused unsure of how to ask his next question. "Have you spoken to Gloria lately?" He hadn't wanted to bring Duke into the details of his null and void marriage, didn't want to discuss the annulment with anyone, but wondered if he was the last person to know about Lauren's latest maneuvers.

"That's a very personal question, man, even coming from you. Don't take this the wrong way, but I'm trying to handle my business without interference, if you know what I mean."

"Duke, listen, we've been joined at the hip since university days, man. You know that I don't give a damn who you date, sleep with, or squire around town."

"I'm sorry. I know you are not out to get into my thing, man. It's just that since I started seeing her, my head is not on straight. She's terrific, but it carries a lot of tension, you know?" Duke almost seemed relieved to have someone to discuss this with, and Michael realized that aside from business, they still had a lot in common.

"I was just wondering. You know Lauren keeps in touch with her and all. Look, I'm going to get off the phone because I need to concentrate on all this stuff on my desk. I don't know how I am going to handle this, but I will." He'd changed the subject swiftly, knowing that Duke would be able to uncover the truth of his inquiry if he continued. They'd always had an uncanny connection, one which defied the privacy of their own issues. After all, they were best friends, partners. At the moment, they were both knee-deep in solving a major company mystery. It also seemed to him that they were both emotionally involved with women who were very unpredictable.

"No doubt, buddy. You do your thing. If I hear anything further that I think might be of use to you, you know I have the digits. In the meantime, take it easy."

"You do the same," Michael replied, turning once again to the papers spread out across his desk. He picked up the annulment papers, read and reread them, and then picked up the phone, dialing the law firm's Manhattan offices.

The phone range several times, and was picked up by someone with an efficient, yet impersonal tone. Michael hung up immediately. There were no answers to the questions he had. Not at that number, anyway. He needed to speak to Lauren if he were to even begin to scrape the surface. Only she would be able to tell him what he needed to know.

Picking up the phone, he made reservations to New York for the next evening's Worldwide Airlines red-eye into John F. Kennedy Airport.

Chapter Twenty-Six

Lauren arrived at her mother's townhouse armed with a resolve to see her parents through a crisis.

They placed a joint call to her father, but he had left the base half an hour before. After leaving a message, they comforted one another with the fact that he'd spoken with Eva the night before, had sounded calm and in good spirits, and was committed to getting through the prescribed series of treatments.

Lauren did not share her personal dilemma with Eva. She couldn't rationalize adding additional drama to what was an already tense situation. On the surface she appeared calm, even unusually low keyed. Her mother attributed her odd behavior to the strain they were both operating under. Colin's illness had come as a shock to them. Only Lauren knew that the timing could not have been worse.

Lauren's nerves were like a tightly coiled spring, waiting for the torque to reach its highest level. She knew the paperwork had been delivered to Michael by this time, knew he would reach out to her, knew that no matter what, there would have to be a final accounting of her actions.

Until that moment came, it was as if she were waiting to be called to the guillotine. She methodically made phone calls, researching her father's illness, and made sure Eva was remaining calm throughout.

The telephone rang once, then stopped and both women exchanged puzzled looks. Then it rang again, and Eva walked quickly across the room to pick it up. Lauren prayed it would be her father. She knew she was not ready, perhaps would never be ready, to speak with Michael. As luck would have it, it was Colin.

"Colin, Lauren is here. Yes, I spoke with her last evening, and she insisted on coming down so we can all figure out what we should do going forward. Yes, she knows everything. Here, talk to your daughter," Eva added, holding the receiver out to Lauren.

"Dad are you okay?" With that question, she almost broke into tears again. Out of deference for her father's pride, she held back, knowing that he would want her to be strong for him.

"Lauren, I'm fine, or at least I will be." His voice was softer than usual, more reserved. But she could also hear the resolve in it, and knew that he would fight this disease as he would anything that threatened his existence or his way of life.

"Dad, I've done some research and I want to talk with you about getting a second opinion. There's no reason to accept a final diagnosis or course of treatment just because one set of physicians has said certain things. Mom wants to talk to you too. . . ."

She couldn't go any further because her throat had tightened up. She knew she was an emotional wreck, on the brink of breaking down, and wanted to avoid that at all costs. She gave the phone to her mother, indicated the list of information she'd compiled, and left the room.

Eva watched her daughter and knew that she was trying

to remain in control of her emotions. Lauren put up a brave front, but Eva was sure that having to deal with her father's illness would present a challenge to her, as it would to all of them. Eva read off the fifteen or so specialists that Lauren had gathered and then offered her ex-husband the support and consolation any woman who still cared about someone would. The realization that she still loved him came to her without fanfare. No bells, whistles, or special banners accompanied this knowledge, yet she knew it to be true.

"Eva, I can't tell you how much I appreciate both you and Lauren doing this for me. I don't know what I would do without you two in my corner. It's a wonderful thing to have a family . . ." his voice trailed off.

"You never lost us; we were always here," Eva added her voice heavy with emotion.

"I know that now. I didn't always, you know?"

"Well, what's important is that you know it now. Now and always is what counts," Eva replied firmly, hoping that it would give him the courage to get through all that was to come.

"Thank you. I guess I haven't always made the right decisions when it comes to you and Lauren. Even when were in Barbados, I guess I kind of made a mess of things," he admitted.

"No, not really." Eva turned, to be sure that Lauren could not hear the conversation and continued. "You know, I would have come to your room if you had asked me. The thing that made it unacceptable was that you felt you needed permission. That made me feel as if it wasn't right. After I left you that night, I tossed and turned the entire night. It was an awful way to celebrate our daughter's marriage."

He chuckled into the phone. "Now you tell me. You know, the anxiety of knowing you were only a stone's throw away bothered me to the point of distraction. I didn't have a peaceful sleep for the next two months. At first, when I started to feel so tired, I actually attributed it to that. But then it was time for my annual physical and they called me back for additional tests after some of my blood work came back. Thank God I had it done when I did."

"Yes, thank God. From what I understand, prostate cancer is one of the more slow growing cancers and as long as we caught it early, we're in luck. Please don't worry, Colin. From everything I've read, the odds are definitely in your favor."

She finished giving him the remaining information Lauren had gathered, as well as some additional doctors she had researched. They made a pact to talk again later that evening.

"Eva, I don't want to belabor the point but I just wanted to let you know that I was serious when I said those things in Barbados. You knew it too, which is probably why you ran away from me."

"Colin, it was never a question of how serious you were. It was more that I wasn't altogether ready to give up everything I had gone through to return to our former way of life."

"Eva, I know now is probably not the right time to talk about it, but I want this on the record. At our daughter's wedding, I realized how wrong I had been about letting you get away from me. I hadn't been happy for months before that. When you stood there looking so beautiful, so calm, so peaceful, I realized what I had done by leaving you both. I had walked away from my life. And for what?"

After a long moment, Eva sighed, then gave a small laugh. "You know, I had no idea you were going to make a pass at me. That threw me off something terrible. It actually scared me in a way, because it made me wonder what would happen if I took you up on your offer. I wasn't prepared to handle that, so I turned you down."

Her explanation delivered, they each had much to think about, knowing that the past had just been put to rest. They would move forward and deal with whatever was thrown their way as a family.

Eva placed the receiver in the cradle and began making a fresh pot of tea for herself and Lauren. The phone rang again, and she picked it up thinking that Colin had probably forgotten something he needed to discuss.

"Hello, Mrs. Traynor. This is Michael."

"Hello, Michael, how are you, dear? And more importantly, how is California?" she asked, sounding tired.

"It's unusually cloudy here today. The sun is nowhere in sight, which, believe it or not, is sometimes a good thing." He wanted to add that the weather reflected his mood, but did not want to alarm his mother-in-law. Knowing Lauren, she had probably kept her in the dark about the annulment. It would come as a shock to Eva if he were to divulge any of the details of what he'd only recently discovered. He cleared his throat and forged ahead. He only had a few hours before he had to board a plane, and knew it would save time to connect the dots now.

"Actually, Eva, I was wondering if you knew where I might find Lauren. I called the house a while ago and there wasn't any answer. I figured she probably decided to take a drive down to visit you." He neglected to say that he'd also been calling all of the day before, the night before, and that morning without getting an answer. He didn't want to scare Eva. His only intention was to locate Lauren.

"Actually, Michael, she's here. Hold on for a moment."

He breathed a sigh of relief, sat back into the leather chair and realized how tense he'd been since receiving the papers notifying him of the dissolution of his marriage. His initial reaction, aside from shock, had been total denial. It was difficult for him to believe that Lauren wanted to end their marriage.

He'd stared at papers for hours before the full impact hit him. It was only then that he began to wonder if there were ways he could contest it. Michael had phoned a trusted colleague, asked a few questions and hung up disgusted.

He waited, knowing that to speak with Lauren wouldn't be enough. But he needed to make that connection anyway. No matter what was said now, he knew he had a fight on his hands going forward. She'd set it up that way, but he was ready for the challenge.

"Hello?"

"Hello, Lauren. Is this your idea of a joke?" Michael asked firmly.

"No, Michael." She was tired, more tired than she'd ever been in her life, but she knew he was waiting for an answer, so she gave the only one she could think of. "The reality is that we don't have a marriage. It's been a long-distance affair."

"Have you lost your mind?" he asked, raising his voice. "I was just there with you. We talked, we walked, we made love. Then I return to my work here on the West Coast and you file for an annulment? I don't understand you, Lauren. But then maybe I'm not supposed to." His annoyance was clear.

"Michael, I realize it came as a shock for you to receive those papers, but I tried to tell you how I felt, tried to warn you. Remember, we had an agreement. You said that if either of us was unhappy and wanted to end the marriage, there would be 'no strings attached.' I decided to cut the string before it became a noose around my own neck. It was better for me to walk away now before any further complications came up." Lauren's chest heaved as she revealed the emotions she'd been hiding for so long.

There was silence on the other end for a moment, then Michael's voice came through sounding more frustrated than she'd ever heard it. "Lauren, I don't think I have ever been so disappointed in someone in my entire life. I have been sitting here for the past few hours trying to make heads or tails out of what it is you think went wrong, and for the life of me, I cannot put my finger on it. When I told you that I loved you, I meant it. The need to come out here came up unexpectedly, granted, but that should not have signaled an end to the marriage. In fact, whenever this stuff is straightened out, I'll be even more solidly entrenched in my own life, because my company concerns will have been addressed. You made a huge mistake, and used even worse judgment," he shouted, ending his tirade.

Lauren sighed, her head pounding, her heart racing. She knew that Michael was angry, and rightfully so. She'd ended their marriage and left the marital home. At that particular moment, she couldn't justify all the reasons for her actions, nor did she have the strength to try. Her mother was right, she should have talked to her husband before doing something so drastic. She felt drained from the tears she'd shed, first for her failed marriage, then for her father who was probably facing the toughest battle he'd encountered in his life.

"Look, Michael, I know you feel this way now, but believe me, I probably did you a favor." She didn't mention the woman who answered the phone in L.A., didn't mention the nagging suspicions she had. "One day maybe you'll even understand what it is that I was trying to do," she said, her voice lowered to a whisper.

Michael's heart sank, hearing the defeat in her voice. He'd never understand how she had come to this place, wanting to end their marriage when she so obviously still loved him. He changed the subject, knowing if he continued to press, Lauren would clam up.

"Your mom answered the phone a while ago. She didn't sound like herself. Is everything else okay?"

"Mom is fine. She's just taking care of a couple of things right now," Lauren answered. She wanted desperately to avoid discussing anything even remotely associated with her father's illness. She feared she would still break down if the conversation continued, so she hurried to end it.

"Uh, Michael, would it be okay if I called you back another time? Now is not really so good for me." She sounded exhausted and thoroughly overwhelmed. He wanted to reach out to her, to rekindle, and reconnect. Then he looked at the papers laying across his desk and realized she had severed that right.

"Lauren, I don't know what's happening, but bear one thing in mind: I love you, and have from the very first day I laid eyes on you. I am a patient man, but I won't wait forever for you."

His words echoed in her ears. She wanted to respond, but couldn't. She hung up and stumbled to the guest room, her vision clouded. She lay across the bed, one arm thrown across her forehead, a constant flow of tears rolling from her eyes. The ceiling became a blur, her life disintegrating into small, finite pieces as she willed herself to breathe.

Lauren reminded herself that she had to be strong, had to continue to be there for her mother and especially for her father. Her marriage to Michael aside, there were more important things that had to be tackled. The days ahead were filled with uncertainty, but Lauren was determined to overcome this latest hurdle in her life.

As if on cue, Lauren realized that her return to Worldwide Airlines was the perfect diversion. She was scheduled to work the maximum hours allowable for the entire month and looked forward to being able to turn off the constant thoughts of her personal life.

Three thousand miles away, Michael gathered his briefcase and his paperwork, and headed back to the hotel. His wife's sudden and disturbing behavior was at the forefront of his mind. Michael realized with that thought that Lauren was now his ex-wife, and it angered him immensely. The fact that she hadn't even consulted him before initiating that kind of betrayal was painful; but he also realized that it had taken an awful lot of determination to move her forward. He wondered if she realized how final the documents she had sent could be, then chastised himself for underestimating her. Lauren would have checked it all out, would have had numerous conversations with the legal representatives she'd approached.

What he did not understand was why. Barring something that even he could not put his hands on, he simply did not understand her motive. He'd made it clear to her that he loved her, made it undeniably plain for all to see that he wanted to spend the remainder of his life with her. With that kind of commitment and devotion, what would possibly make her back out of their marriage without even so much as an argument?

The questions kept coming, but the answers remained elusive as Michael prepared to arrive in New York armed with determination.

The agreement he'd used to coax Lauren into marriage had no basis in reality. He'd only constructed it to entice her into feeling less pressure to marry him. Thinking back he knew it was a silly, almost childish agreement, but he'd been determined to get her down the aisle any way he could.

Anger bubbled within him, but even more disturbing was the disappointment he felt. There was no doubt in his mind that Lauren loved him. He also knew she was probably as miserable as he was, but he also recognized that she possessed a stubbornness that would carry her through this as it had during the other tough times she faced.

Michael Townsend was a man in turmoil. He'd gambled and lost, but the final hand had yet to be played.

Chapter Twenty-Seven

Flight 325 on Worldwide Airlines was the second leg of Lauren's trip. She'd reentered the world of airline transportation weeks earlier, and was doing her best to adjust to the routine. En route from Atlanta's Hartsfield-Jackson airport to Logan International in Boston, the flight held a full roster of passengers eager to arrive in a city that held much of the country's history.

She winced, thinking of the changes she'd made in her life of late, and wondered how she had made so many mistakes so quickly.

There were no more tears to shed, no more regrets to express. She'd turned her back on all the life she knew for that short period of time, and was once again eager to establish her own destiny, even if it hadn't yet been clearly defined. She missed Michael, missed their home, missed their marriage terribly, but was determined to move forward. She did her best to ignore the constant ache she felt in her chest on most days. Her appetite was diminished, and she realized that she had probably lost a few pounds.

Her father's surgery had gone well. He was now scheduled to begin undergoing radiation therapy which would, they hoped, be over in the next few months. He and her mother communicated often, exchanging the support necessary to get him through this health crisis.

Lauren felt they both seemed happier, although she avoided asking the obvious question. In her eyes, the mere fact that they had reestablished contact was a beautiful thing. Apparently, time had healed many of the wounds inflicted in their divorce and separation. There had been no real mention of reconciliation, each was simply content to be accepted by the other.

Lauren expected no such resolution of the conflicts she and Michael shared. She lived, breathed and endured the devastation she'd initiated with the break-up of their short-lived union. Thankfully, her daily routine rarely allowed her time to focus on anything other than her duties as a senior flight attendant.

Surprisingly, Michael had seemed to accept the inevitable. There'd been no late-night telephone calls, no unexpected arrivals, and none of the expected showdowns. Lauren experienced a mild degree of disappointment, having expected him to at least offer a minimum show of resistance. Then she remembered the phone call she'd placed to his room early one morning and fresh tears entered her eyes. The woman who answered, her voice crisp and professional, had not even tried to pretend.

"I'm sorry, Michael is in the bathroom right now," she'd said. Lauren's words had become trapped in her throat. Unable to speak, she hung up the phone, felt the bile rise in her mouth. She made it to the bathroom just in time.

Even now, as she thought of that fateful day, she was overcome with anger. She hadn't thought if possible, but it was obvious that Michael was capable of more than she'd ever given him credit for.

Moving back into the apartment she'd shared with Gloria

had been somewhat awkward. She'd tossed and turned for several nights, unused to the unfamiliar environment. After the first few days, she'd relaxed into a static, if not comfortable, routine, and realized she would somehow get through this transition. Going forward, Lauren vowed to rise above the temptations that marriage to Michael had taught her she was obviously receptive to.

There were times since she'd moved out that she thought of Michael, but knew it would defeat every action she'd taken if she reached out to him. The pain in the middle of her chest which she'd been carrying finally began to subside. Lauren immersed herself in the very real new life she'd created, and hoped that, in time, she would overcome her feelings of failure and disillusionment.

Walking back to the galley to begin the in-flight refreshment service, Lauren noticed the flight attendant call bell flashing at seat 14A. She approached the row, automatically reaching up to switch the call indicator to the off position.

"May I help you?" she offered with seasoned professional calm.

"Yes, you may. I'd like a copy of *The New York Times*. Are there any on board?"

The passenger looked nothing at all like Michael, but in Lauren's emotional state, the fact that he was tall, dark, and authoritative rang a familiar bell, one which produced an overload of unexpected emotions. She blinked, swallowed, and then stammered, "Why, yes, I can bring you a copy in a moment." She fled, hoping she'd avoided coming across like an idiot.

She instructed a junior attendant to deliver the newspaper, not trusting herself to handle an additional encounter.

The flight ended without further incident, but Lauren had been spooked sufficiently to stand far in the back of the aircraft as the passengers deplaned. She wanted no further contact with people who could bring her to tears with the mere sound of their voices, or a slight gesture of their hands. For the life of her, she couldn't figure out how to avoid it going forward.

The Novotel hotel in Boston's Quincy Market area was small, efficient, and sleek in its contemporary design. Lauren checked in with the other members of the flight crew, but declined their invitation to dinner. She was exhausted. All she could think of was a hot bath, room service, and an early night.

She fell asleep instantly after eating a light dinner of soup, salad, a small container of rice pudding, and iced tea.

"What on earth are you doing? Lauren asked, laughter in her voice and pure joy in her heart as Michael tied a scarf over her eyes and whispered into her ear seductively.

"I am surprising my wife," he answered as he led her slowly into the bedroom. After coming home unexpectedly, he'd turned down the bed, plumped the pillows, and prepared the room for an evening of lovemaking. Candles gathered in clusters of three adorned the room, their faint light enhancing the darkened interior of pulled blinds.

"What's that music I hear?" she asked softly, recognizing the strains of an enticing rhythm.

"You're listening to Kemistry. We seem to have a lot of that don't we?" he asked as he touched her slowly, excruciatingly, in all the places he knew would elicit the responses he loved.

"Oh, so now we're making music," Lauren answered, instinctively moving close to him. She could feel him, could smell the remnants of the cologne he used each morning, but he moved out of range.

"How much do you really want me?" he asked her boldly.

Lauren responded by touching the buttons on her blouse hesitantly. She heard the light chuckle he emitted as she moved her hands to each button, then removed the silk blouse she wore.

"Does that answer your question?" Her breasts rose with each breath she took and strained against the sheer lacy fabric of her brassiere. Michael's breathing became labored but he was determined to see the game through. Lauren felt his hesitation, and pushed the envelope. She removed her chinos, stepping out of them gingerly. The panties with a lace tulip embossed on the front panel matched the bra she wore. The fact that she was still blindfolded only enhanced the allure of what she was doing. Lauren began to walk slowly toward where she felt Michael was standing. Within three steps, she felt him before her, his arms rock hard and immovable.

"Are you ready to stop playing games?" she asked.

"Yes, but now I want the prize," he answered, sealing her lips with a scalding kiss. Their lovemaking was demanding, each attempting to extract the highest possible response from the other. Lauren's body felt as if it were on fire and Michael was determined to extinguish the flames. Much like the candles that continued to burn all around their bedroom, the temperature rose higher and higher until they were each consumed with the heat of passion.

Lauren reached behind her, pulled off the silk scarf and took the band off her ponytail. Her hair fell loose, and she shook it, allowing its fullness to frame her face. Michael reached out to her, urging her to come closer. Her body felt solidly soft, pliant in all the right places, and seemed to mold itself to his instantly. They fell onto the bed with Lauren on top. She looked down at him, his tie still tied, his shirt still buttoned, and placed her palm on his chest. His sharp intake of breath signaled his response, and Lauren smiled knowingly.

"I think you have on too many clothes to be a prize winner in my game, Mr. Townsend."

Lauren awoke to the television's gray light shining brightly in the darkened room as she stumbled to the bathroom, where she vomited most of her dinner into the white porcelain bowl. She removed a washcloth from its rack and washed her face with cold water before brushing her teeth. The thoughts which marched across her mind were not to be acknowledged. Instead, she vowed to never eat rice pudding again.

She tossed and turned the remainder of the night, visions of gray eyes, a rich voice, and curly black hair on her mind.

Chapter Twenty-Eight

Duke's phone rang six times before the answering machine came on, but Michael did not leave a message. Instead, he dialed Duke's cell phone. He knew he'd answer that. True to his character, Duke picked up on the third ring.

"Yeah, this is Duke."

"Hey, buddy, what's going on?"

"You, my man. You got it. Where the hell have you been? I've left messages at the house and on your office line. I haven't seen you since you got back from California. What's up with that?"

"Man, you don't even want to know. I've been working from home until I can get my head together. What's going on with you, dude?" he asked, hoping that Duke's response would not confirm Morgan's prying questions.

"Hey, nothing, nothing at all. I finished my part of the assignment, but everything was cool on this end. Nothing out of the ordinary at all. I turned it in to Morgan. I think the guy was disappointed, or at least he appeared to be," Duke added, surprise evident in his voice.

"Yeah, well he wasn't disappointed with the stuff I uncovered, I can tell you that. Man, there are some serious things going on at WJZZ. Mind you, this only started since the acquisition, so it had nothing to do with our end of the company. It's almost as if the station was chosen specifically because it was the newest part of the organization."

"Wow, so that's why he wasn't singing out loud when I came in with nothing. He was looking for a bug all the time, and neither of us knew it."

"Right. Okay, look, man, I have to tell you something. I don't want you to take this the wrong way, but Morgan is on to you and Gloria, so be on your guard. He suspects something."

"Thanks for the heads-up. Morgan doesn't worry me, though. His kid sister has a mind of her own. We're grown folks, so he needs to step back. The sooner he understands that, the better off he'll be. I'm not looking forward to that conversation, but I know it's only a matter of time. By the way, what gives with you and Lauren?" Duke asked.

Michael's defenses rose immediately. "What do you mean?" He wanted to avoid discussing their marriage. That it had already been dissolved was too painful an acknowledgement for him to make, that he hadn't seen Lauren since his return to Manhattan was ludicrous.

"Well, if you must know, Gloria mentioned that her former roommate had taken up residence again. I didn't want to ask too many questions, but needless to say, I was shocked. Man, what's going on?"

Michael hesitated, then took a deep breath. "I wish I knew. We're no longer married. She had it annulled while I was in California."

"What?" Duke said, genuinely shocked. "You've got to be kidding. Gloria didn't say anything about an annulment. She just said Lauren was back at the apartment. Damn, man I am so sorry."

"Yeah, so am I," Michael managed to get out, his mind

turning, his heart pounding, its efforts to keep him alive were only physiologically effective. In all other aspects, he felt dead, buried, and forgotten.

"So, what's next?"

"What do you mean what's next?" Michael answered, anger flaring immediately. He couldn't even fathom the next two hours, let alone the next week, month, or anything further. For Duke to ask what was next was almost insulting in his book. This was not to be business as usual, not for a long time.

"Take it easy, man, I know you," Duke responded, sensing his partner's anxiety. He continued, knowing that some things needed to be said, even if Michael wasn't in the best of moods. "Look, you are positively still in love with Lauren, even though she's behaving like someone you probably don't even *like* right now. So, what's your next step? You're not going to sit back, relax, and allow her to get away from you, are you?"

Duke didn't wait for an answer, launching into another speech. "Look, she obviously loves you too, man. I watched you two at the wedding, and you guys are ridiculously in love. She obviously just needs to get her head together."

"You seem to have it all figured out," Michael responded, unwilling to buy into Duke's theory at the moment.

"Not really. Women . . . And you wonder why I'm not married." Duke ended the statement with a chuckle, but there was no disdain in his voice. He sincerely felt for his partner, knowing he'd gambled and possibly rolled snake eyes.

Duke's statement stayed with Michael, although he remained silent. He'd been so hurt, so immobilized by Lauren's actions. But Duke was right, at least about one thing. He did still love her.

"So, you say she's at Gloria's," he said finally, his voice deep.

"I guess you know she's flying again. I don't know anything about her schedule, but that shouldn't be too hard to get—I speak with Gloria every few days. What do you say I drop a few pertinent questions, then get back to you with the details?"

"Man, your subtlety is about as intact as my pride is right now, but do what you can. Meanwhile, I'm going to find a way to get Lauren back."

"Now that's my partner talking. You handle your business, my man. I'll call you in a day or so, hopefully with something you can sink your teeth into."

"Thanks, man. Here I made the call to alert you and instead, you've given me the heads-up. I appreciate it, Duke."

"No doubt you do. Hey, that's what friends are for. You'd do the same thing for me now, wouldn't you?"

"Absolutely."

Michael hung up then. For the first time since learning of the dissolution of the marriage, he did not have a headache.

Later that same evening, Michael was startled when the phone rang as he was preparing a light dinner.

Duke's next words confirmed his worst suspicions. "Your bride is on a pretty tight schedule. There also seems to be a hitch."

"What's that supposed to mean?"

"Well, it seems her father is ill. That and some kind of a stomach virus seem to have caused her a few problems. I could only ask a few questions because I didn't want Gloria to become suspicious. If I were you though, I'd check on her. It didn't sound like she's been feeling too well."

Michael was suddenly alert, his intentions forming. "I don't know what to say, man. Thanks."

"You don't have to thank me, just do something, man. I know it's hard, especially when she's pulled the rug out from underneath the marriage, but maybe she felt she had reasons. And if she's worried about her father too, man, that's got to be heavy. Anyway, I knew you'd want to know, so I thought I'd better get back to you quickly."

"Duke, you're the best."

"Yeah, that's what they tell me," he replied, suppressed laughter evident in his voice.

Chapter Twenty-Nine

Lauren entered Gloria's apartment in a fog. After leaving Dr. Garcia's office, every function she'd carried out had been done on automatic pilot, her conscious mind short-circuited by the physician's words.

She'd felt tired for weeks, but assumed her run-down condition was somehow connected to everything going on around her. Periodic visits with her father in Colorado, as well as her new flight schedule had taken a toll on her, but Lauren was determined to stay on top of his doctor appointments. Those she was not able to make were handled by her mother.

Thus far, he was doing fine, with his physicians offering a good, strong prognosis for the future. Both women had been there while he underwent surgery. The Denver Cancer and Research Center had been their choice, and two weeks earlier, he'd undergone the operation successfully. Colin Traynor was now recovering and scheduled for the required course of radiation to begin sometime in the coming month after he'd had adequate time to heal from the surgery. Already his strength surprised both his ex-wife and daughter, confirming what they'd known all along: he was definitely a trooper.

Lauren had not eaten since the night before, a tuna sandwich with a glass of orange juice having been her dinner. She decided to make a cup of tea, then took out some crackers and cheese, and sat down to have a lunchtime snack. She was only halfway through her meal when the phone rang. Thinking it might be either her mother or father, she picked up the receiver.

"Hello, Lauren." His words turned her world upside down, and threatened to make her gag on the food she'd just put into her mouth.

"Hello, Michael." She wanted to say more, but knew if she attempted to, all the emotions his voice evoked would come spilling out.

Lauren's heart beat rapidly in her chest. She wondered how long he had known where to find her. Then the anger which had filled her heart and mind for the past months rose to the surface and she was immediately ready to do battle.

"How are you?" His simple question seemed filled with underlying insinuation, and Lauren's guard immediately went up. Seconds passed and both knew the true agony of missed opportunity.

"I'm fine, just fine," she replied nervously.

"Lauren, I need to talk to you, but I am not willing to do it over the telephone." *Click.*

She panicked then. A surge of bile rose in her throat and she raced to the bathroom, bringing up all her food. The effort left her weak and trembling. She washed her face, brushed her teeth, and lay across the bed wondering how he dared hang up on her. She willed herself to calm down and lay across the bed. *Men,* she thought to herself.

Lauren fell asleep, and was awakened by the doorbell. Gloria was out of town, but had keys, so the sound startled her. She walked to the intercom, pressed it, asked, "Yes, who is it?" Her voice sounding soft and deep from her recently interrupted nap.

"Lauren, it's Michael. We need to talk."

Her first reaction was panic, then anger, and finally resolve. If this was what it took to bring everything to a conclusion, then so be it. She rang him in and waited. Smoothing her hair back from her face, she realized she looked tired and worn. She also realized that she didn't care. This was not a beauty pageant; it was her life. And Michael had been a part of that life until she had evicted him from it.

Lauren opened the door and the breath literally left her body. He too looked worn and haggard. Her heart cried out as she realized the pain she'd caused him. She wondered if she'd ever come to terms with the love she still felt for him. Lauren was wary as she realized Michael had not uttered a single word. Instead, he stepped into the apartment without invitation, determined to have his say.

Lauren followed him to the living room, wondering how they would get through this final confrontation.

"I'm not sure what brings you here, but if you think this is going to do any good, I applaud you for your courage. Can I get you anything? Some tea, a beer, a cold drink?" she asked wanting to give herself something to do with her hands.

"No, I'm fine. You don't look well, Lauren. Is everything okay?" he asked suddenly, scrutinizing her slowly. She looked as if she'd lost weight and her cheekbones were more pronounced than ever, lending a slightly gaunt appearance to her face. Even still, Michael realized he's missed her, missed her smile, and, most definitely, missed her presence.

Lauren walked into the kitchen, poured a glass of ginger ale for herself and walked back into the living room where Michael stood by the window looking out.

"You've lost weight," he said without turning around.

"Yeah, probably because neither Gloria nor I ever cook. We eat take-out or we're somewhere in another state, so it's eat on the run," she chattered nervously, sitting on the couch.

She recognized that he had taken the offensive with his simple observation. She also knew that it was just the beginning, so she braced herself for his next statement.

"Look, I didn't come here for small talk," he added turning around.

"No, I know you want to clear the air and so do I. I've already told you that I'm sorry that things didn't work out. I hope you'll forgive me for doing what I did, but I thought it would be easier, no confrontation, no hassles, no ordeal. It seemed to be the right thing to do at the time. . . ." Lauren continued to look into her lap and would not meet his eyes which were filled with anger and pain.

"I see . . . so it was easier. On whom? Did I ever say that I wanted to be anywhere but with you? Did I ever make you feel as if I wasn't thrilled to death to be married to you? What gave you the right to sever the ties that *we'd* made, dissolve the bonds *we'd* formed, and end the vows *we* took?" He stood over her then, demanding an answer, anger, frustration, and love all mixed in one tangled emotional vessel.

Lauren heard the pain and wanted nothing more than to erase the frustration. She raised her head, stood and stepped toward him, defiance appearing suddenly in her demeanor.

"I didn't have to be told, Michael. I knew by your behavior that you were distancing yourself."

"Lauren, do I have to remind you that it was company business that sent me to the West Coast? You can't possibly believe I orchestrated a corporate emergency," he added, his voice rising as the frustration built.

"Michael, I don't know what I thought. It just didn't feel right. It brought to mind all that I had gone through with my dad when he left. Now, he's undergoing treatment for cancer and I feel as if we might lose him for real. . . ." Her voice trailed off then, as she tried to handle emotions kept too long within. Tears welled up in her eyes, and she felt herself losing control.

Lauren stood before Michael filled with unspoken regret,

unable to voice the sadness that filled her as waves of emotion overtook her body. He silently stepped forward, taking her into his arms, holding her gently, as her body quivered.

"You are a hell of a wreck, but you're my wreck. I'm not letting you walk away from me again—not today, not tomorrow, not ever. I'm sorry about your dad, sweetheart. Whatever kind of cancer he has, as long as he's being treated, he stands a good chance of beating it, you know."

"I know that. They've already said he should be fine, but I worry about him so much. My mother is also taking care of him. They've sort of become each other's best friends. It's nice to see them together," she added, her face brightening with the admission that her parents were now somewhat reconciled.

Michael looked at her and saw further concern there, which really saddened him. "Look, I know there are other issues you have which make it almost impossible for you to enter into a long-term relationship that is actually good for you. I'm just trying to get you over that hurdle," he responded.

His honesty sent a concise message that reached Lauren this time, allowing her to ask her next question. She struggled for a moment, then looked up and blurted it out angrily. "Look there's something else we should talk about. I don't know how to say this, but I have to. I called your room looking for you. Someone answered your phone. Who was that, Michael?" she asked, still afraid of his answer.

Michael looked puzzled for a moment, then smiled. Lauren felt extremely vulnerable and prepared herself for his answer.

"It had to be Noelle. I know there were a couple of times when we stayed up late as she helped me go over the reports we were working on. I know she came to my room at least twice. Maybe she picked up the phone, but honey, you've met Noelle. That should not have been a problem."

Lauren blew out a sigh of relief that was quickly replaced

by extreme regret. Her body began to shake and tears rolled
from her eyes as she realized the great mistake she'd made.
"The woman never identified herself," Lauren cried. "I was
so startled that I hung up. I'm sorry Michael, I didn't know
what to do. It added to my suspicions as to why my new husband *volunteered* for an assignment that would put him three
thousand miles away from me." She ended breathlessly, her
defenses down now that her explanation was on the table.

Michael watched her shoulders slump forward, and realized that she'd carried the burden of thinking him unfaithful
for all this time. It was absurd, in his mind, but he also knew
that when love is on the table, any disruption of the norm can
be devastating. He watched her struggle with her error then
leaned forward.

"Listen, woman. Noelle doesn't even exist in my world. I
don't care about anyone but you. You are the one I am committed to, who I live for each and every day. I did feel that I
was the best person for the assignment and that is why I said
I'd go. At the time, I thought we needed space, time to get
used to the idea of marriage. I couldn't have been more wrong.
No one realized it would take the time it did to straighten out
the reports, so I do owe you an apology for that. The fact that
some numbskull assistant answered the phone and then didn't
even have the communication skills to identify herself, or to
tell me about the call, is irrelevant. You are my most cherished possession, partner, and the one I want to spend the rest
of my life with. Understand?" He wrapped his arms around
her. The anger in her voice was gone, replaced by a genuine
need for love and understanding.

"I guess I've made a mess of things, haven't I?" Lauren
asked, looking into his eyes for the faith and hope she
needed to sustain her.

"Honey, you have to be strong and be willing to cope
with stuff in this life. We're going to get through this together. And just so you know, to me, those papers you filed

are not worth the sheets they're printed on, Lauren. We consummated our marriage over and over again. There is no way you can annul it."

"I never thought about that. Somehow, I thought that if I removed myself from your life, the pain would go away. I was wrong though; it only made it worse," Lauren admitted for the first time, thinking back on how miserable she had become.

Michael looked into her eyes and touched his lips to hers gingerly. The warmth of his body seemed to seep into her skin, scalding her and bringing her to life all at once. "You were too eager to give up, Lauren. We're in this together for the long run, so you'd better get used to it."

After seeing all that her parents had gone through, and watching them emerge as two whole but separate human beings, she felt she now had a better handle on life's ups and downs. Relationships, in particular, had a way of working themselves out, she'd ascertained.

"Say it. Say we're in it together," Michael coaxed, his arms around her, his body against hers, making Lauren feel as if she were being reborn. Desire flooded her, and she reached her arms around his neck and leaned into him, relishing the feel of his body against hers.

"Yes, we're in it together, forever," she said softly, finally. Her voice had turned husky as tears washed them both rekindling the love each felt. Michael picked Lauren up and carried her into the bedroom, slowly removing her clothing between kisses. There was no hesitation, no delay, their lovemaking providing a union they each hungered for. They made love as if it were the first, the last, the only time. When the storm of desire that engulfed them subsided, they lay tangled in each other's arms, exhausted physically and mentally.

"You know I'm not leaving here without you," he stated, surprising her with the determination in his voice.

"Michael, are you serious about this? I mean, what I did was pretty drastic."

He looked at her then, her hair tumbling wildly about her shoulders, her body flushed from the lovemaking they'd just enjoyed and he knew he didn't want to spend another day without her.

"I'm dead serious. There's nothing you can say to me that would change my mind. I want you now, I wanted you then, and I'm going to go on wanting you."

"I know that now, Michael. I just hope you know what you're in for." There was the very slight beginning of a smile playing about her mouth as she tried her best to keep a serious look on her face.

"Now what's that supposed to mean?" he asked, noticing the look of pure mischief.

Lauren watched him carefully. This time, somehow, she knew their union would be for all time. Something in the weeks that had passed had caused her to realize that if Michael came back to her after all they'd been through, their marriage would last. "Are you sure you want to know," she asked, her eyebrow arched, a smile lingering about her lips.

"I think I do. You've lost weight, I also see that you've developed some very definite curves. The same kind you had the last time your tried to run away from me," he added meaningfully.

Lauren nodded. She could not believe that he could be so perceptive. She'd done her best to hide the truth even from herself, the shock of Dr. Garcia's diagnosis hitting her full force just that morning. She'd had to sit down, with his nurse giving her a glass of water, as she'd tried to come to terms with his prognosis.

"So you are pregnant. I knew it. I hope you realize that this means we're also going to have to get remarried, miss. Right away," he added, kissing her on the tip of her nose, his heart beating rapidly with excitement. "I love you," he added, his arms pulling her into an embrace which was both strong and tender.

"I know, and I love you too, but it was almost as if there was a tape playing in my head that's stuck on dialogue that continued to tell me it would never work. I'm just now coming to understand that I should have erased it long ago," she whispered softly, kissing him. "Michael, I think there's something else you should know," she said, causing his heart to stop. After all they'd been though, this was not the time for additional foolishness. He gave her a look that spoke volumes.

Lauren smiled, continued looking him directly in the eyes, and said softly, "We might be having twins."

Michael looked at her, a shocked expression on his face. "Twins," he repeated wistfully. "Double trouble!" he shouted, then covered his mouth with one hand, his excitement clearly evident in his demeanor. He regained his composure, looking at his wife with love shining from his eyes. "I love you Lauren, forever, for always."

And for the first time, Lauren had no lingering doubts that their love would last a lifetime.

EPILOGUE

Gloria's apartment was a hub of activity. Duke arrived right on time, bearing flowers and wearing a grin that he seemed unable to stop displaying. Morgan arrived next. He quickly took on a look of total disbelief as he came face-to-face with what he'd suspected all along.

"So, I suppose you two are something of an item," he stated with a raised eyebrow, his voice filled with challenge.

Gloria calmly walked over to Duke, looked directly at Morgan, and realized she was actually relieved to finally set the record straight. "Yes, and if you don't mind, I'd rather you didn't make a big deal of it. We're both adults. If Duke is good enough to be partners with you in business, I can't see why he's not good enough to date your sister," Gloria stated firmly. The challenge had been issued, and it was now Morgan's turn to respond.

Instead of issuing an ultimatum, giving orders, or stating an unsolicited opinion, he refrained from doing all three. As his sister stood next to one of the men upon whom he'd come to rely heavily in the past months, he recognized that Gloria was a grown woman. One who could very well make her own decisions, it seemed.

"Forgive me if I don't applaud, but you two do look relatively happy. For what it's worth, I'm glad for you both." With that statement, he walked away and headed toward the wet bar. "I need a drink. Isn't this supposed to be a dinner party? Where's the dinner. Where's the party?" he yelled over his shoulder, solidly ending the discussion.

Gloria looked at Duke and smiled. He seemed a little unnerved, then mirrored her expression. It seemed that Morgan had somehow been tamed. What neither of them realized was that their relationship actually had very little to do with the change in Morgan's demeanor. Noelle Stephenson's entrance into and departure from Morgan's life had deeply affected him. When she resigned three days after her return from California with no explanation, it caught Morgan off guard and his heart ached with the loss of a potential mate. In typical Morgan fashion, he hadn't pursued her but had thrown himself into what he knew best instead: business.

Lauren and Michael arrived next, each carrying a bottle of wine.

"What's all this?" Gloria asked, smiling as she hugged them both.

"Michael insisted we bring two bottles. One for a toast before dinner and another for while we eat," Lauren explained as they entered the apartment.

"Yeah, I figured you'd probably run out at some point. Just making sure we have enough." Michael smiled as he delivered the line. Duke walked over to them, kissed Lauren on both cheeks, and grabbed Michael into his traditional bear hug.

"Exactly what are we toasting to, my good man?" Duke asked, a look of feigned innocence on his face.

"Well, the eviction of a roommate for one thing," Michael

answered, giving Gloria and Lauren a look of complete triumph.

"Oh, that. Well, I want to drink to that also," Duke added, making everyone laugh.

"And there are other things," Michael said, being intentionally vague as he looked over at his wife.

"Such as?" Gloria prompted.

Lauren shook her head, walked into the kitchen and put both bottles into the refrigerator. Gloria was quick on her heels.

"What announcement do you have to make?" Gloria asked her best friend, trapping her next to the fridge.

"Wait until dinner. I'll tell you then. Michael has sworn me to secrecy." She put her index finger to her lips, indicating she would say no more.

Gloria shrugged and went to peer in the oven.

"Need some help?" Lauren asked.

"Actually, everything is pretty much under control. The appetizers are ready. There are a couple of bottles of wine already open, and dinner can be served in about a half an hour."

"Wow, you said you were going to invite us all over for dinner, but I didn't realize you would do it so quickly. Ms. Sorrentino, you are truly a woman of your word." The aroma of Gloria's meal hit Lauren's nose and she sniffed. "What is that? Something smells really wonderful," Lauren added.

"Thanks. I made my mother's recipe for lasagna. There's a spinach salad with artichokes, pimento, and gorgonzola cheese. I also made garlic bread with parmesan. For dessert, we're having the Italian cheesecake I usually pick up from Zabar's."

"Isn't that made with ricotta cheese?" Lauren asked, her mouth already beginning to water.

"Yep, and it's probably half the calories of the regular

kind. Don't tell the guys though, cause they like to think its decadent," Gloria added, laughing as she shut the oven door.

They left the kitchen and entered the living room where the men were engaged in their favorite subject: work.

Morgan adamantly refused to discuss Noelle's abrupt departure. Michael and Duke were puzzled by his attitude, but they knew better than to push. At the moment, they were more than happy to put the past events of Cityscape's financial matters behind them.

The doorbell rang then, and Gloria asked Lauren to get it. Duke smiled and watched as she walked toward the door. Michael noticed but said nothing.

Lauren opened the door, let out a shriek then hugged the two people who stood in the doorway. Michael walked over to her, saw Lauren's parents, and laughed out loud.

"Hey, how'd you guys get here?" he asked then, looking around the room for answers.

Gloria stepped forward and was immediately folded into the older couple's arms. "I knew you'd been worried about your dad and figured it was a good excuse to get them both here," she told Lauren, grinning. "They flew in on Worldwide."

Lauren's eyes were filled with tears, but she managed to find her way toward her friend. "You're the best, Gloria. And boy, can you keep a secret," she exclaimed.

The two young women embraced one another while everyone watched, smiles on their faces.

"Let me get you something to nibble on," Duke said ushering Lauren's parents into the living room. "You must be starving and thirsty. Those airlines don't serve any food to anybody. It's a disgrace."

"You're so right," Colin confirmed. "Eva made me eat something before we left for the airport in Colorado, and she also packed lunch. I could still eat though."

Lauren was thrilled to hear that her father's appetite was hearty. His prognosis was good; having undergone several treatments he was already showing signs of improvement. Eva had been by his side through all of it, and they were still spending a lot of time in one another's company.

Morgan stood then, tapping his spoon against his glass. "I'd like to drink a toast to longevity, health, happiness, and quality of life. Here, here," he added while everyone prepared to join in.

They all touched glasses, then drank the champagne. Lauren had ginger ale.

Michael then cleared his throat and held his glass up high. "I'd like to make a toast as well."

Lauren shook her head, whispering, "I thought we'd wait until dinner," in his ear.

Her attempts to silence her husband were met with cries and protests from their audience. Lauren gave in and tried to take a seat on the couch, but Michael snuck an arm around her waist and pulled her close. He looked into her eyes and she nodded her approval.

"Well, we took our vows again this morning and we are officially husband and wife for the second time. So here's to being married again." The gathering before him cheered and began to lift their glasses to their lips, but Michael stopped them. "I have one more announcement. Lauren's pregnant and we're having twins! Now you can drink."

Eva leapt from her seat, crossing the small room to embrace her daughter and son-in-law. Colin, Duke, Gloria, and Morgan were right behind her.

"This is so wonderful," Eva cried, excited at her second chance to become a grandmother.

After everyone had wished the newlywed and expecting couple their best wishes, the party sat in the living room, enjoying appetizers and good conversation. Suddenly, Morgan snapped his fingers, remembering something.

"Oh, wait. What time is it?" he asked, looking at his watch. "There's a broadcast about CBN on six o'clock news.

Gloria, can we turn it on just for a moment?" His voice was etched with excitement.

"Morgan, this is a dinner party, not a ball game," she said, rolling her eyes at the pitiful look on her brother's face. "Yeah, go ahead, if it's really that important." She suspected Morgan wouldn't dare suggest television during dinner unless it was something very important.

He picked up the remote control to Gloria's flat-screen television and everyone's attention immediately turned toward it. Morgan surfed through several channels and stopped at CNN. His timing was perfect.

"In New York City, the Manhattan district attorney's office today disclosed the end of an ongoing investigation into charges of fraud, racketeering, money laundering, and extortion," the anchorwoman announced. "Sources close to the investigation cited a lack of evidence and the existence of an irrevocable ordinance which states corporate culpability must be proven with prior knowledge of the principal partners before charges may be filed.

"The joint task force, comprised of the NYPD, the FBI and the ATF, each issued separate statements which corroborated the existence of the year-long inquiry. Each department also confirmed the existence of substantive amounts of information, all of which have now been documented and sealed. In an effort to clear the names of those individuals closest to the examination, the statement said that at no time were the principals of Cityscape Broadcast Network ever implicated in any suspected wrongdoing.

"Testimony by an undercover agent assigned to the case was taken in a closed courtroom. The agent confirmed that the state and federal government had ultimately arrived at the conclusion that they had no substantive case."

Everyone in the room seemed to stop breathing. Morgan still held the remote in one hand, his eyes fixed on the screen. *Was Noelle an undercover agent?*

"In a separate statement issued only moments ago, a grand jury has issued indictments for the arrest and conviction of Duane Capparelli and Anthony Sorrentino in conjunction with charges of money laundering and racketeering through several Internet channels. It was disclosed that a sum of close to ten million dollars had been rerouted into a corporate account. The company, which was unaware of the transaction, was not implicated in any wrongdoing.

"This has been the six o'clock report. Stay tuned after this commercial break for additional programming," she added.

Morgan clicked the remote and the screen went black. His expression was one of mixed emotion. The news broadcast answered many of the questions which had plagued him for months. Lifting an empty glass in mock salute, he suddenly said, "It's over." The glint of triumph in his voice was barely audible.

Michael put his arm around Lauren, cleared his throat, and added, "Actually, here's looking forward to new beginnings."

Lauren nodded in consent and returned his gaze lovingly. His statement held special meaning for each person in the room. They all held up their glasses in a mock salute to a future filled with hope and special meaning.

Letter to My Readers:

I want to thank each and every one of you for your enthusi-
astic response to *On a Wing and a Prayer,* my first romance
novel. Many readers asked the question, "What happens next?"
and I too felt the story had not been completely told. Hopefully
A Matter of Time will answer all the questions and serve to
give the sufficient details!

I hope you have enjoyed the return visit!

Peace, blessings, and lots of love!

Linda Walters